BOAT
of
Dreams

Rogério Coelho

TILBURY HOUSE
PUBLISHERS

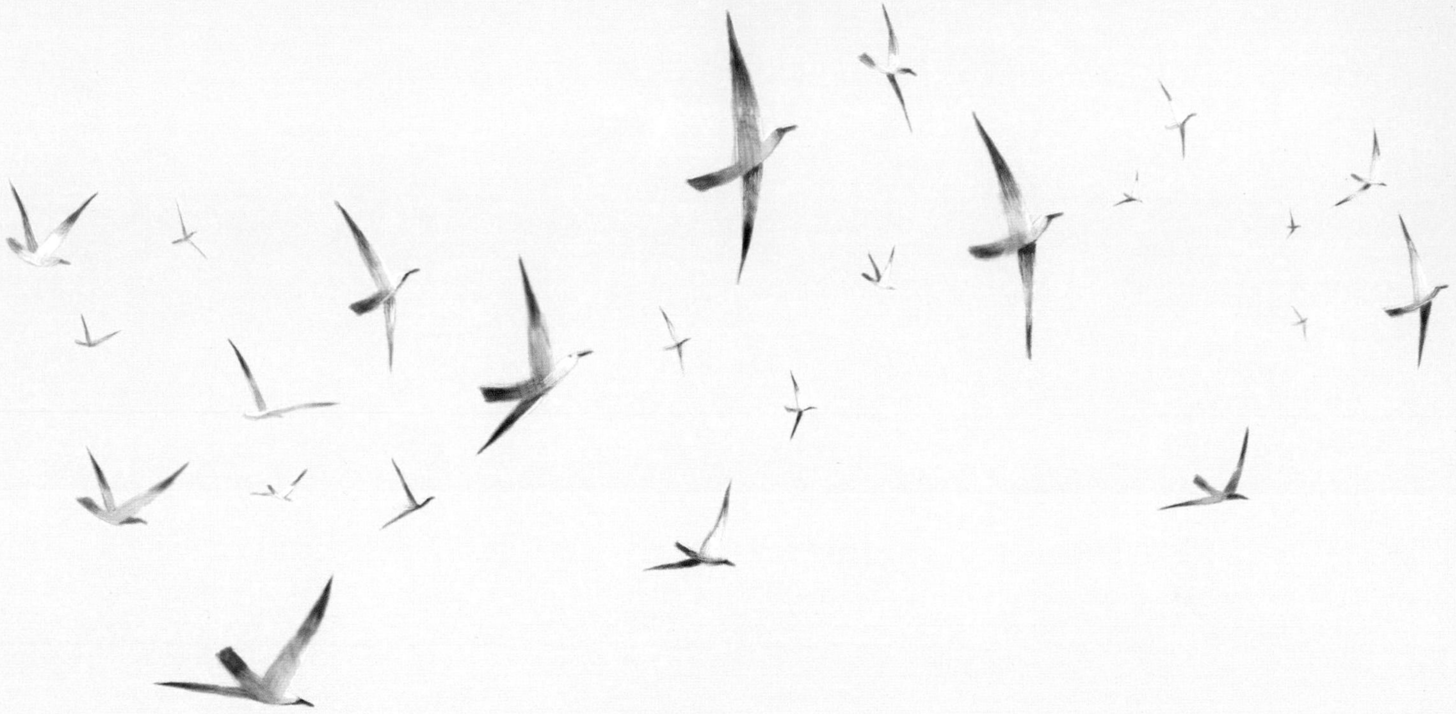

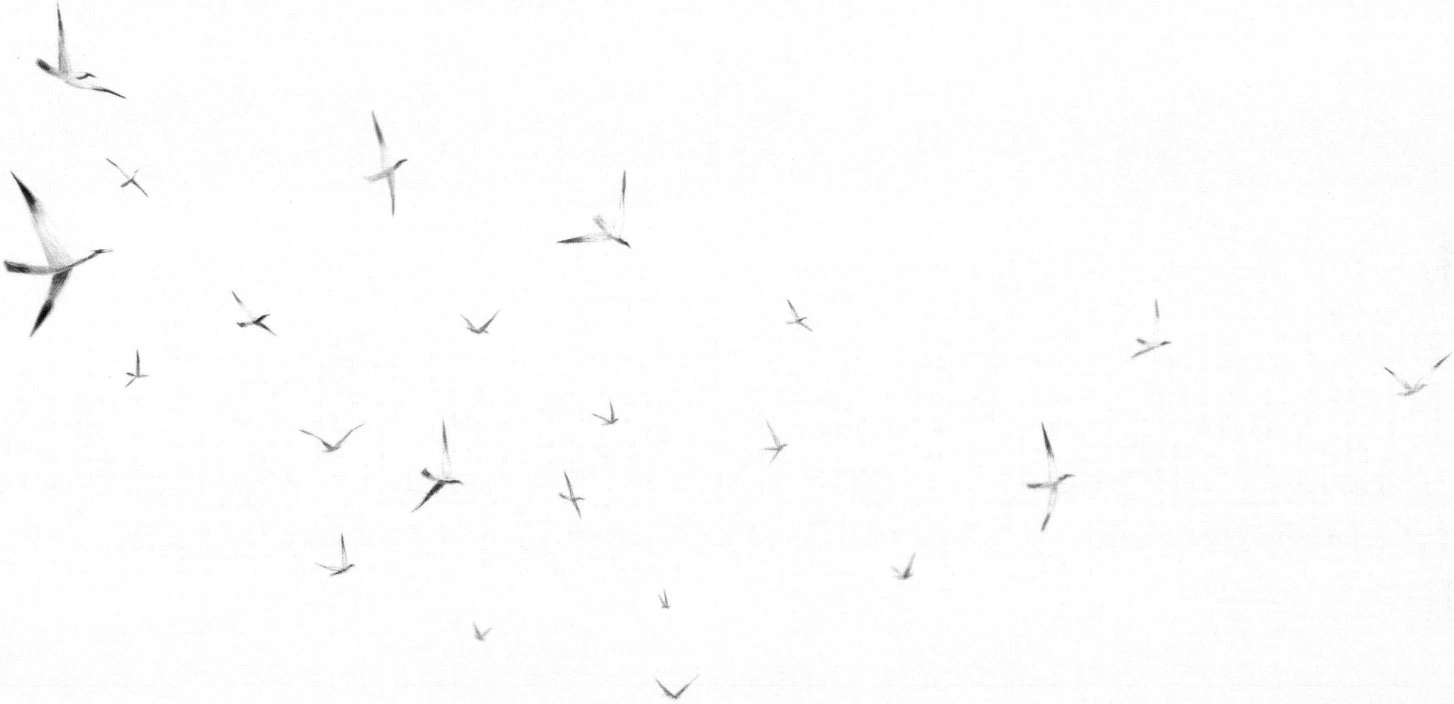

To my father, Orivaldo, for always reminding me that once I was a child,
and to Marcelo and Daniel for not ceasing to hope and believe.

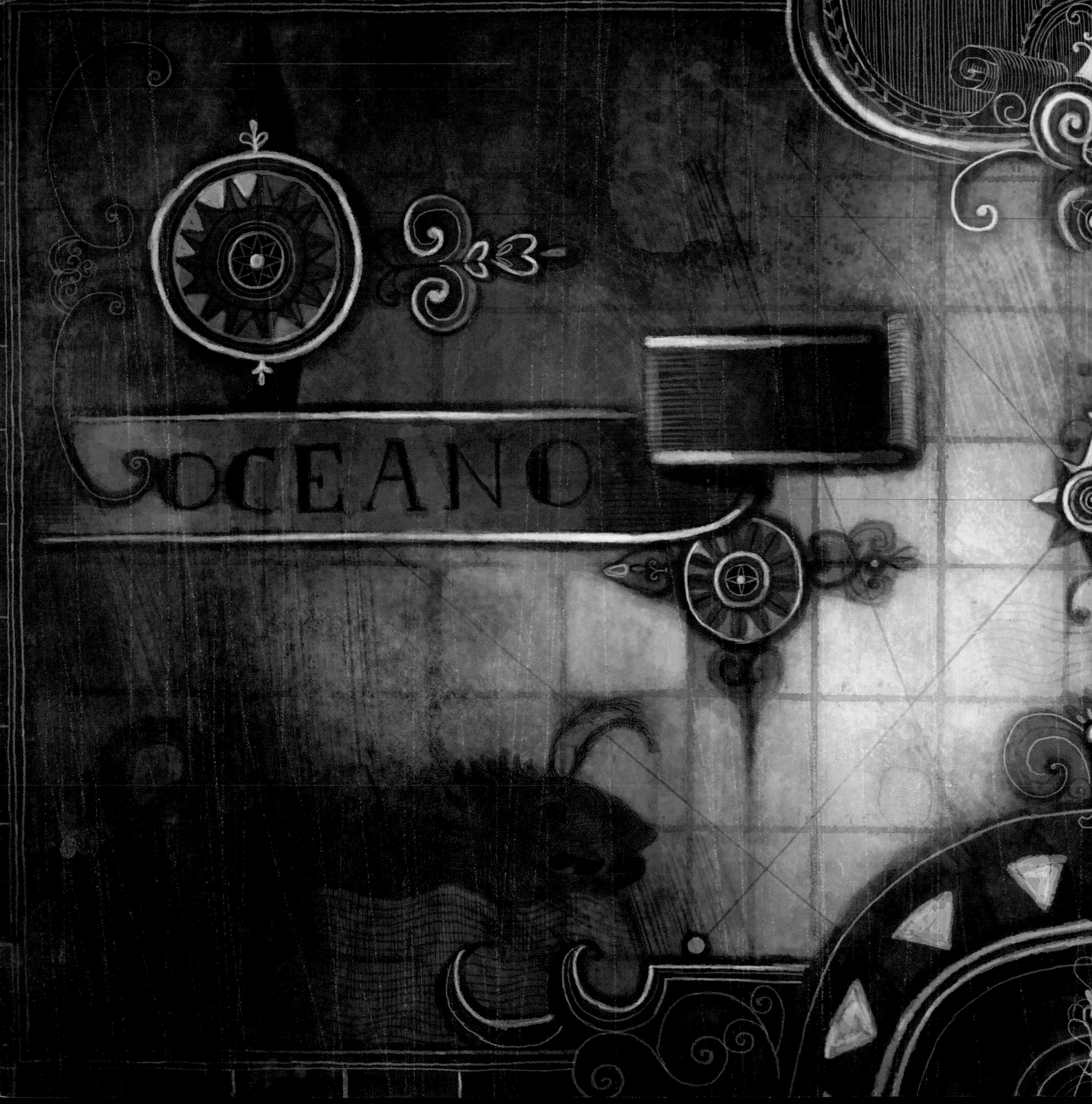
OCEANO

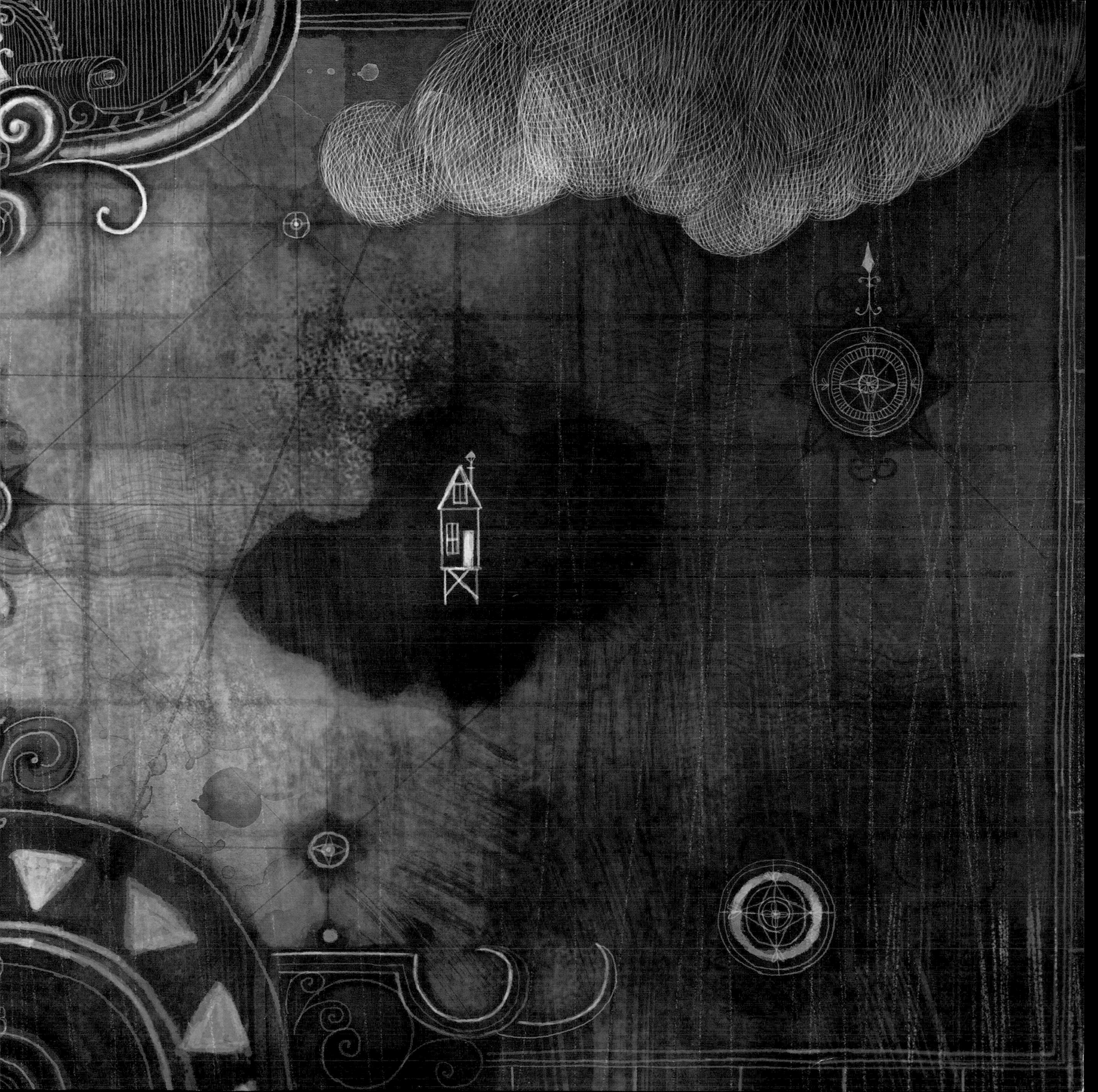

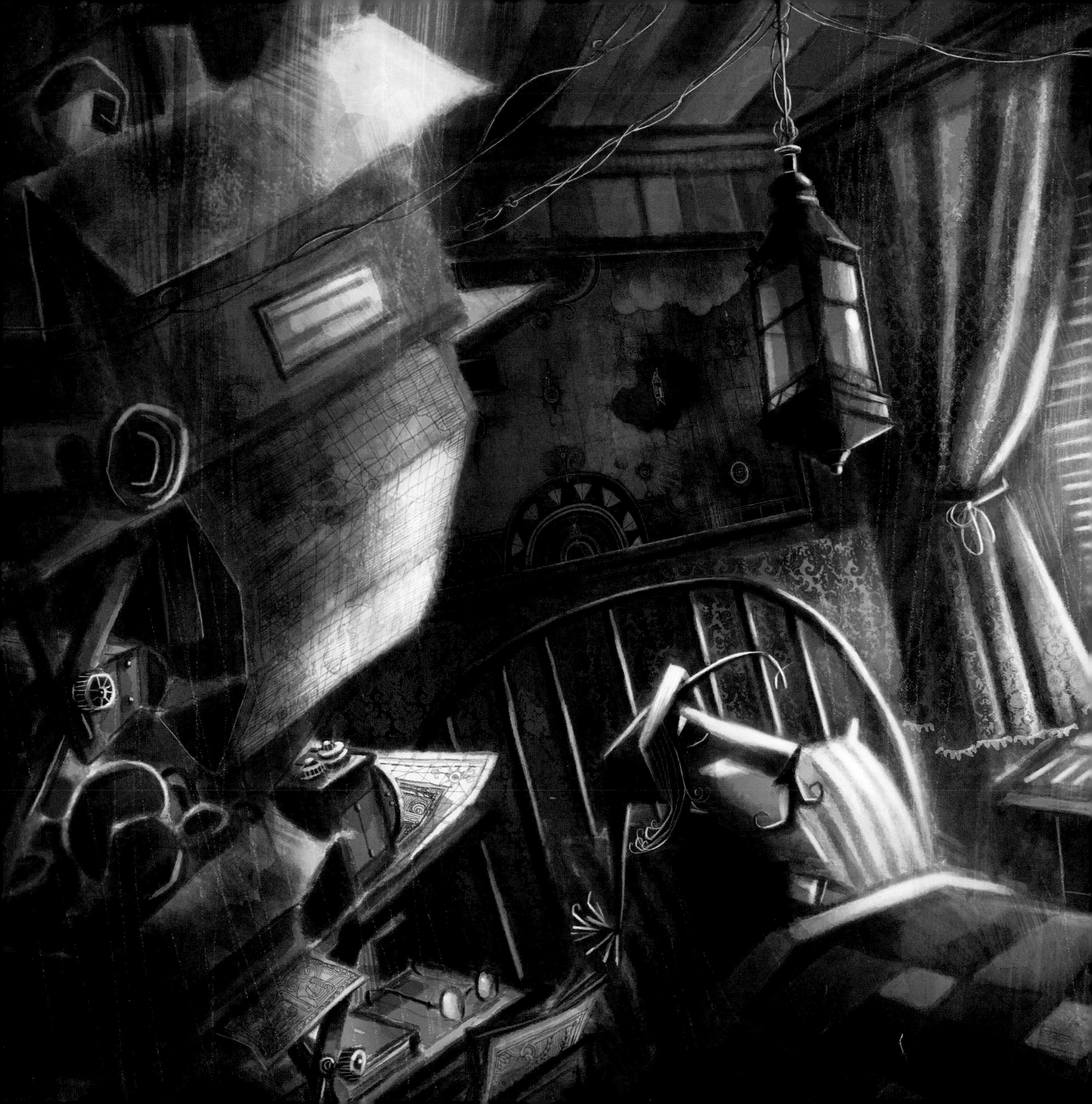

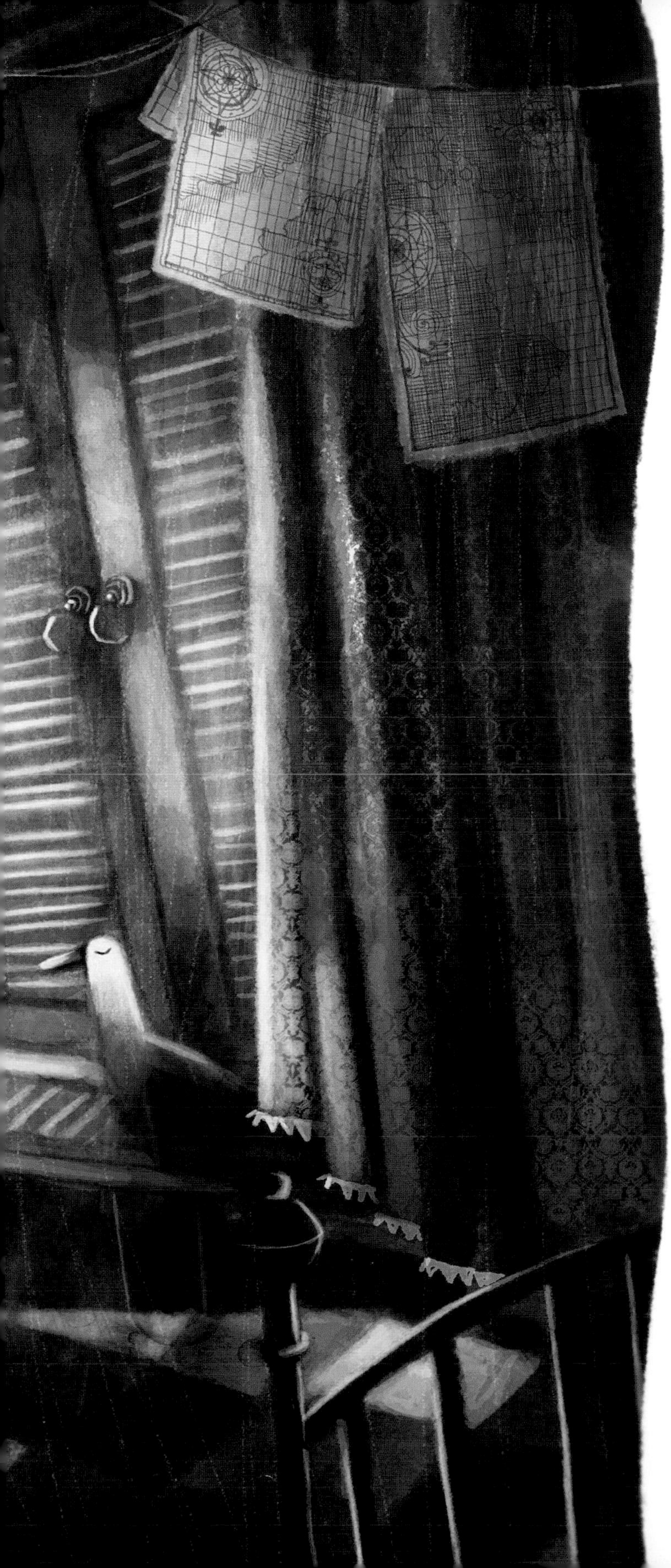
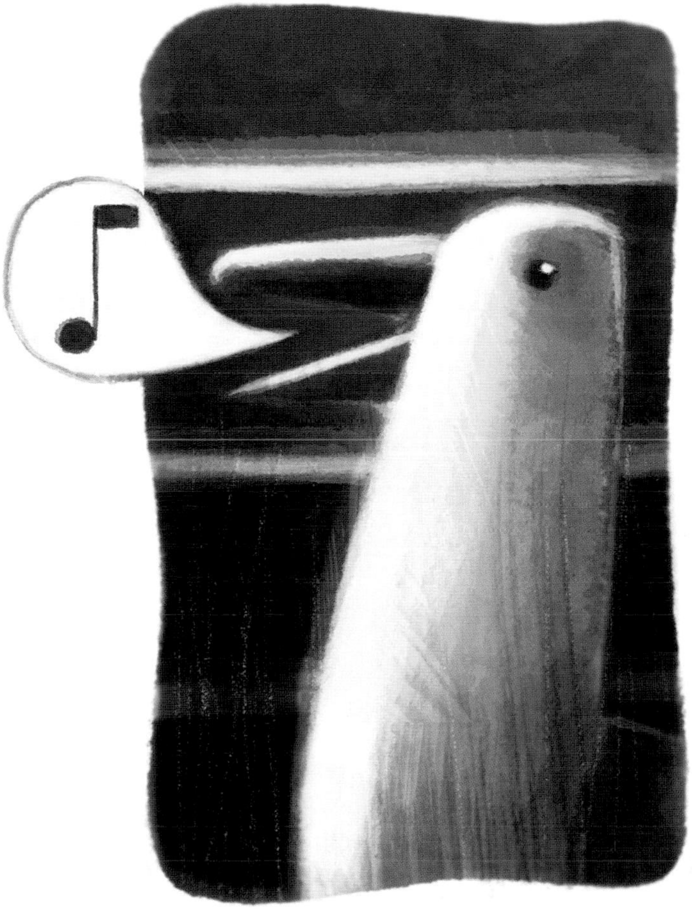

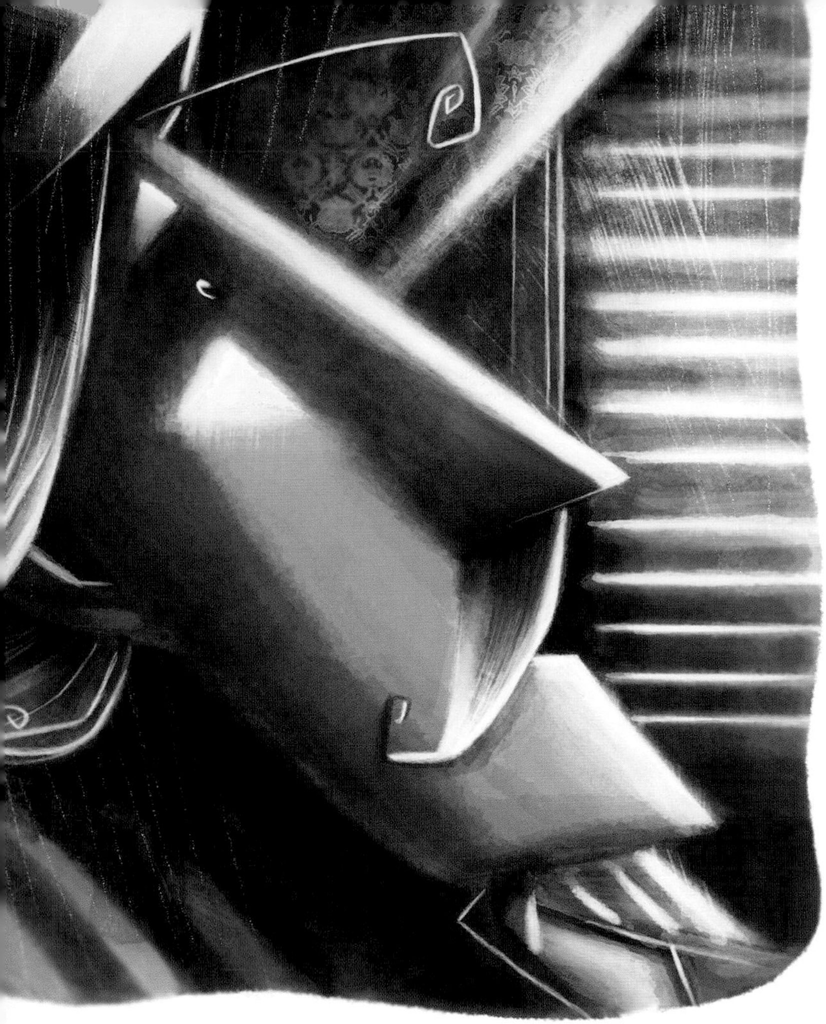

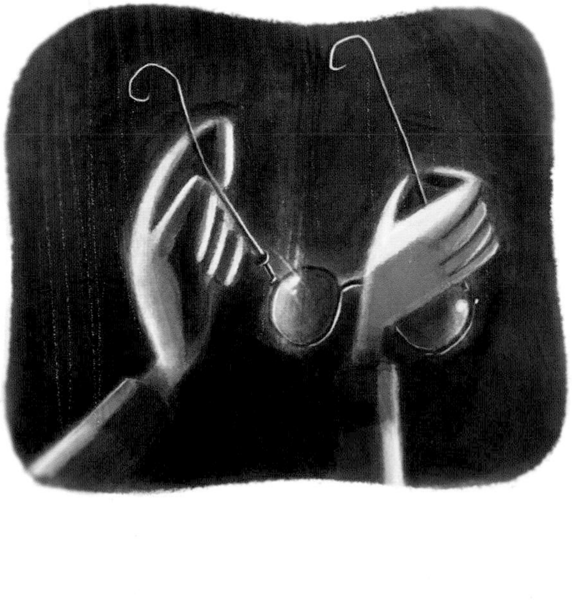

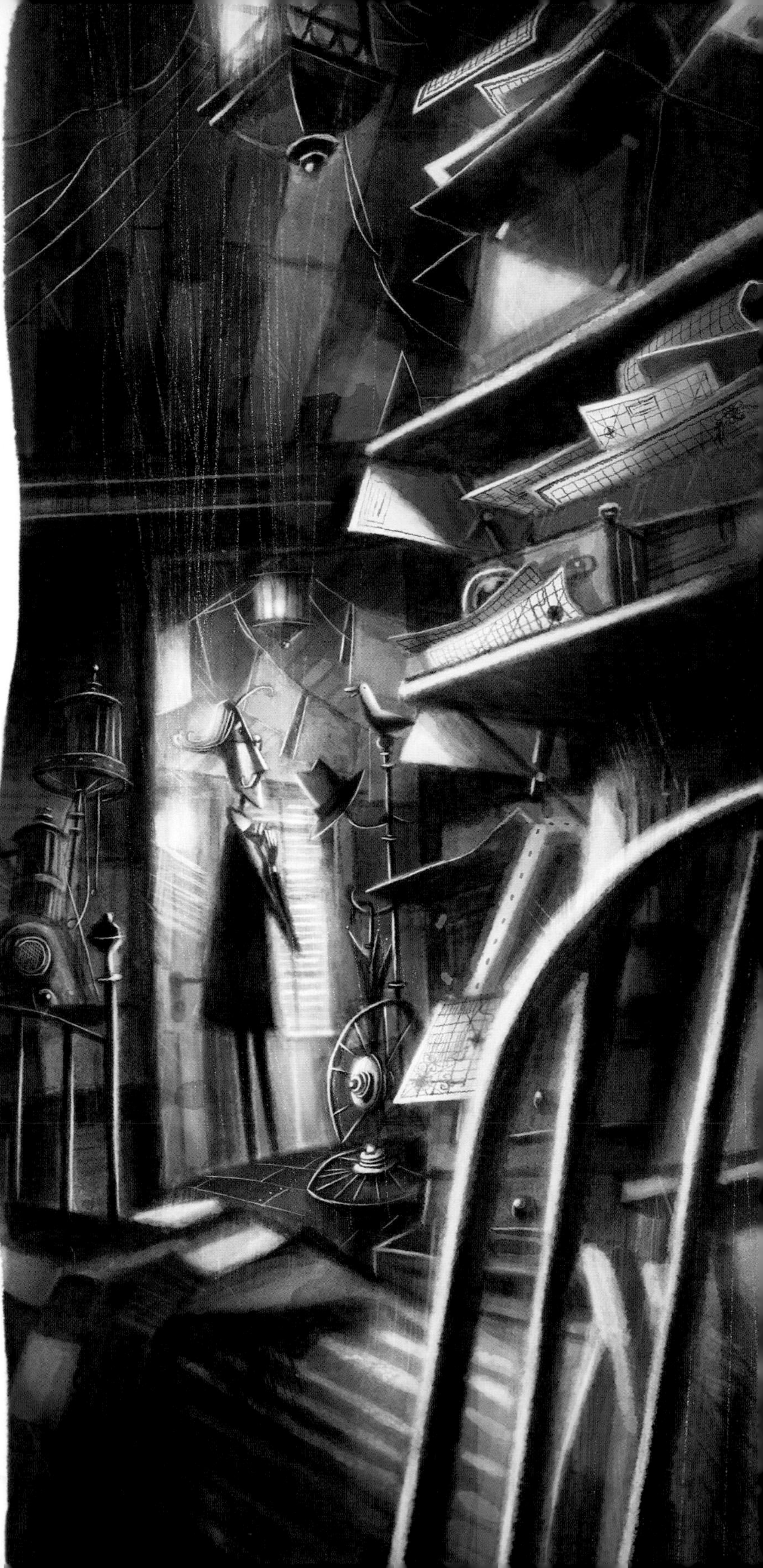

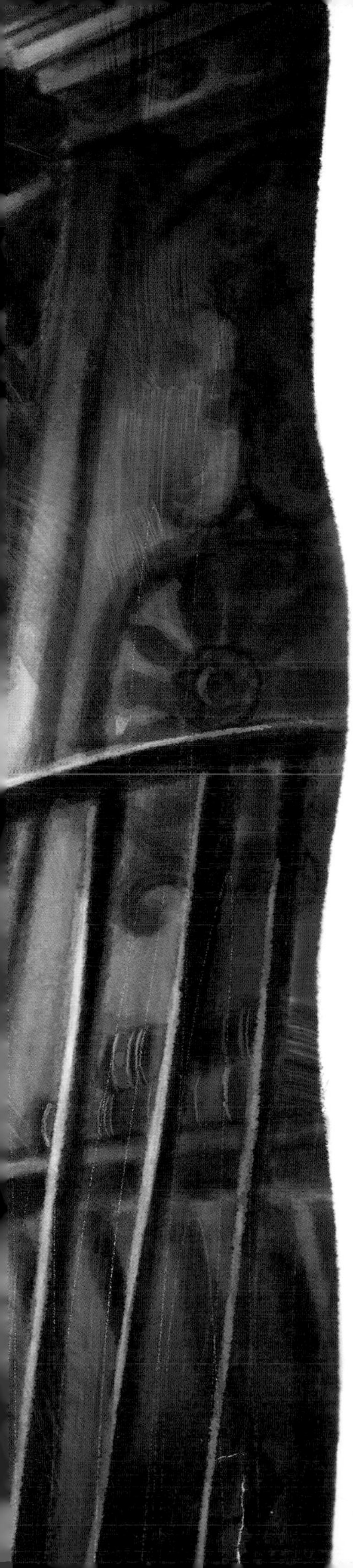

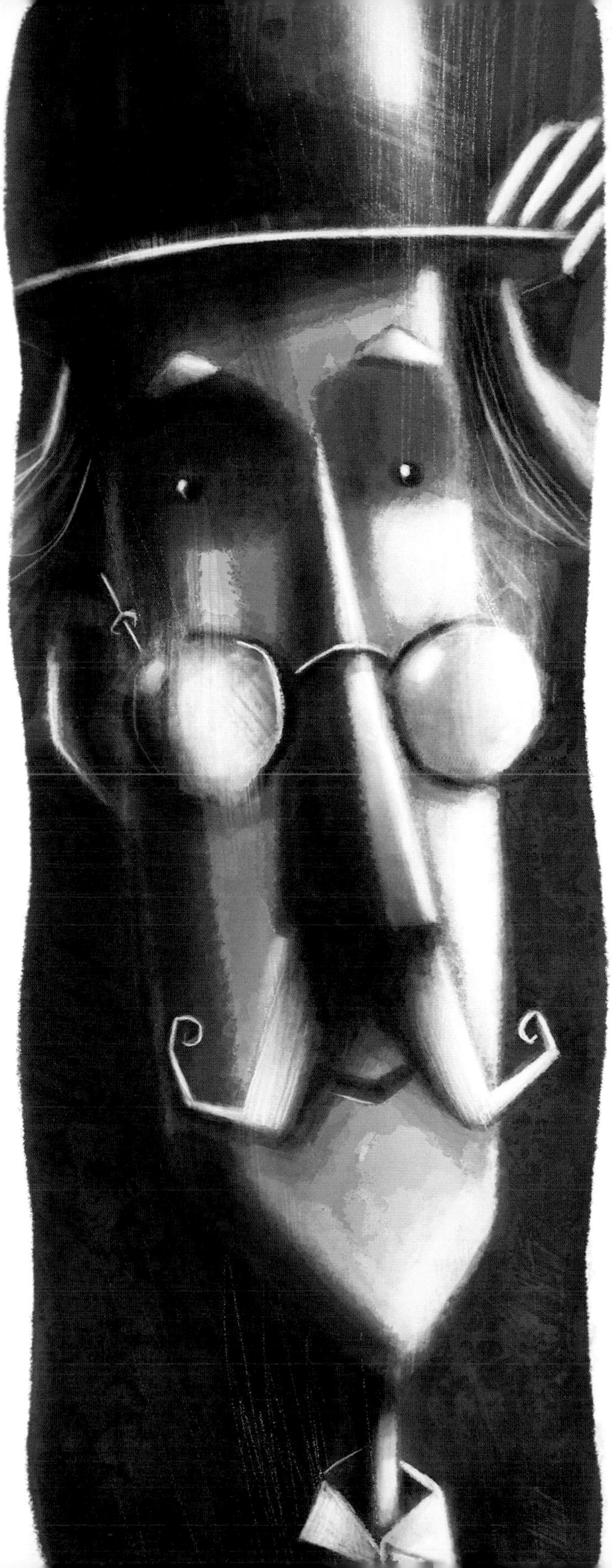

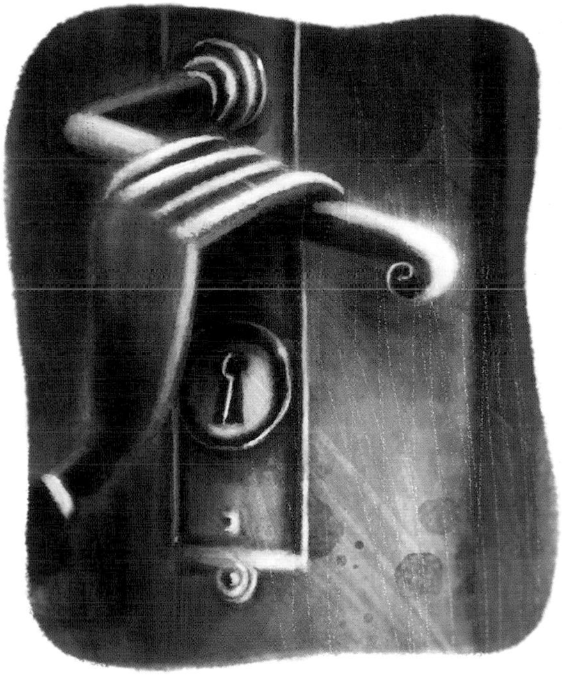

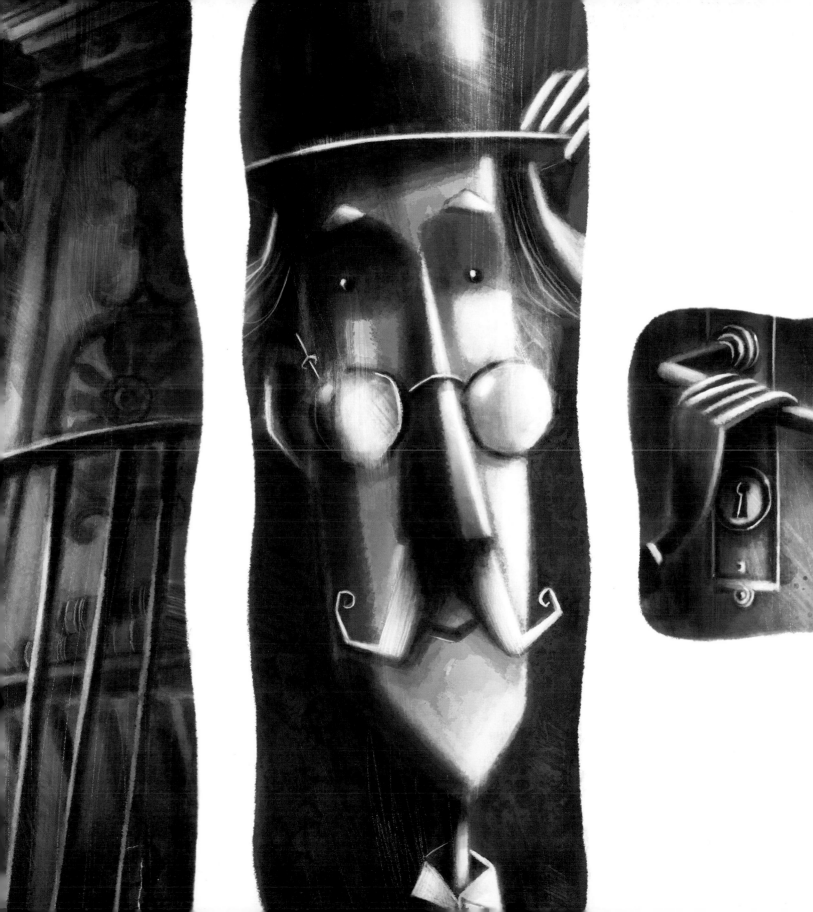

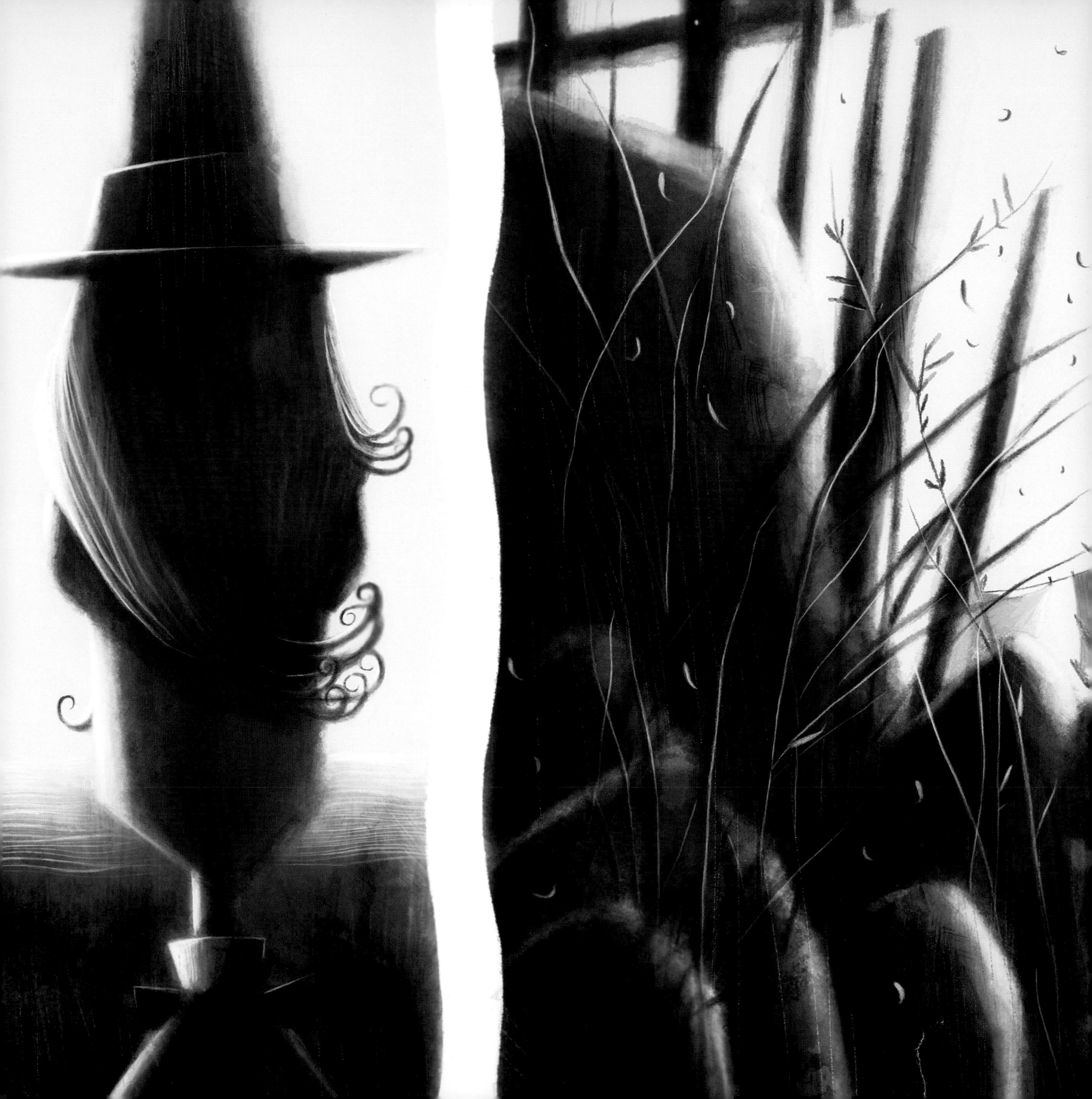

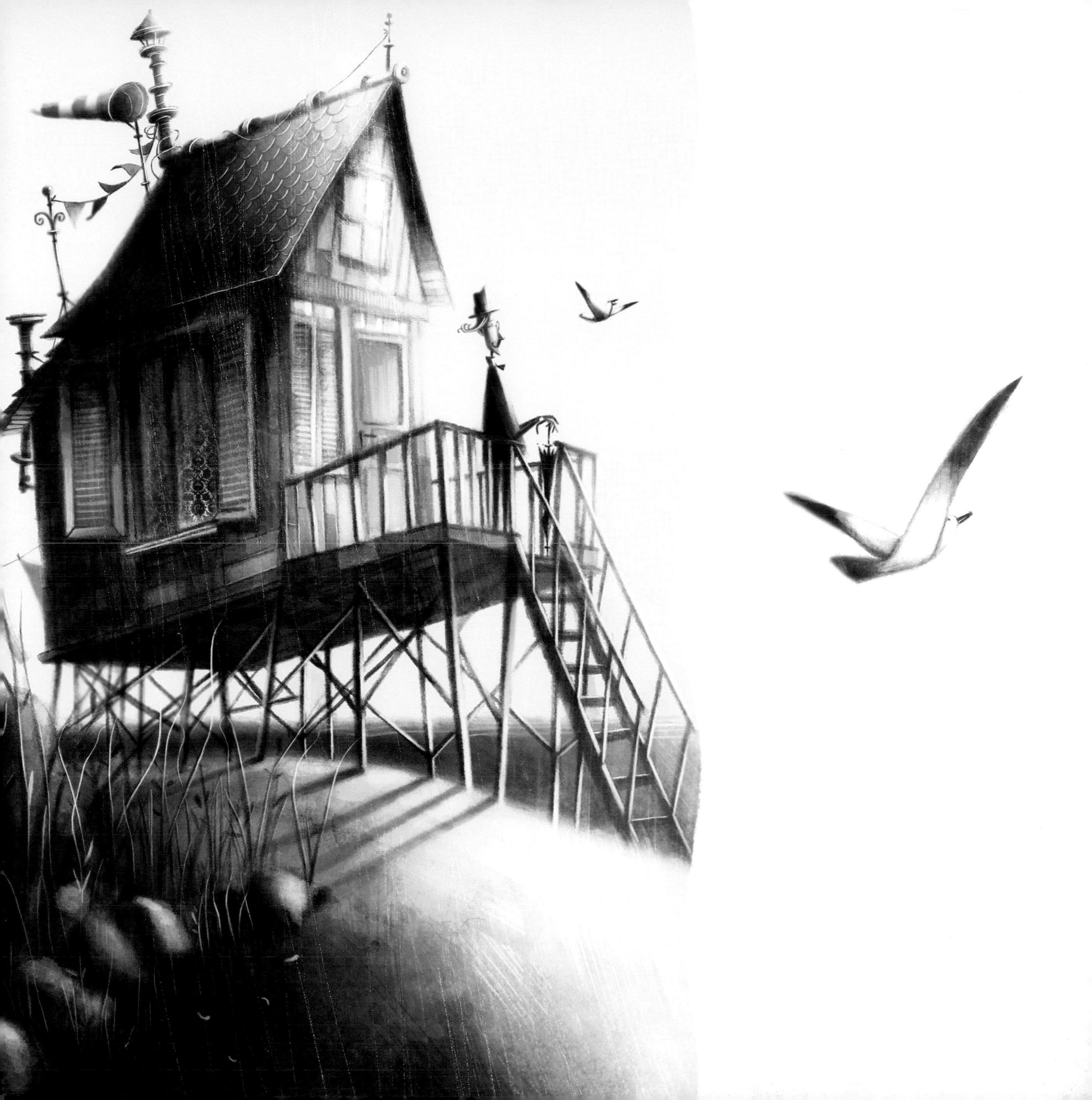

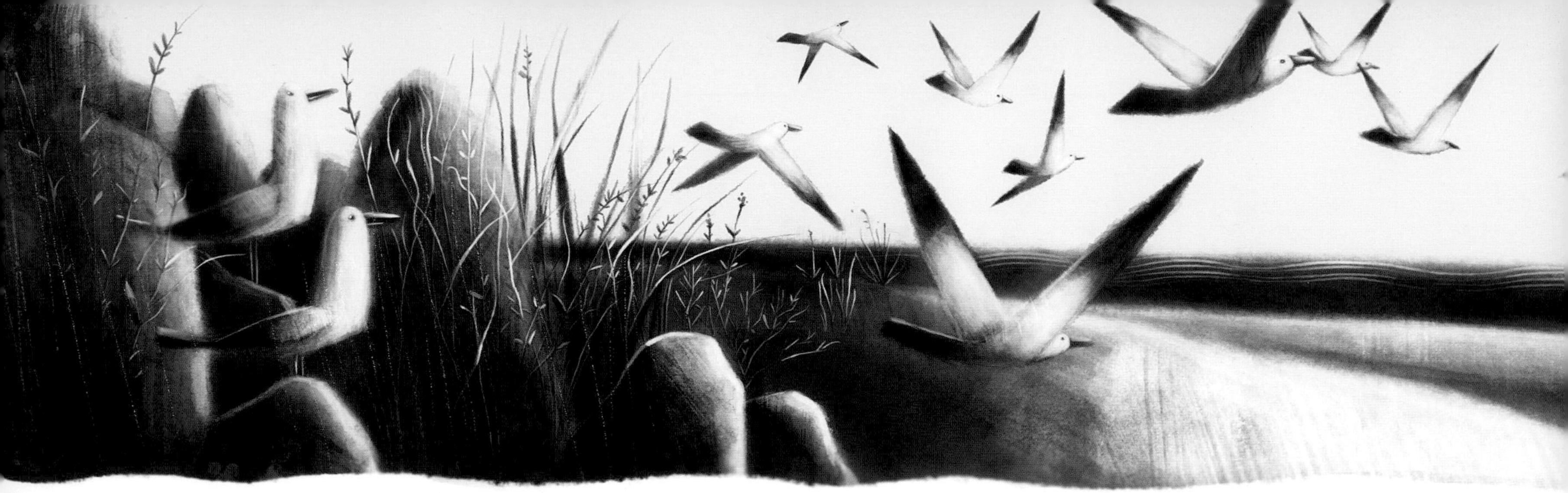

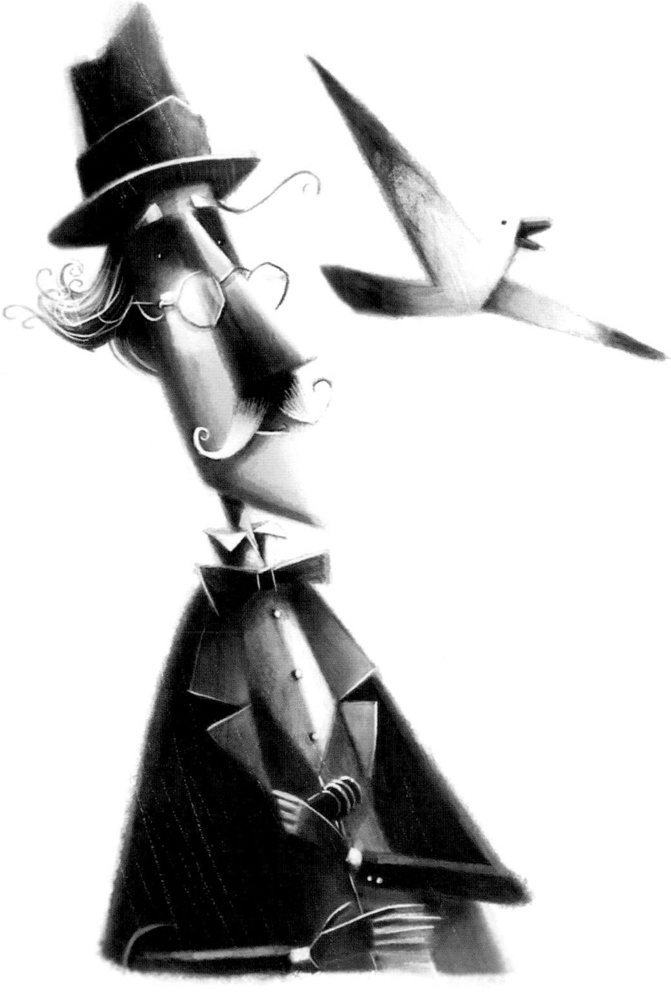

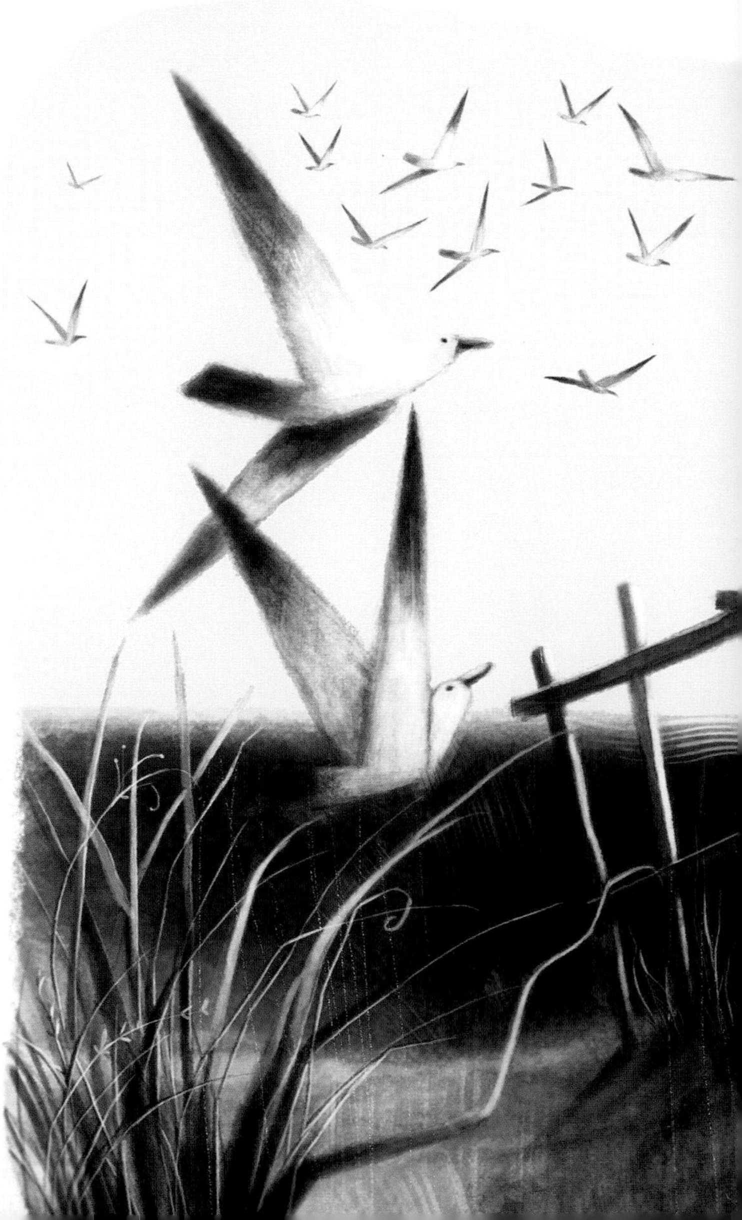

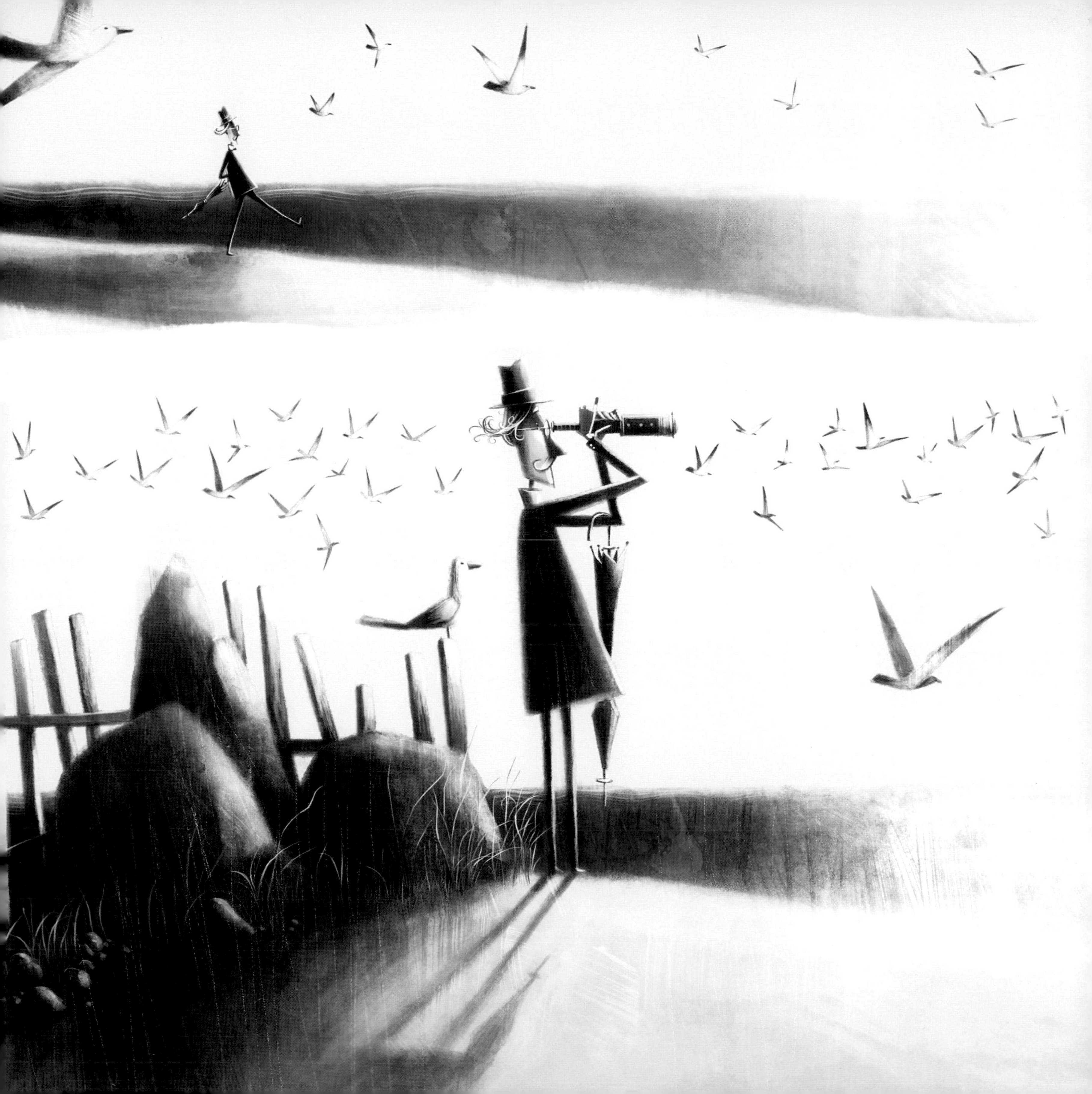

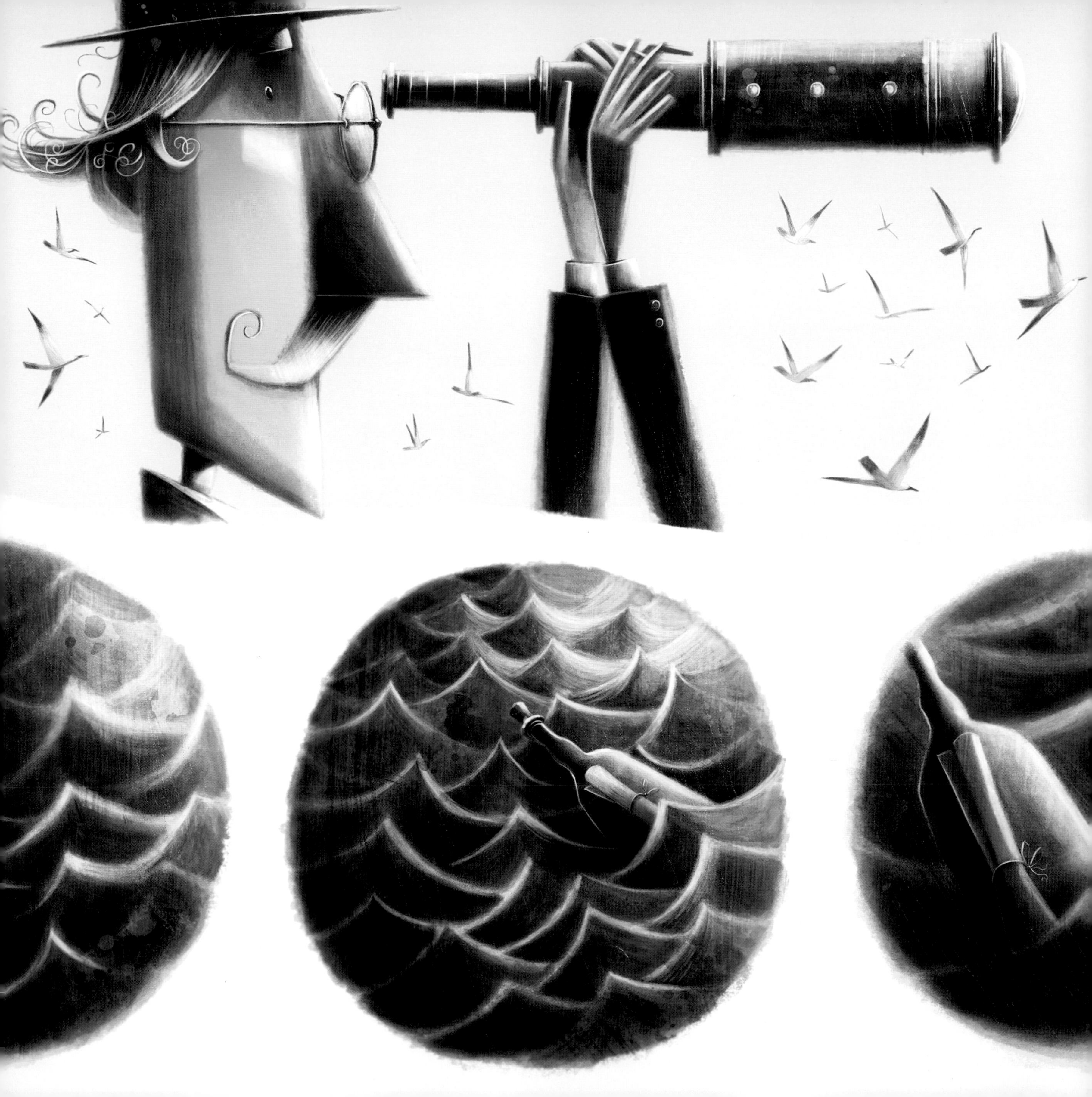

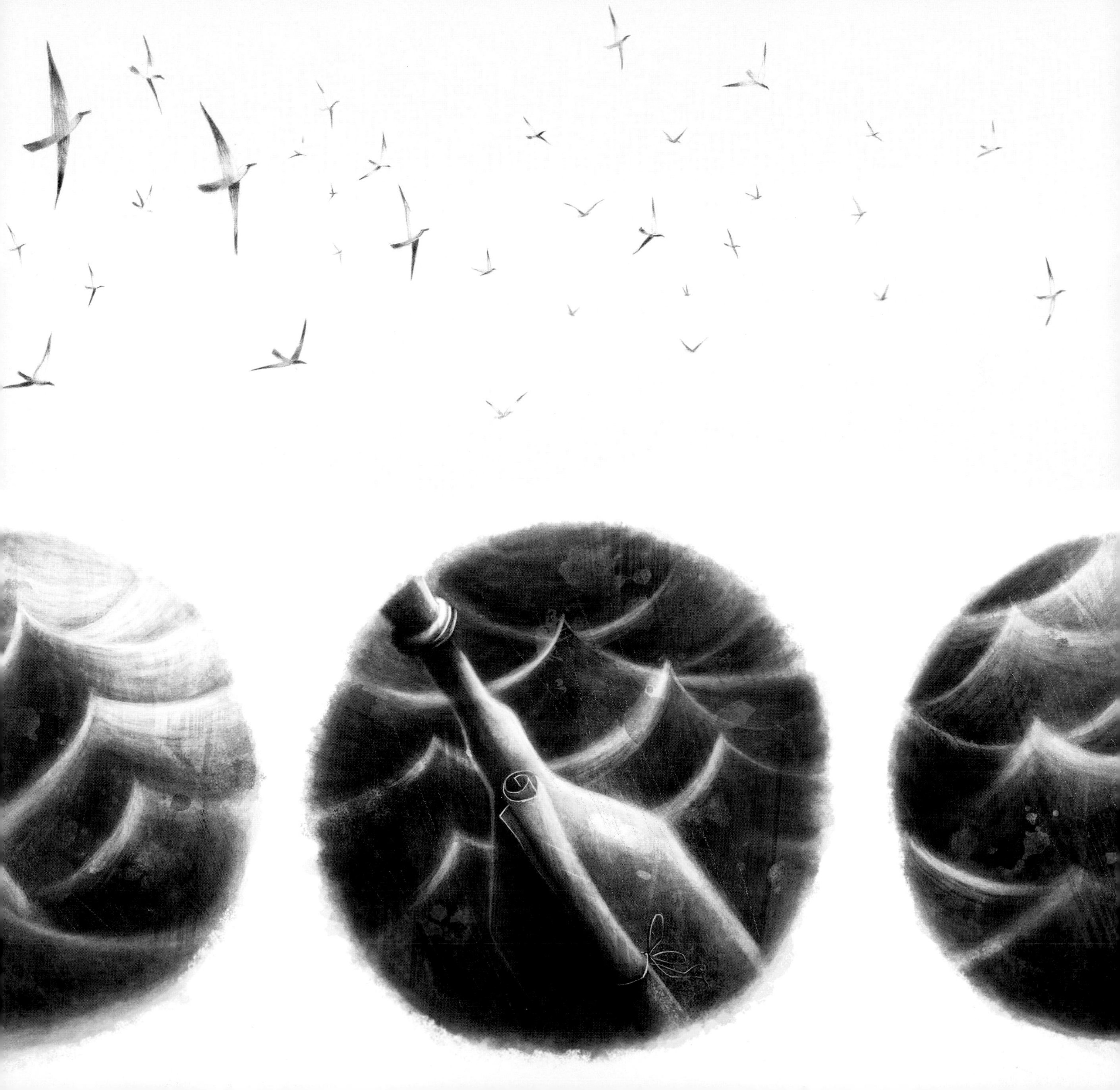

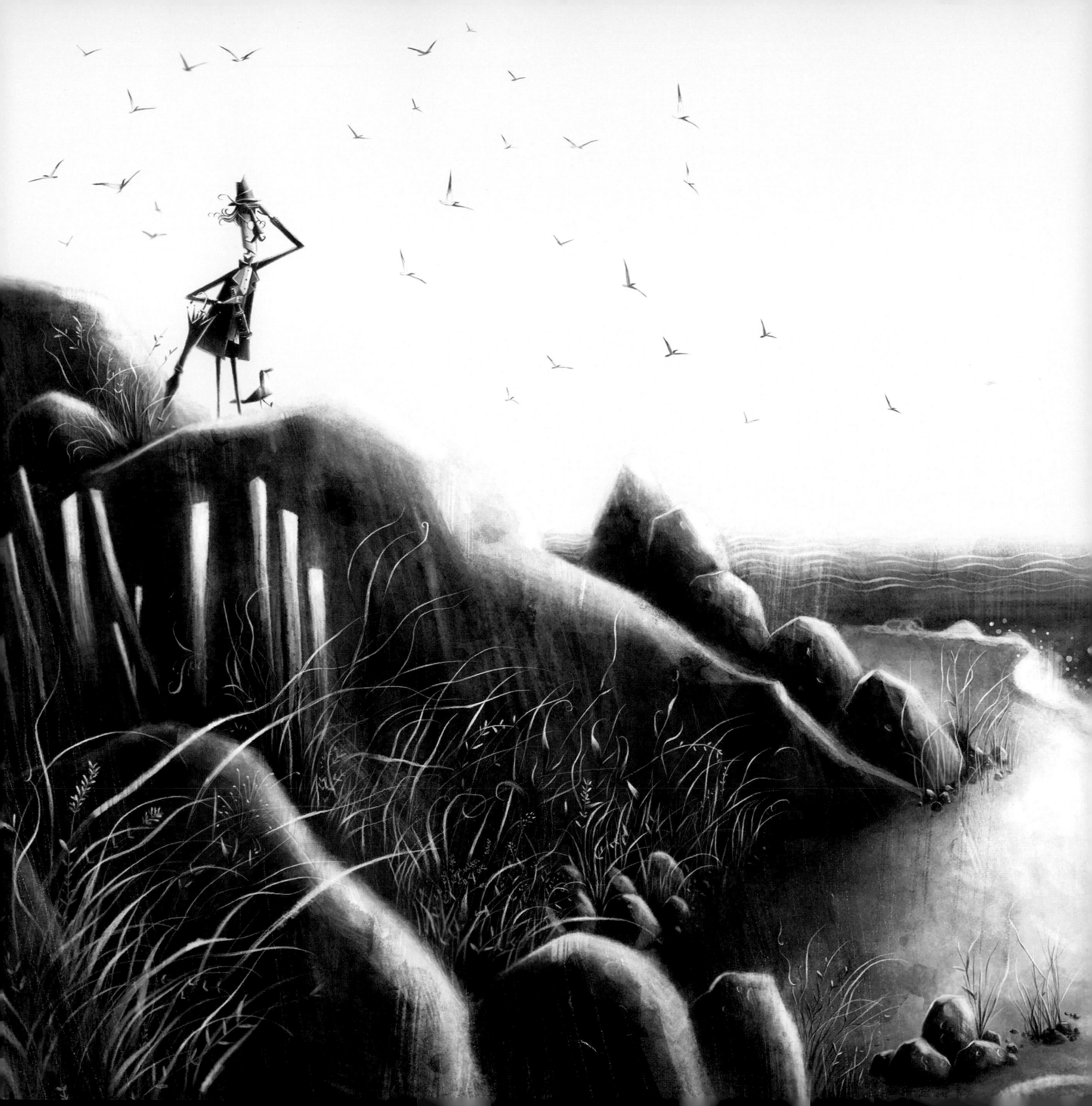

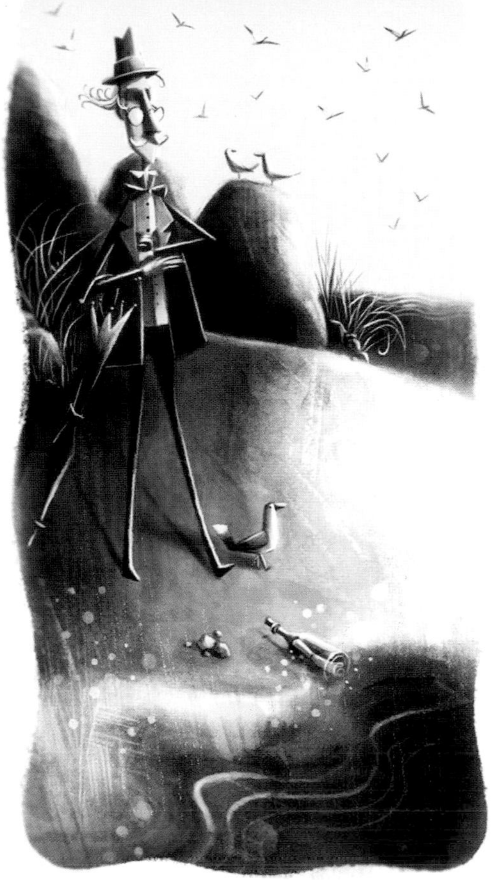
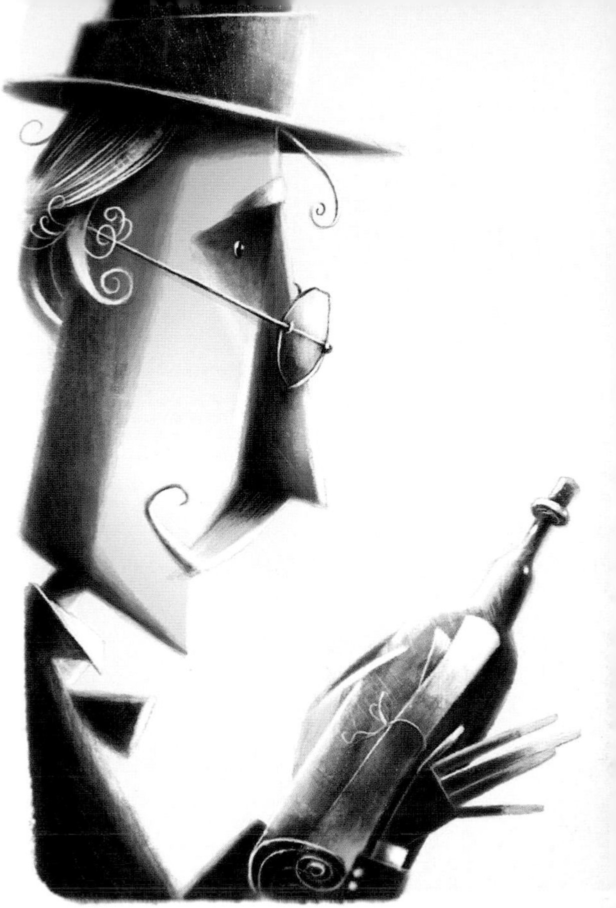
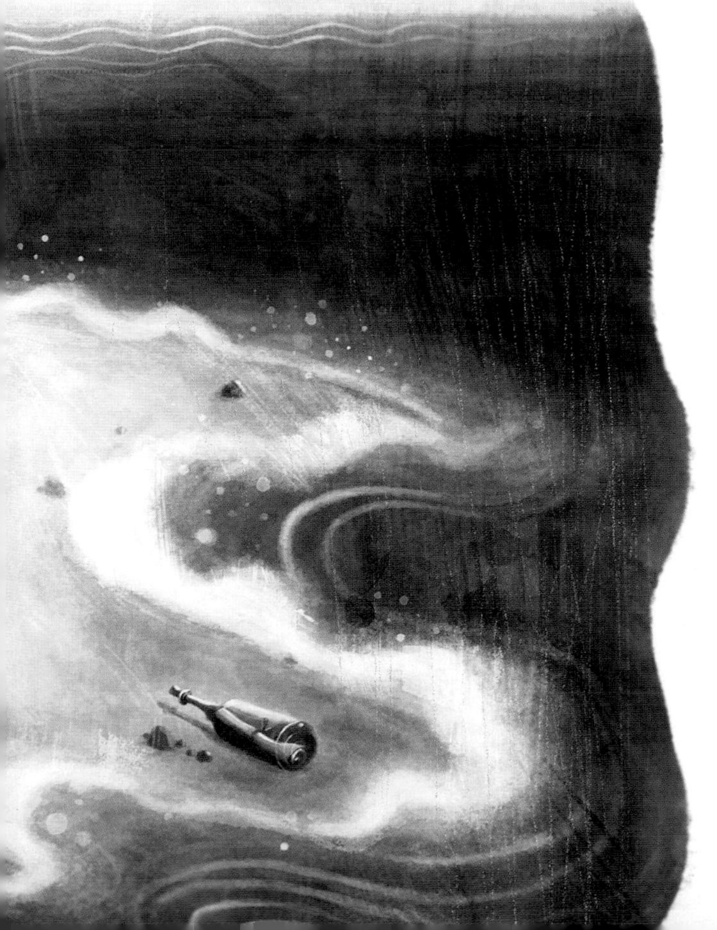
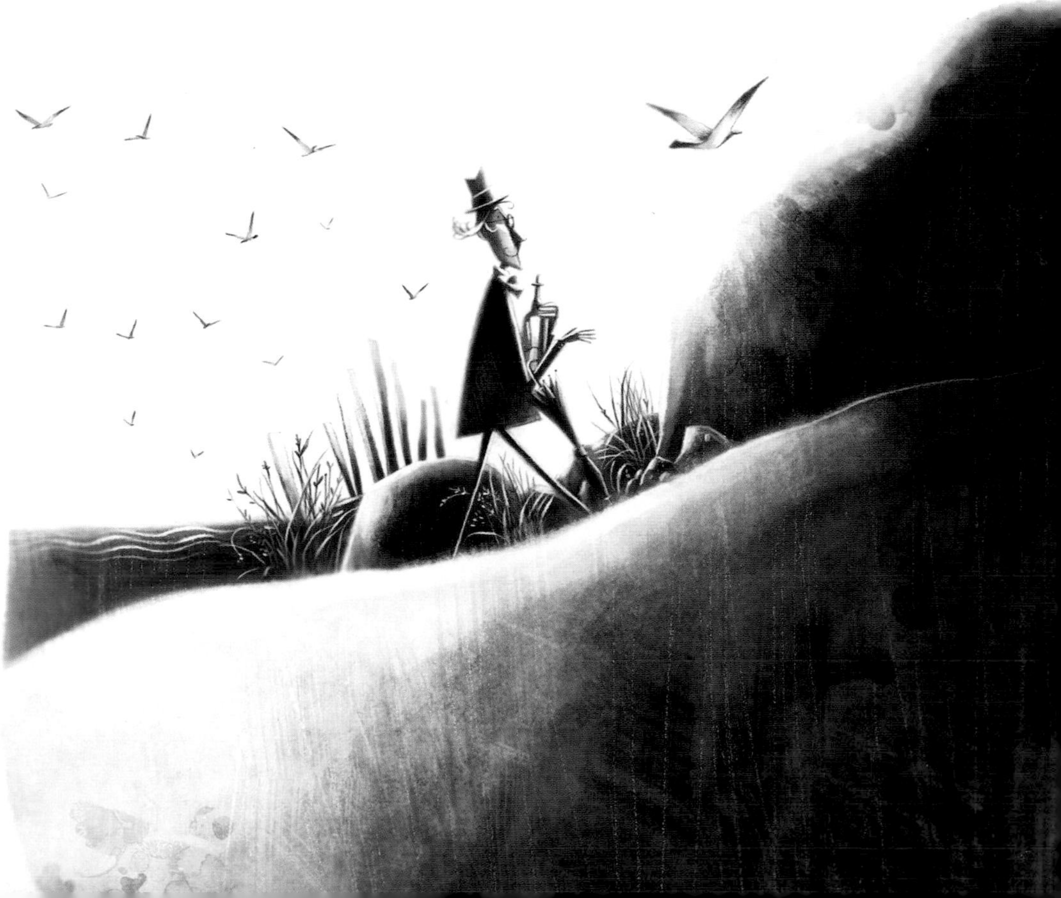

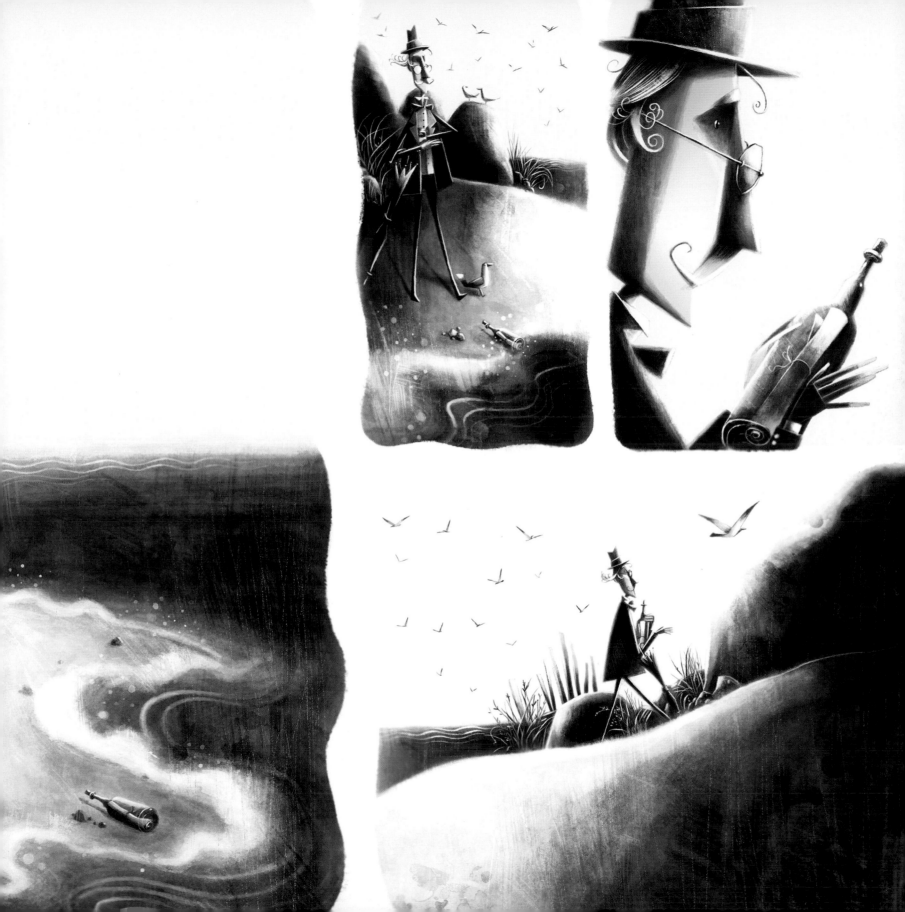

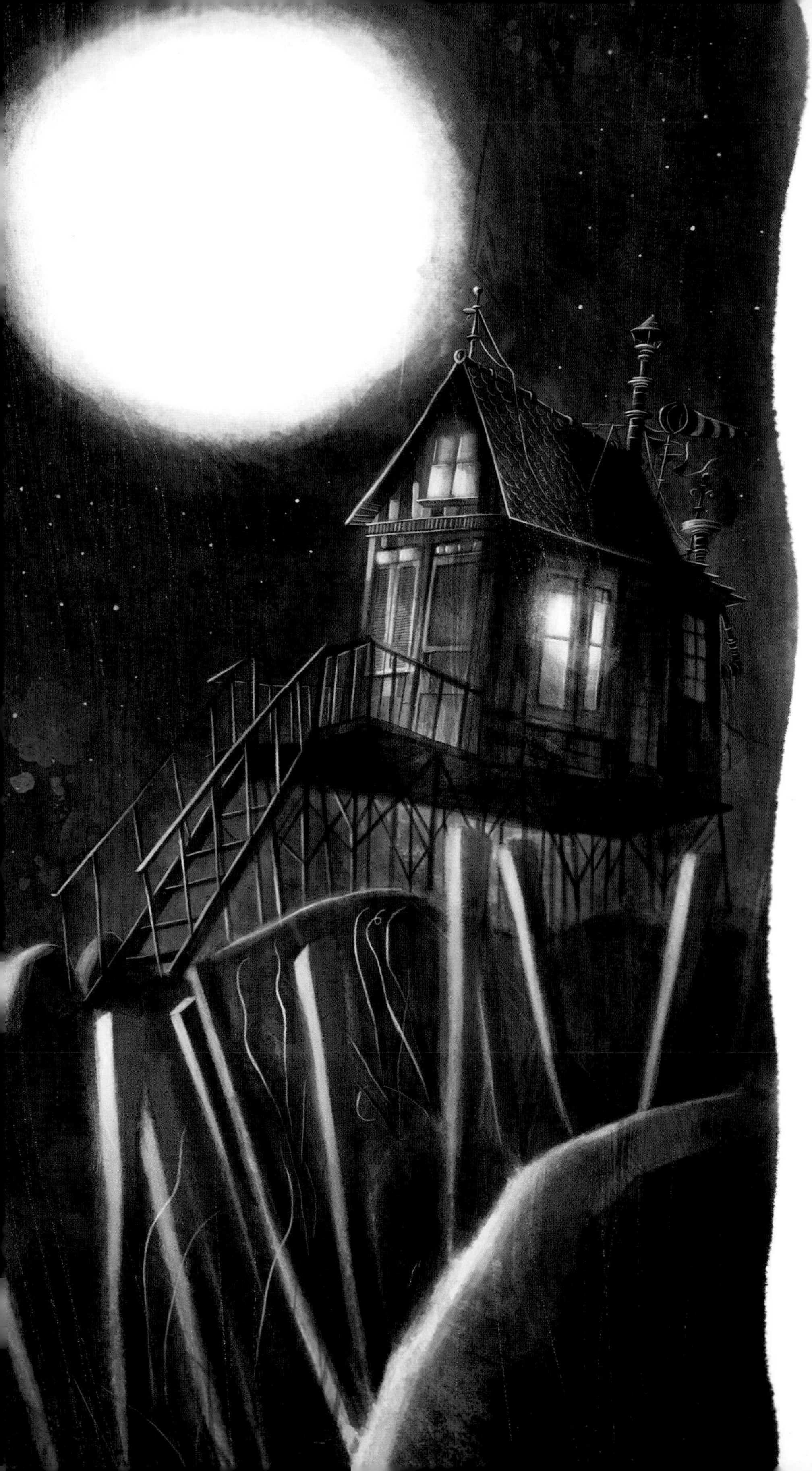

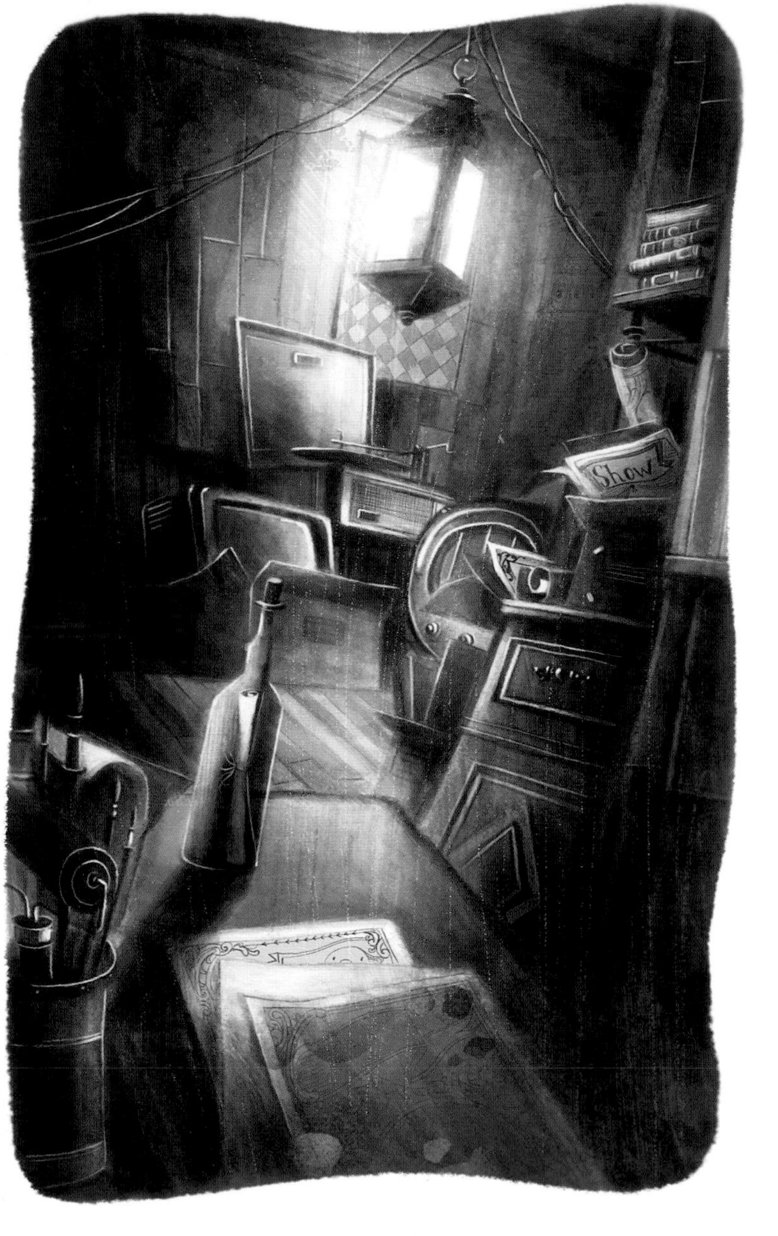
Show

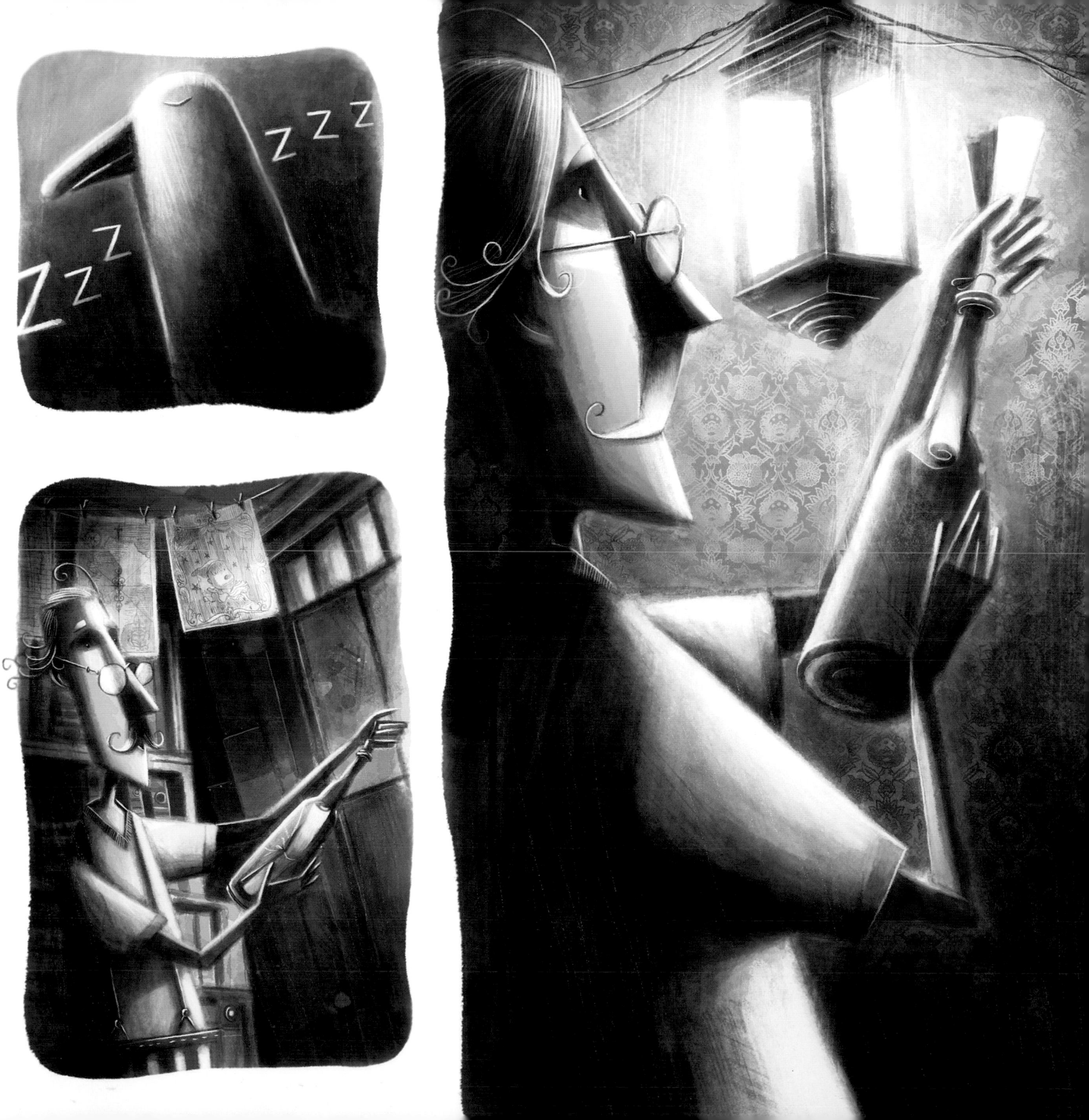
ZZZ
ZZZ

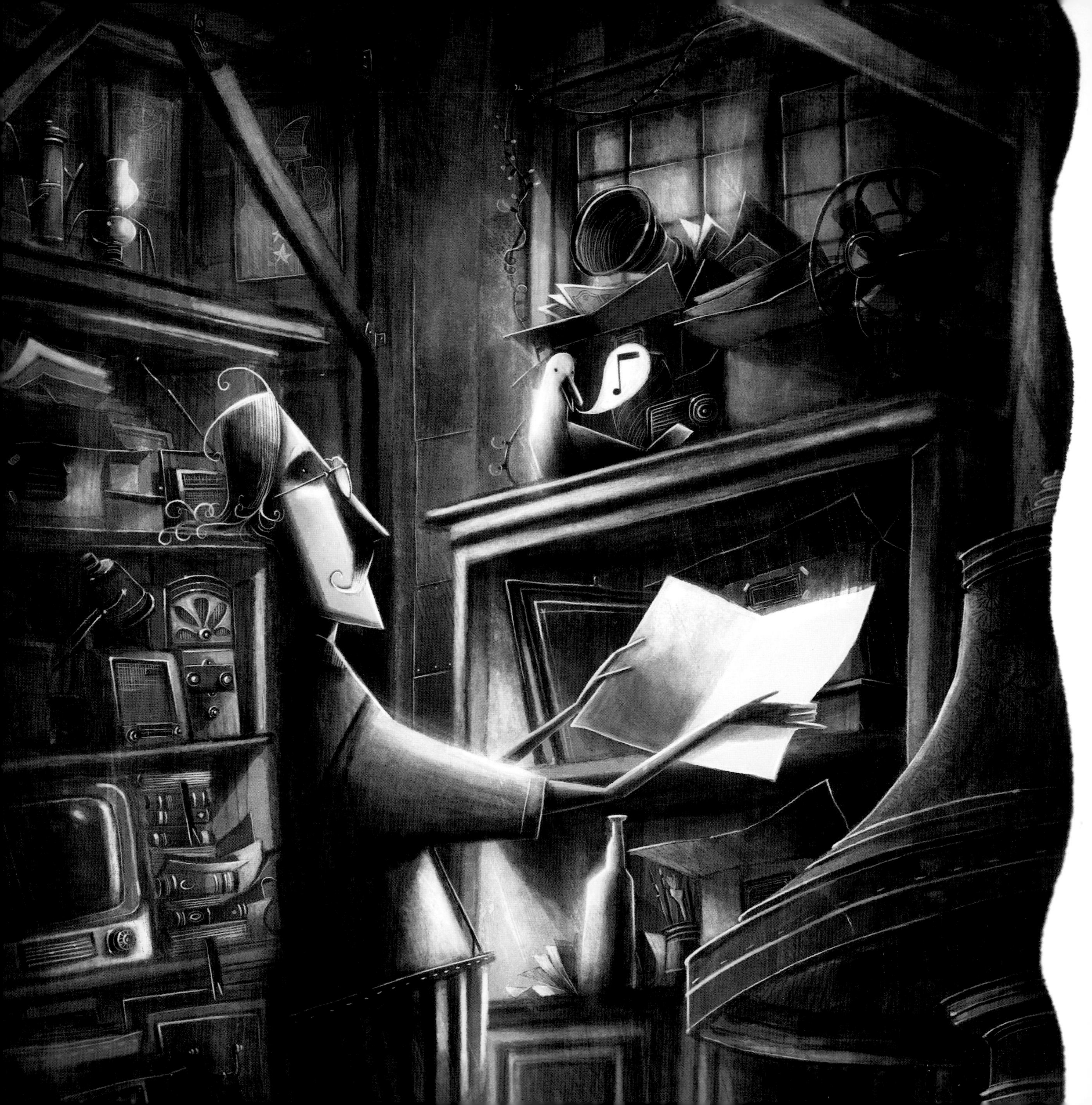

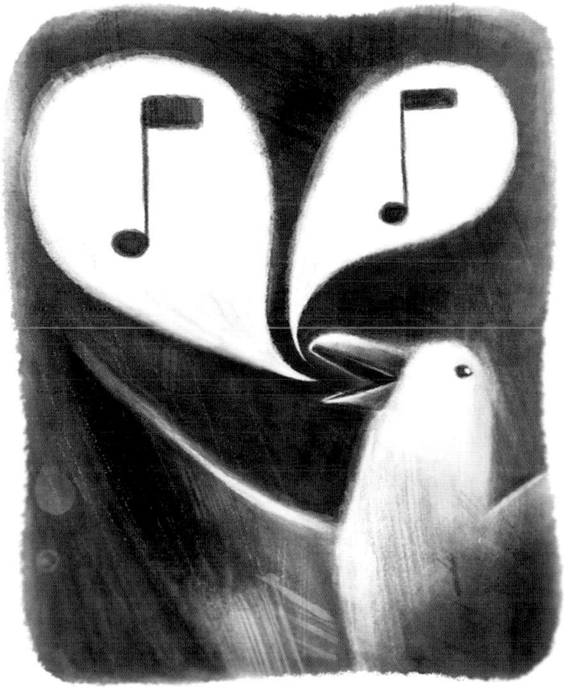

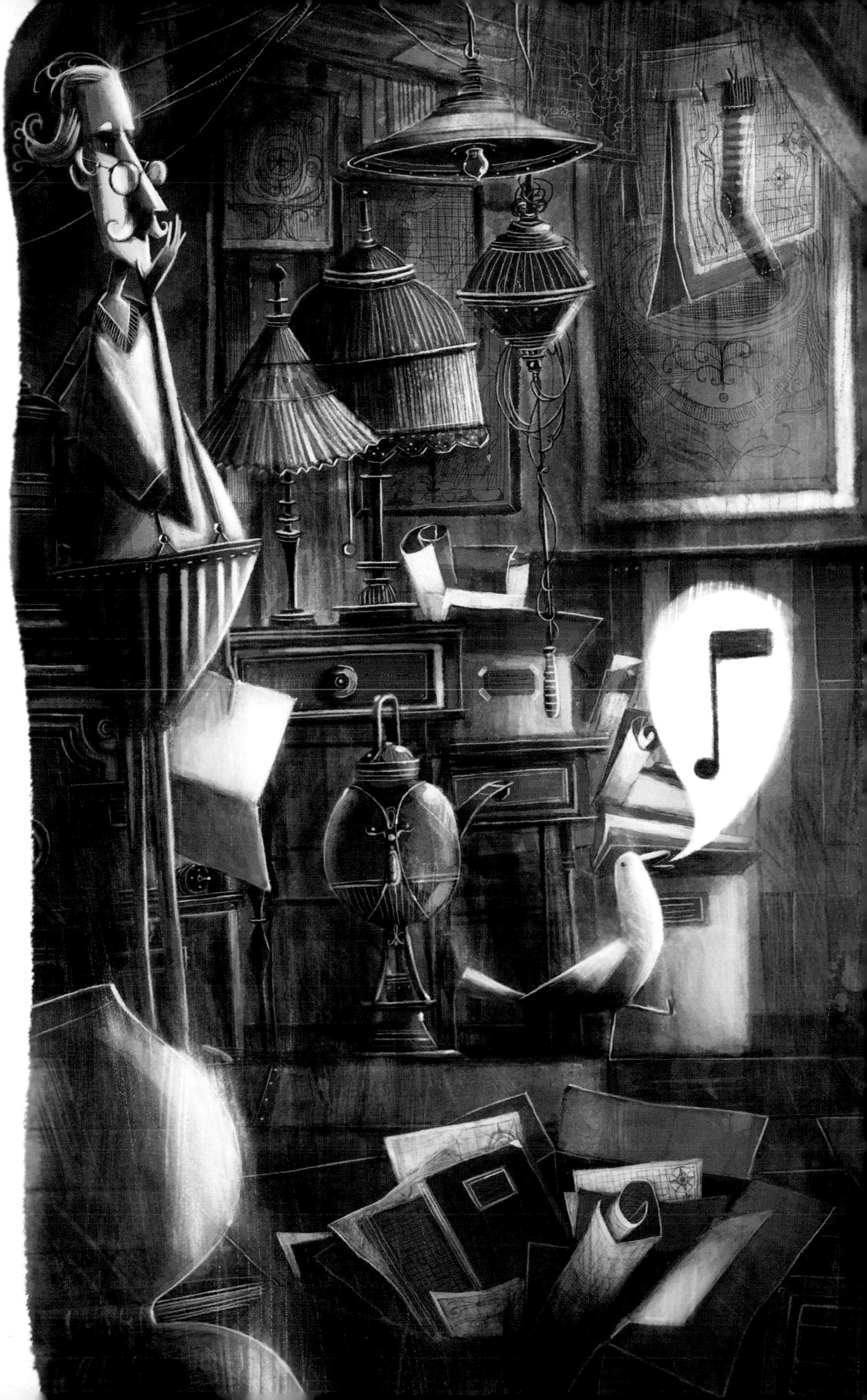

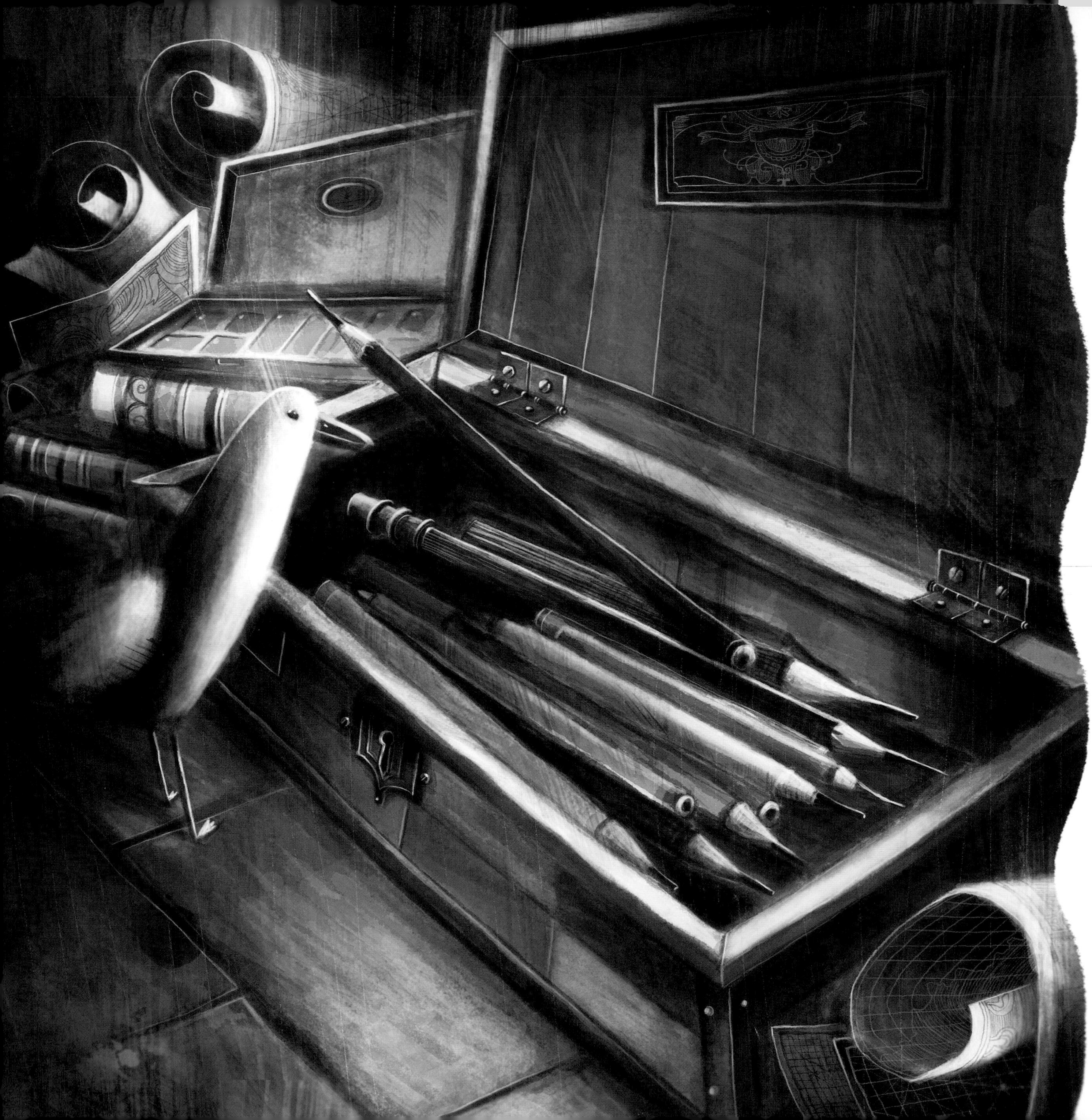

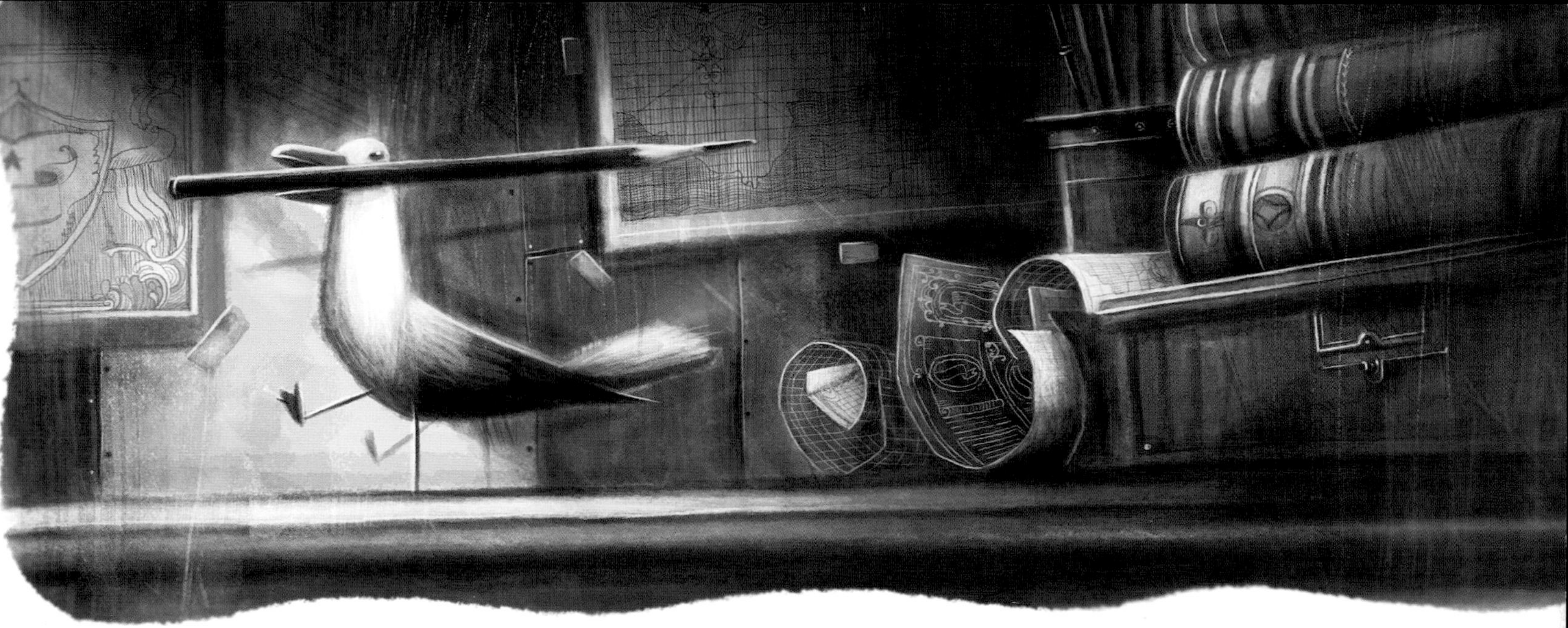

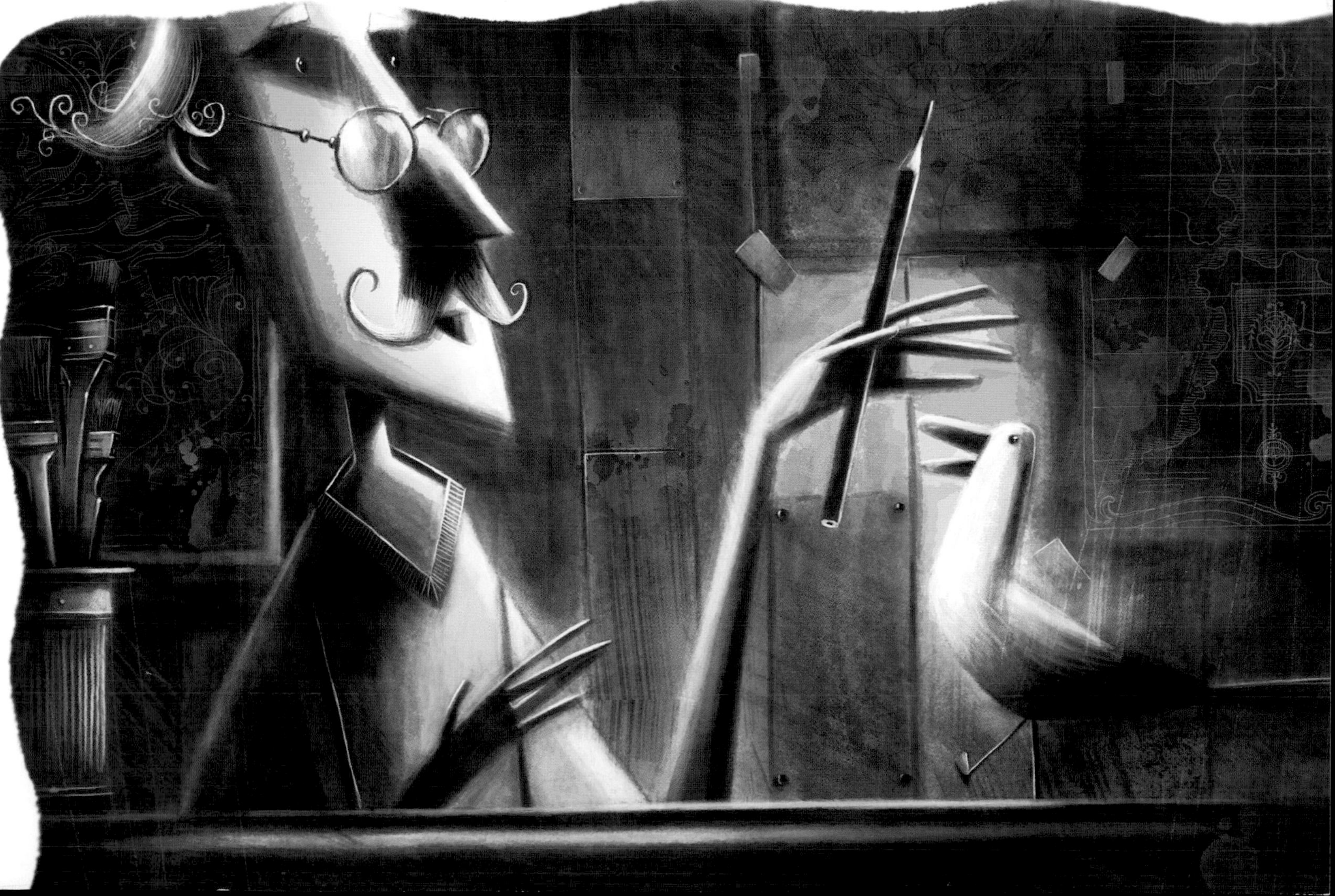

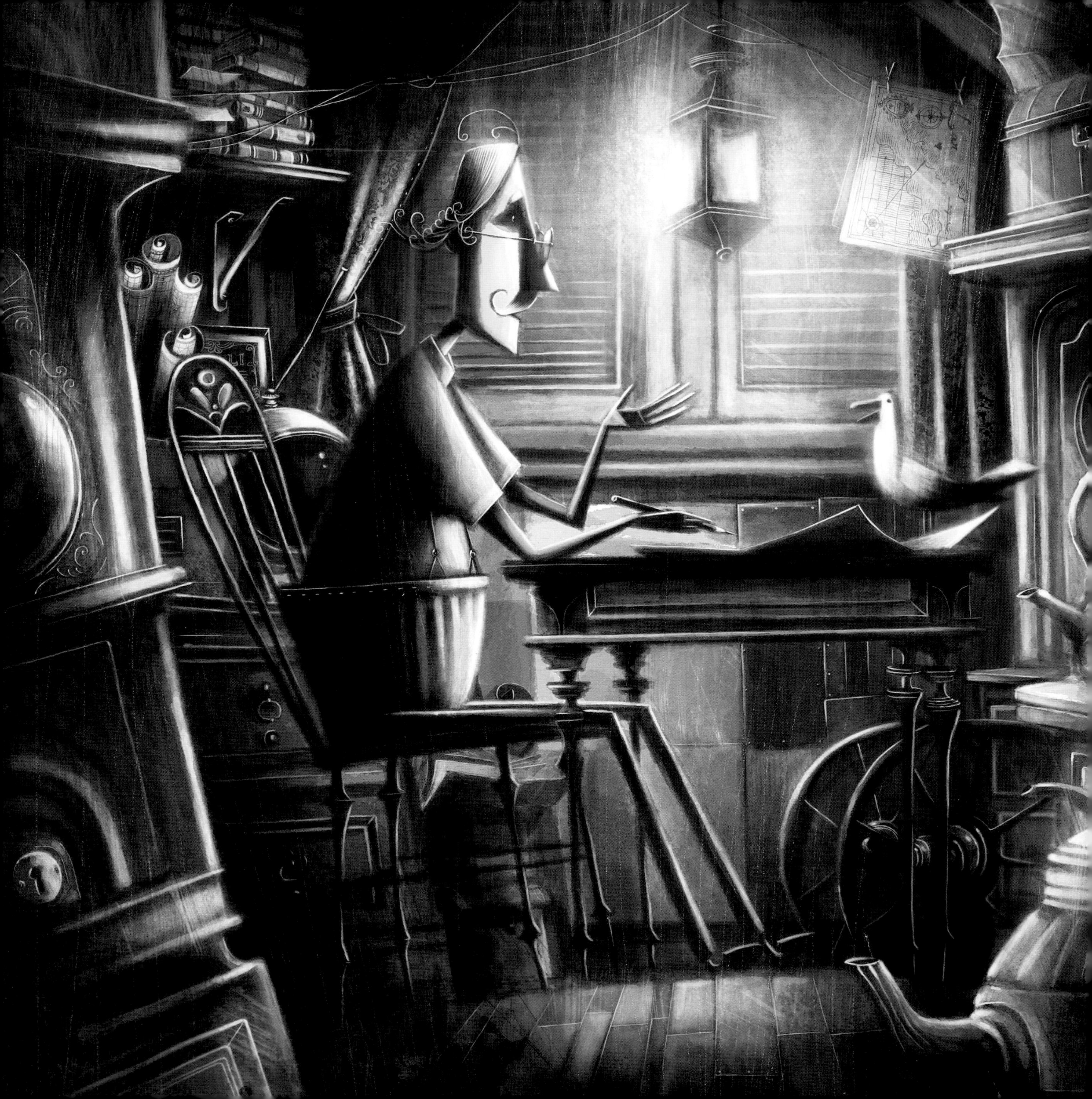

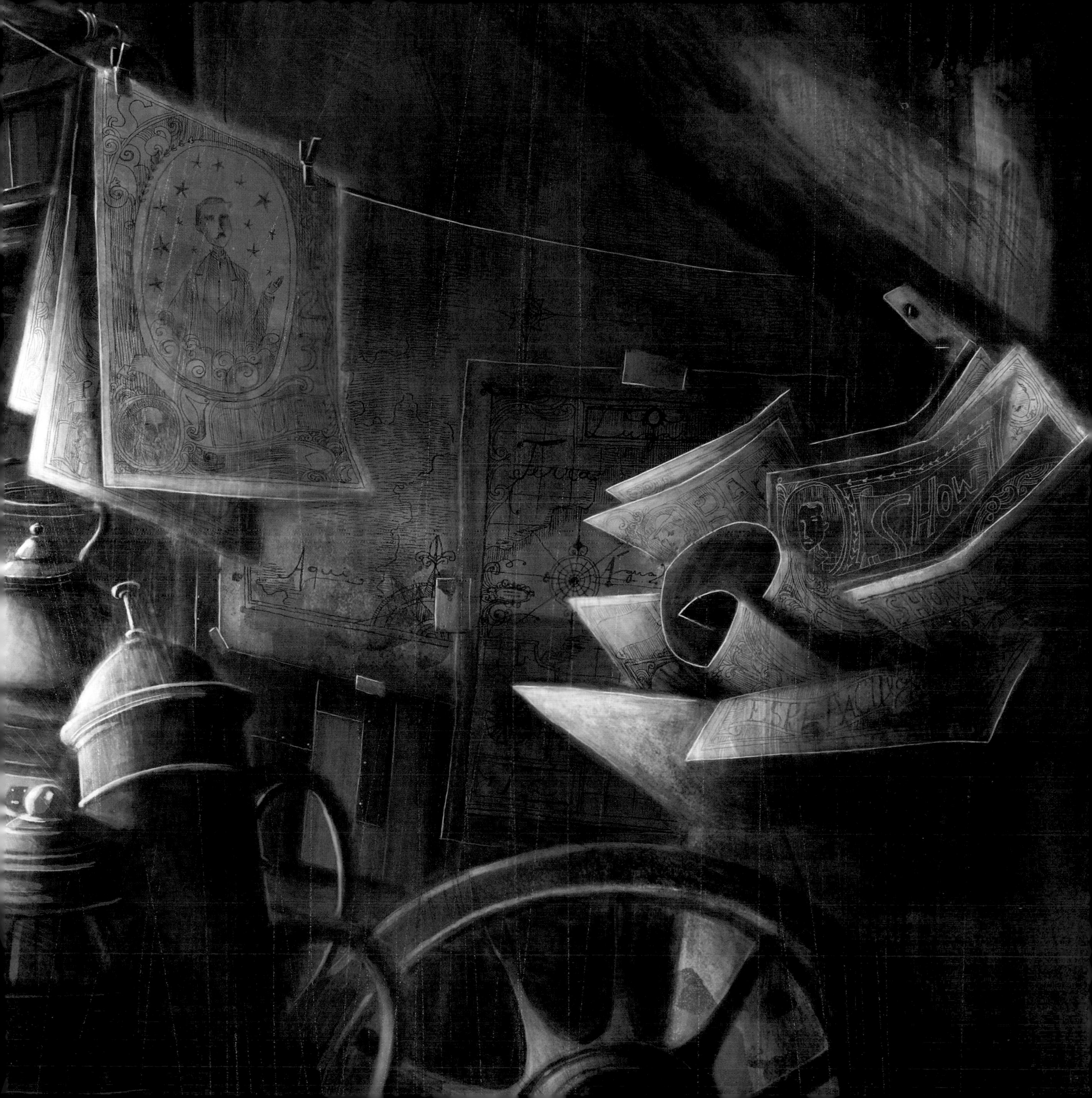

Tierra
Agua
SHOW

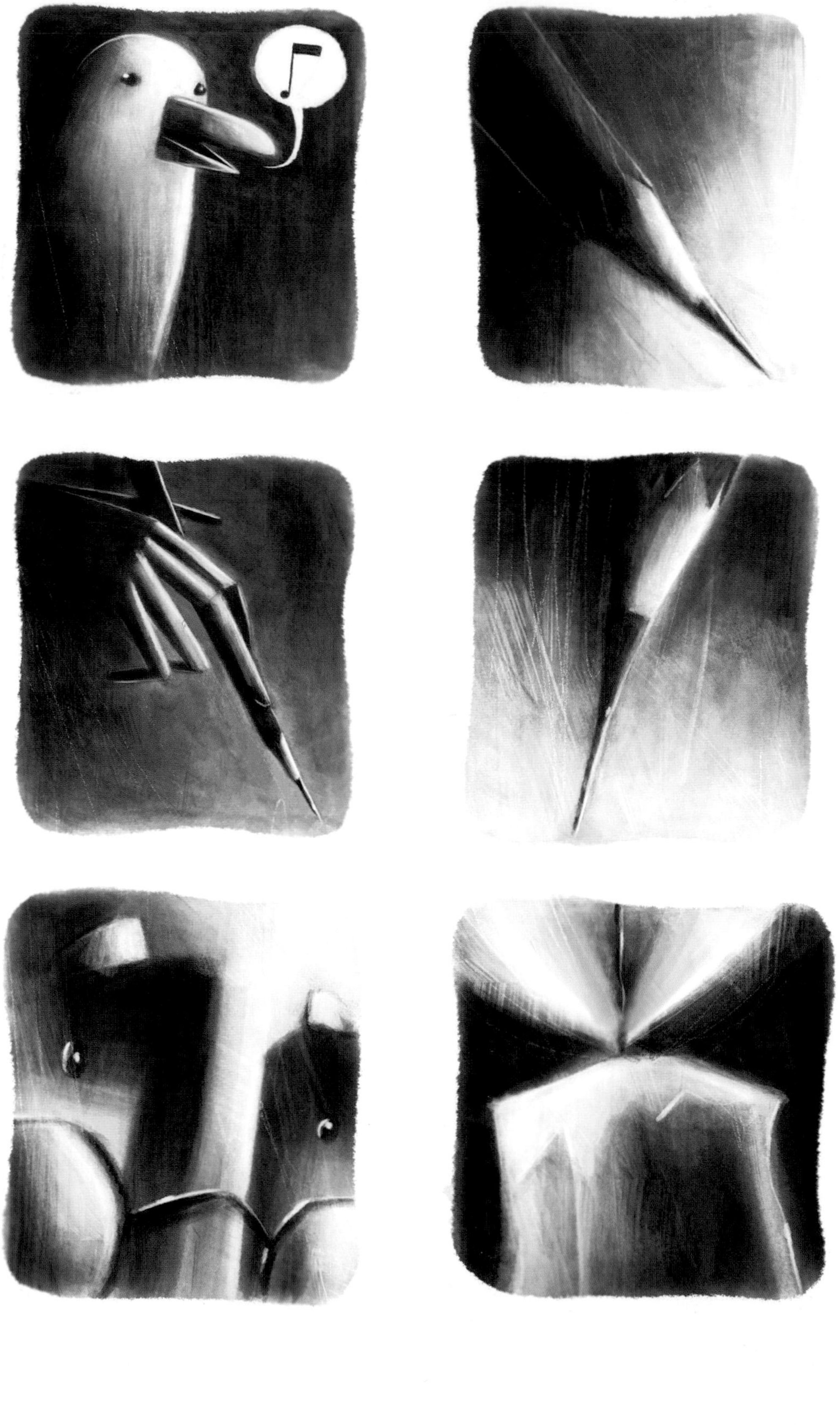

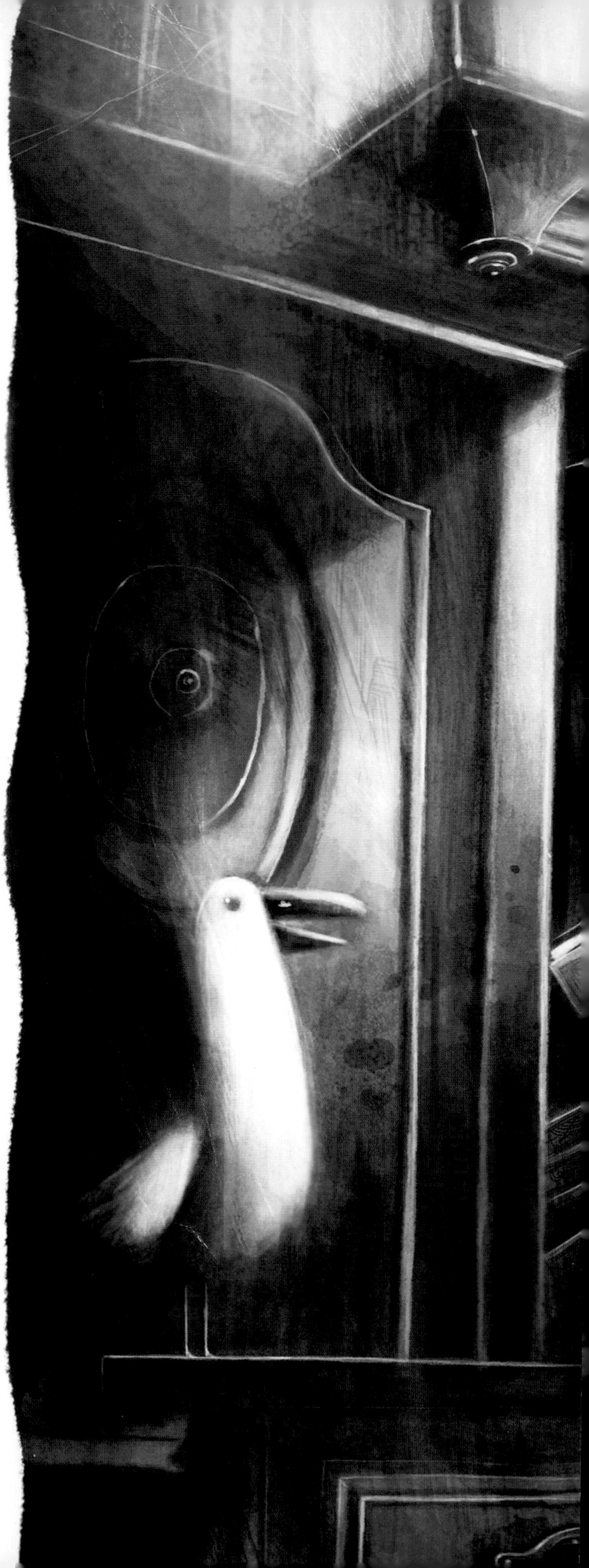

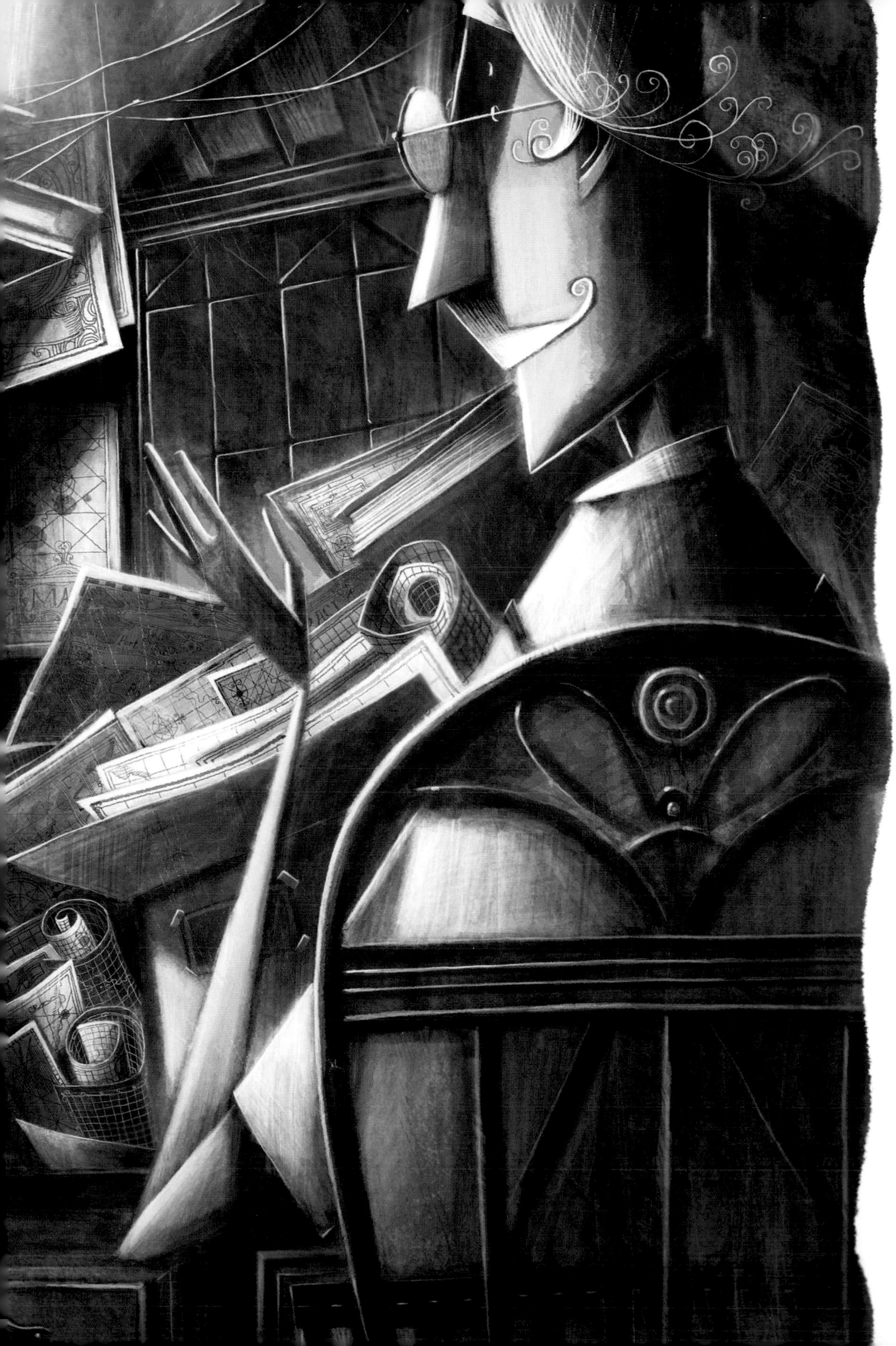
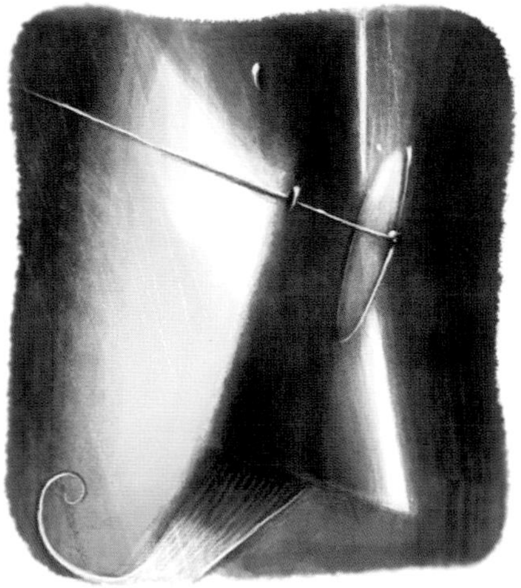
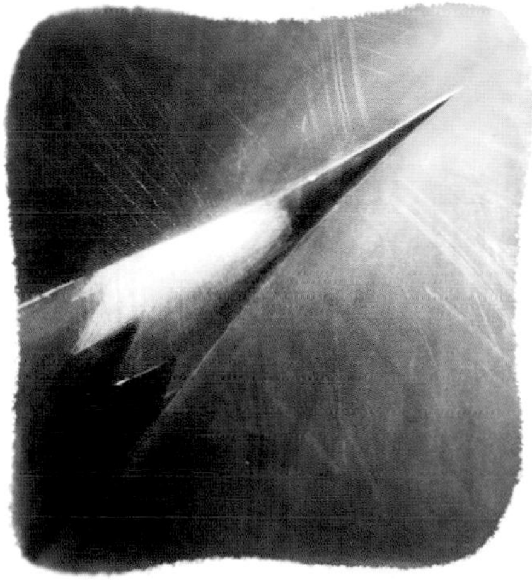
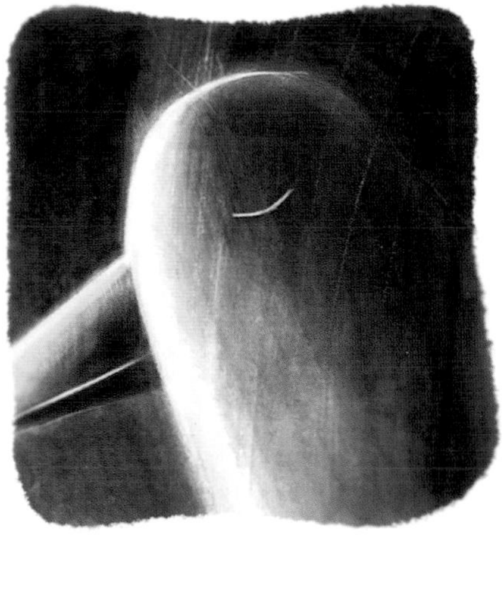

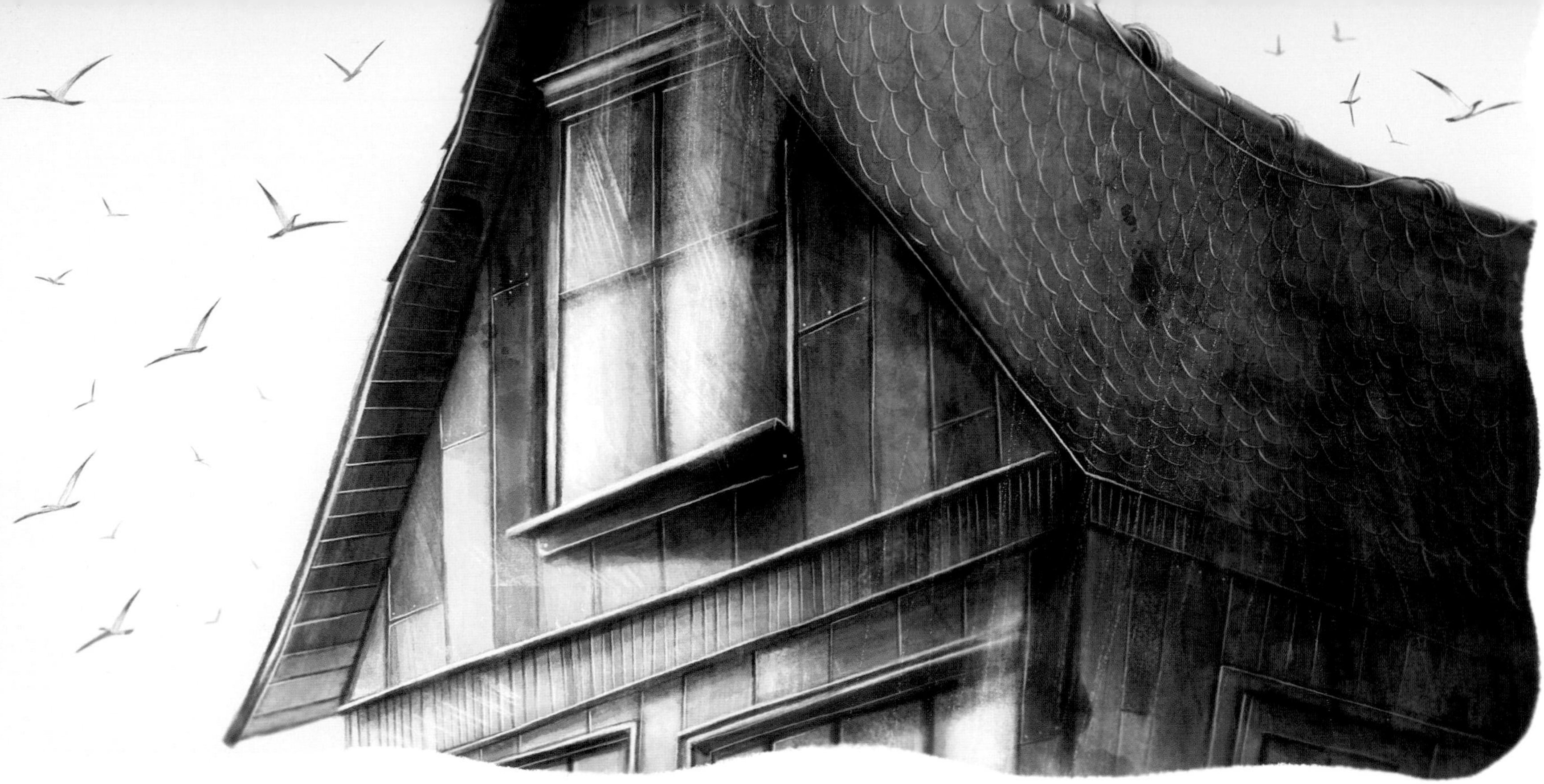

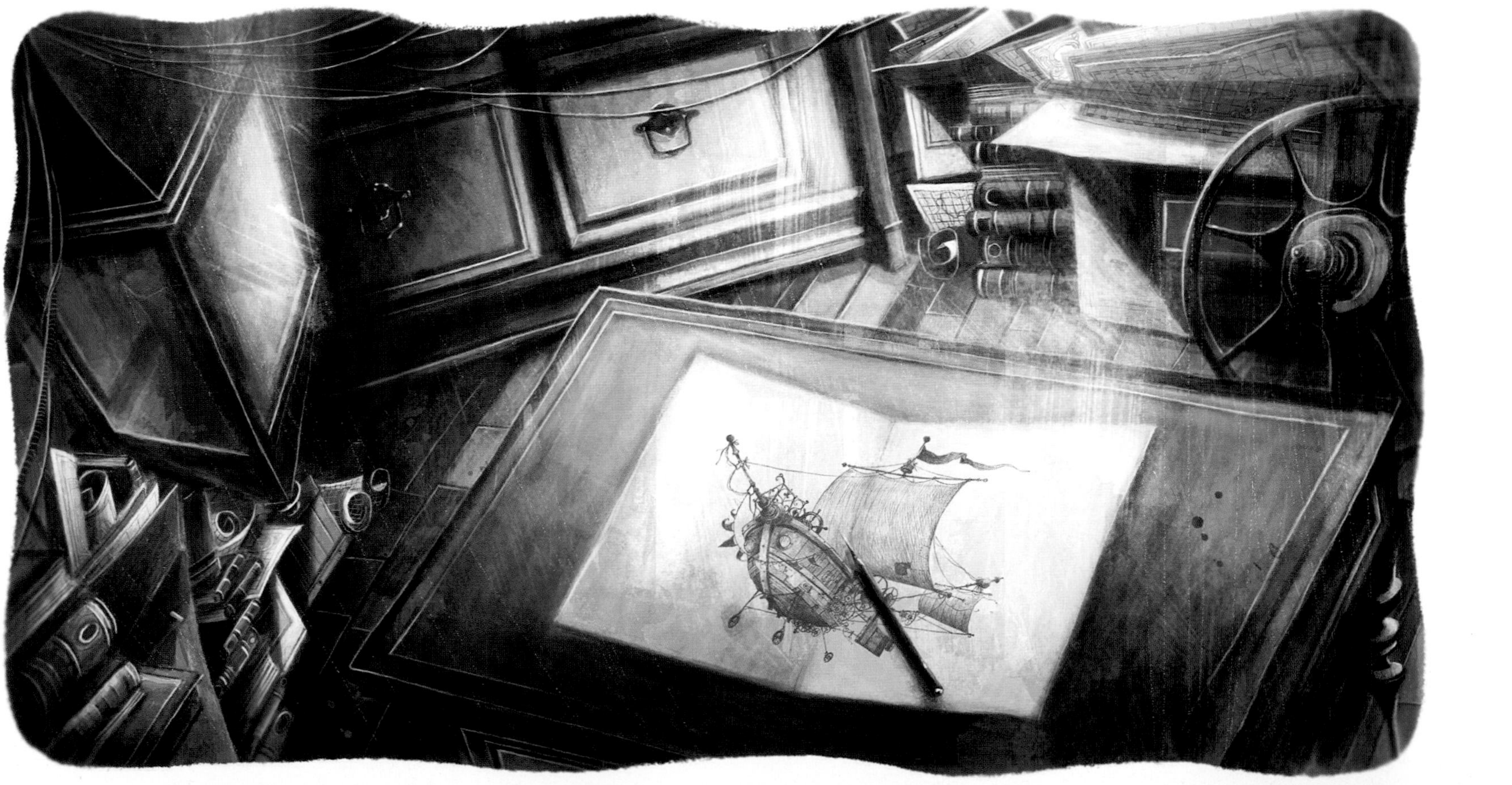

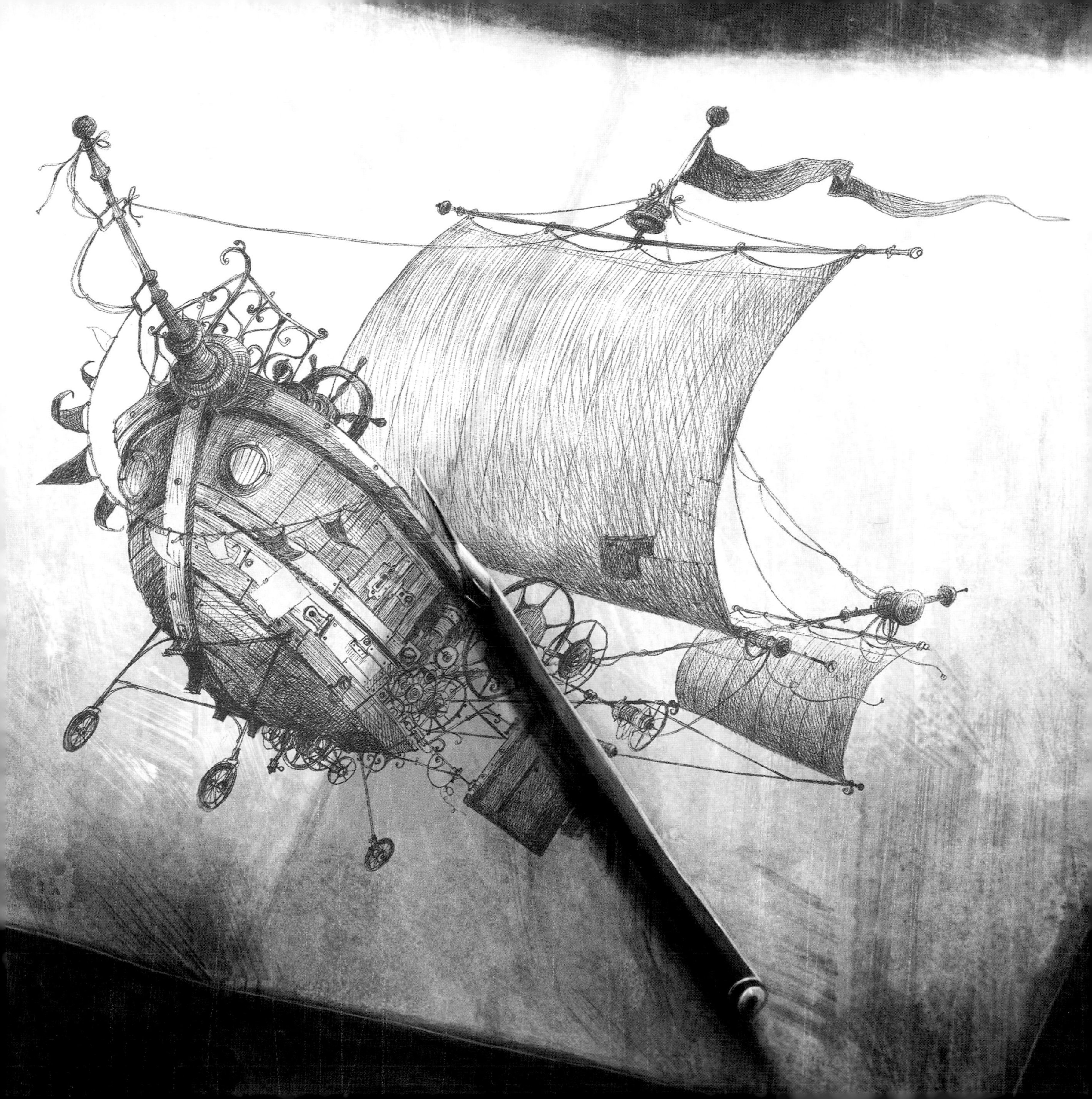

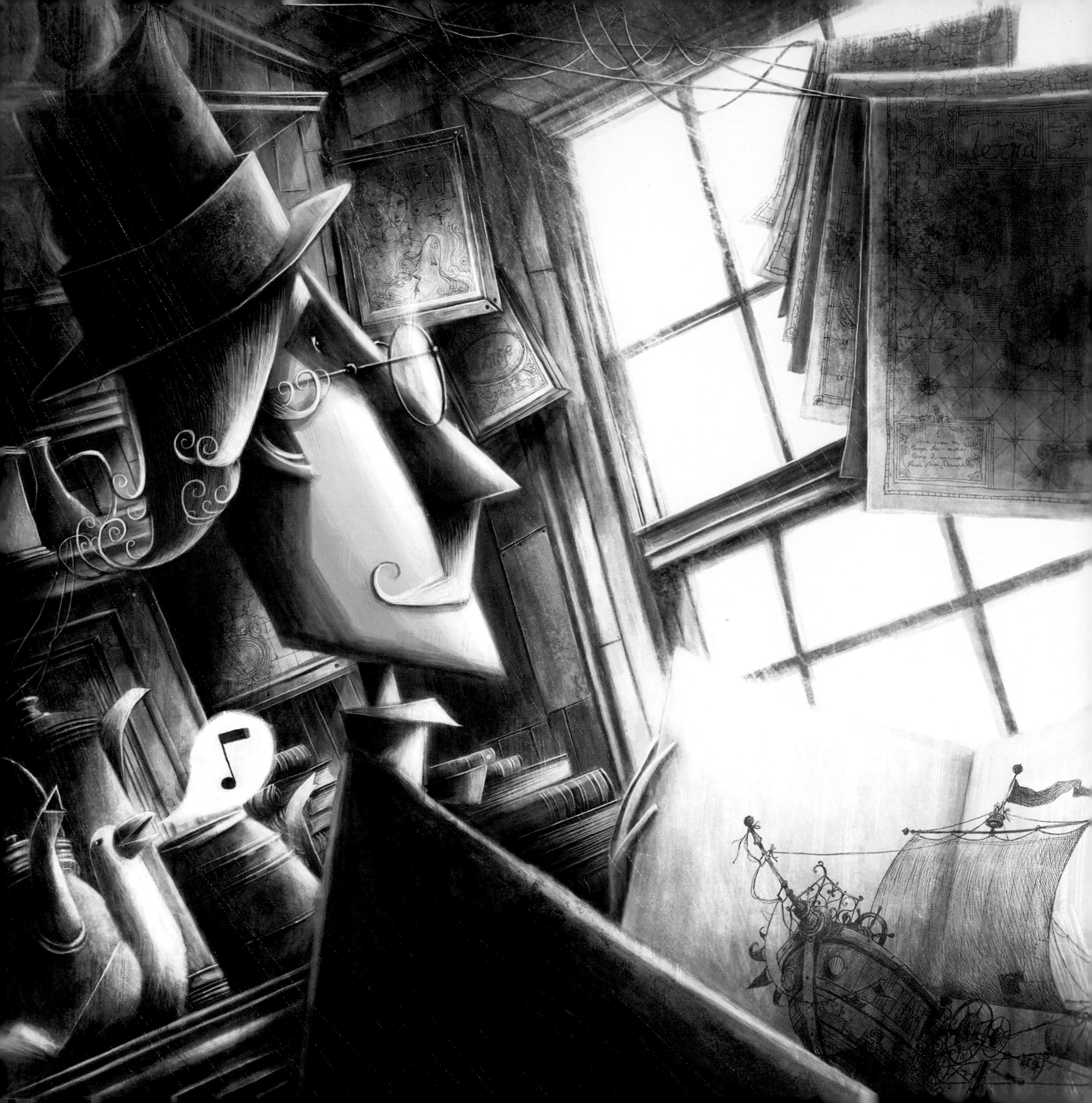
Terra
MAR

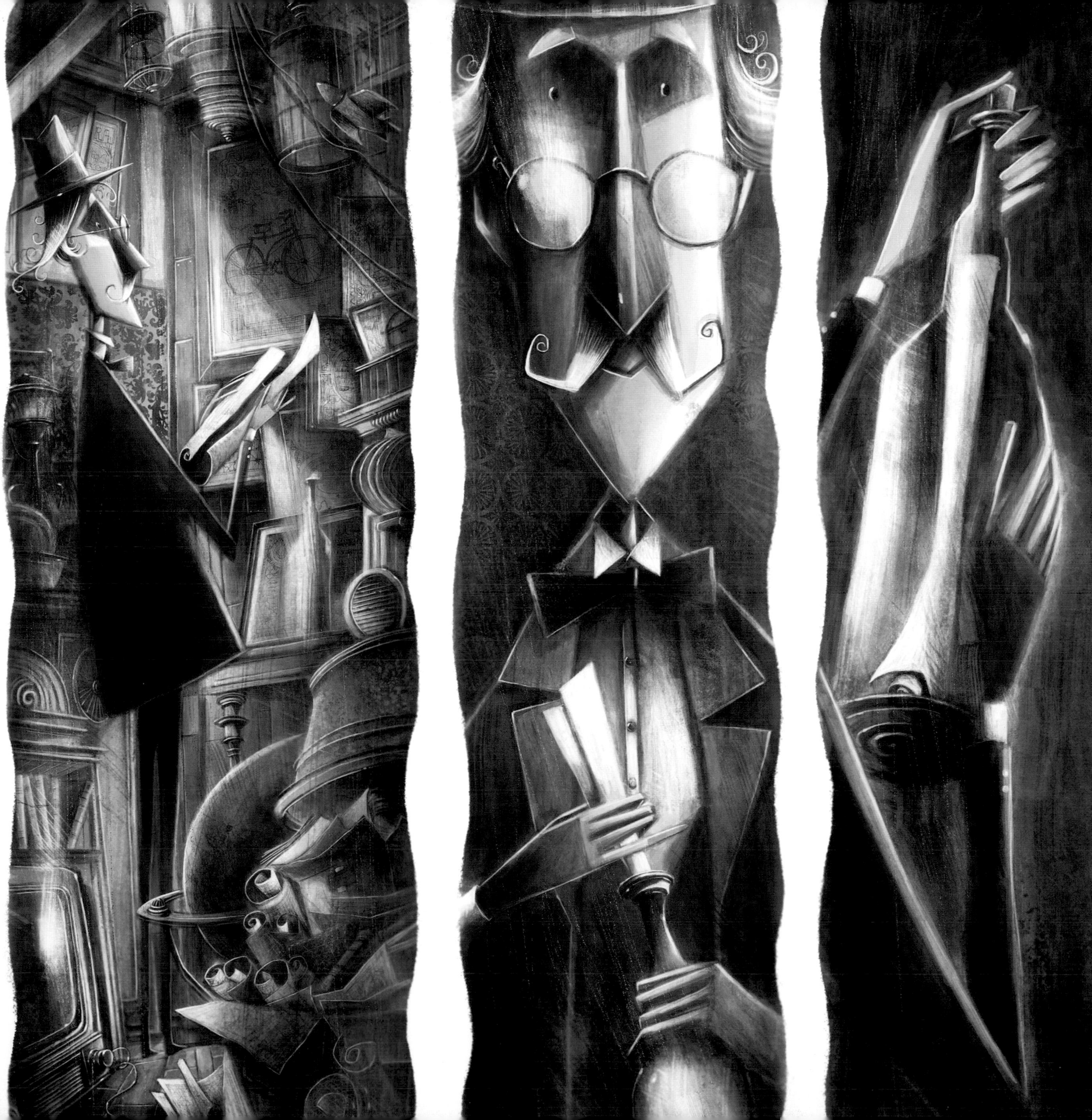

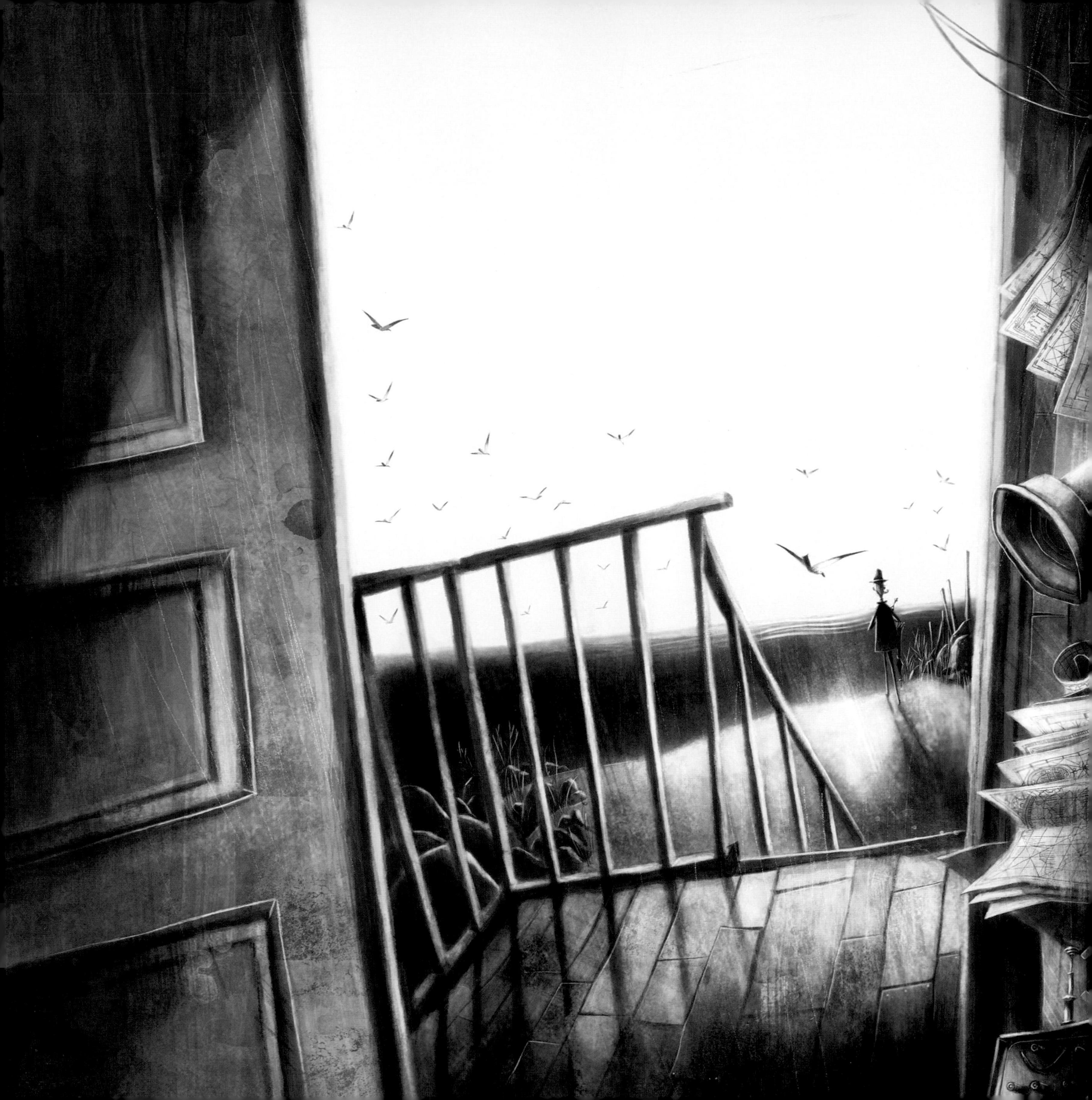

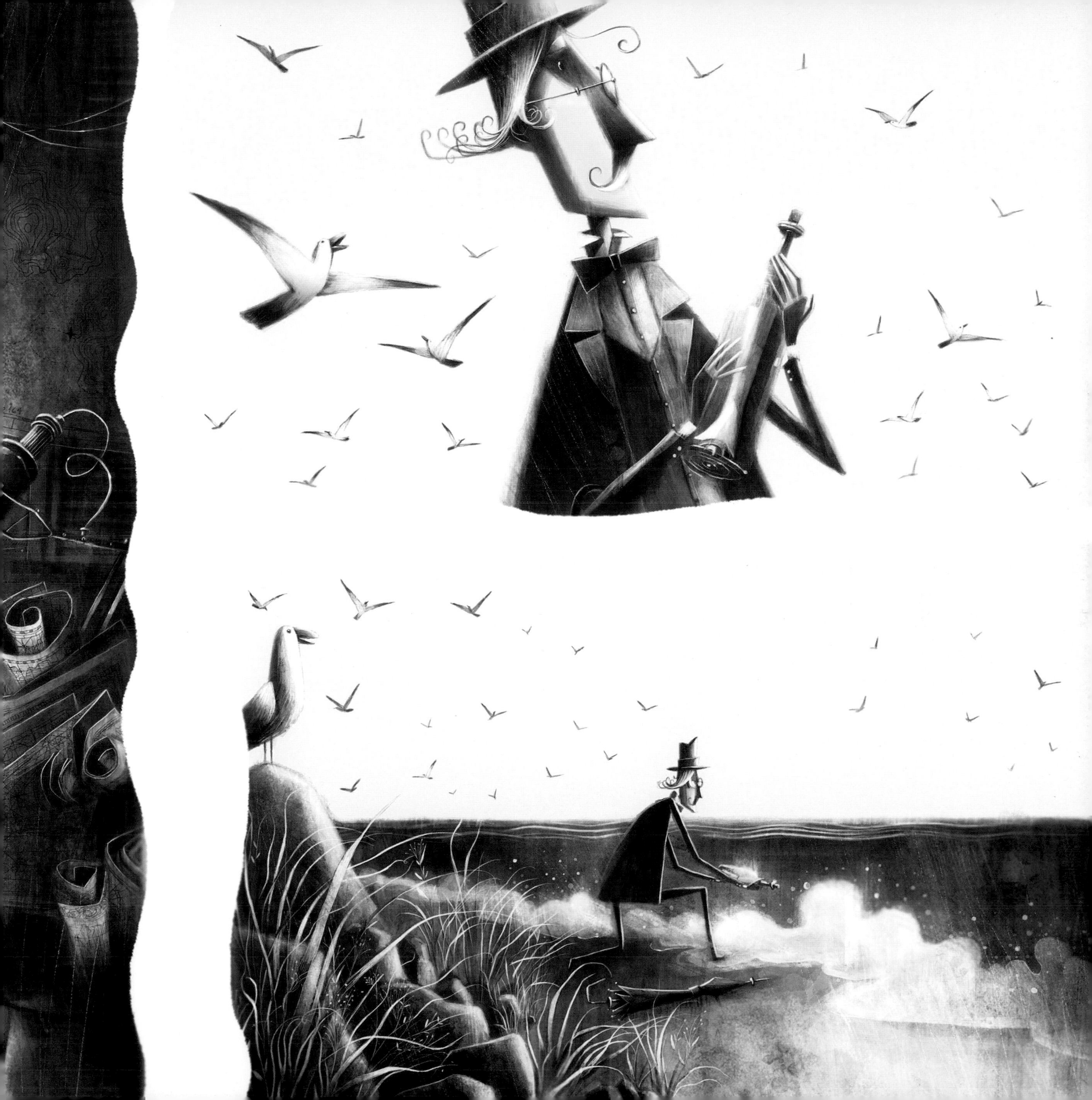

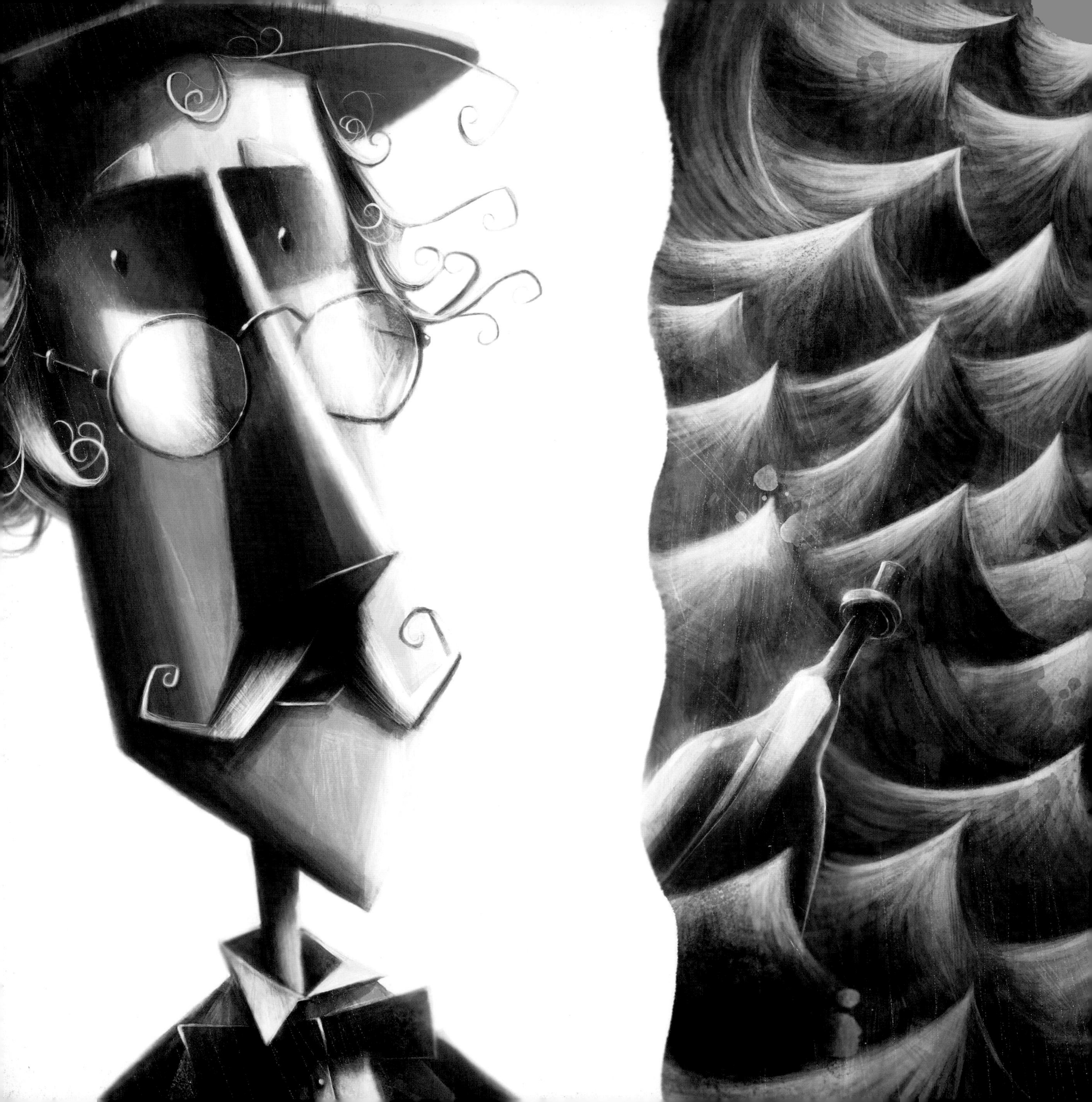

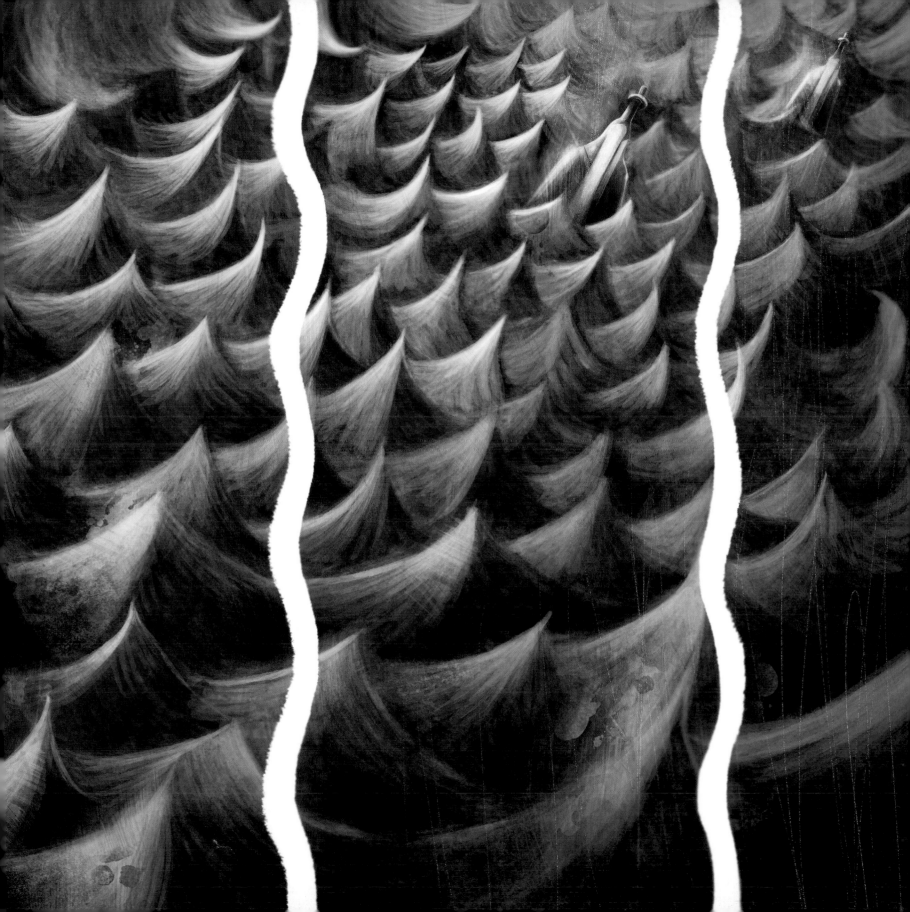

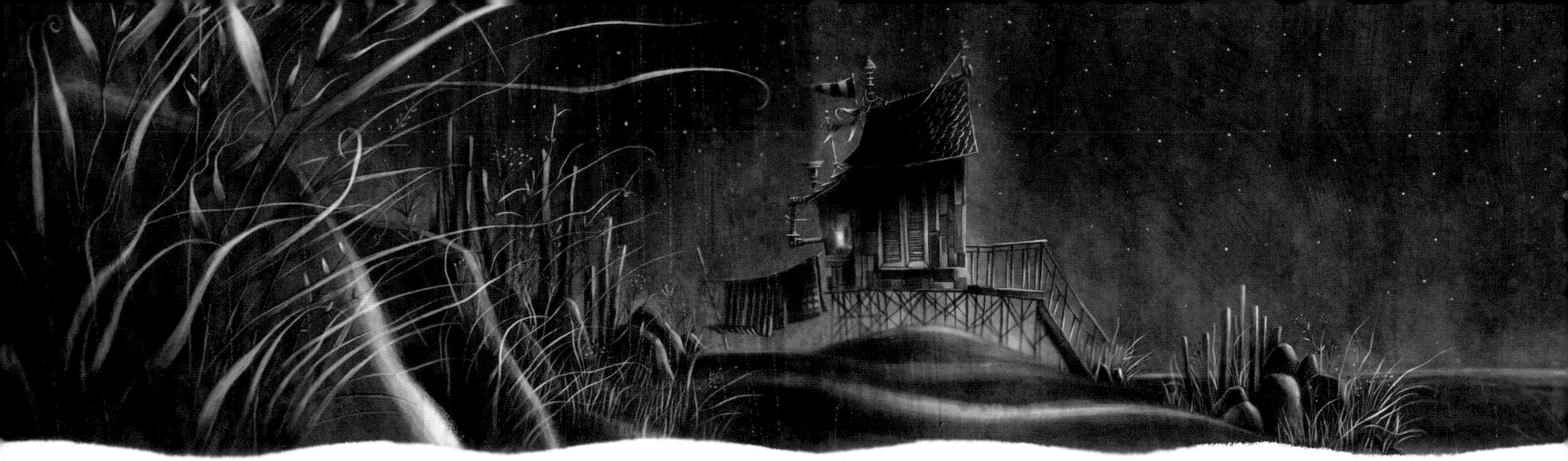
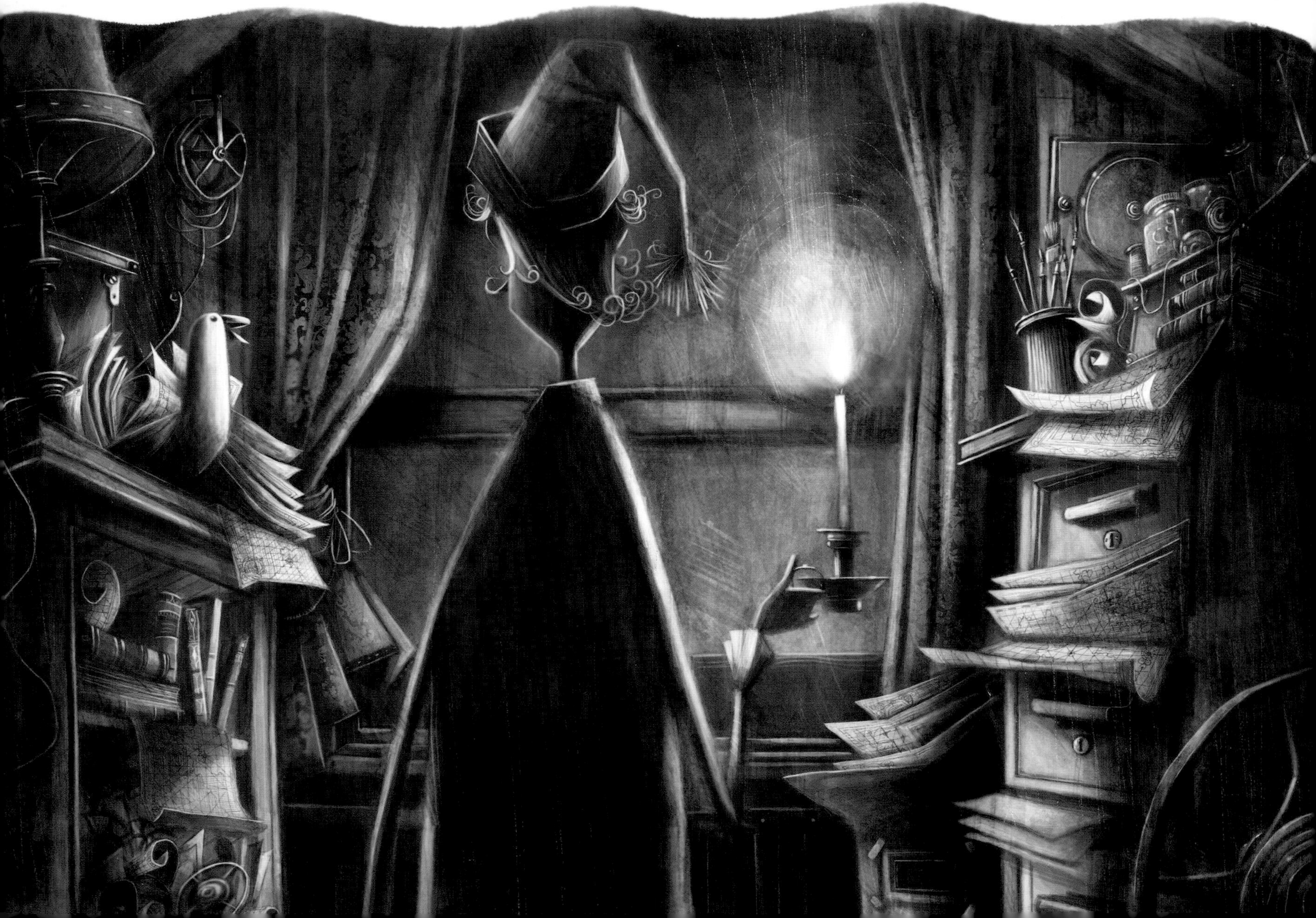

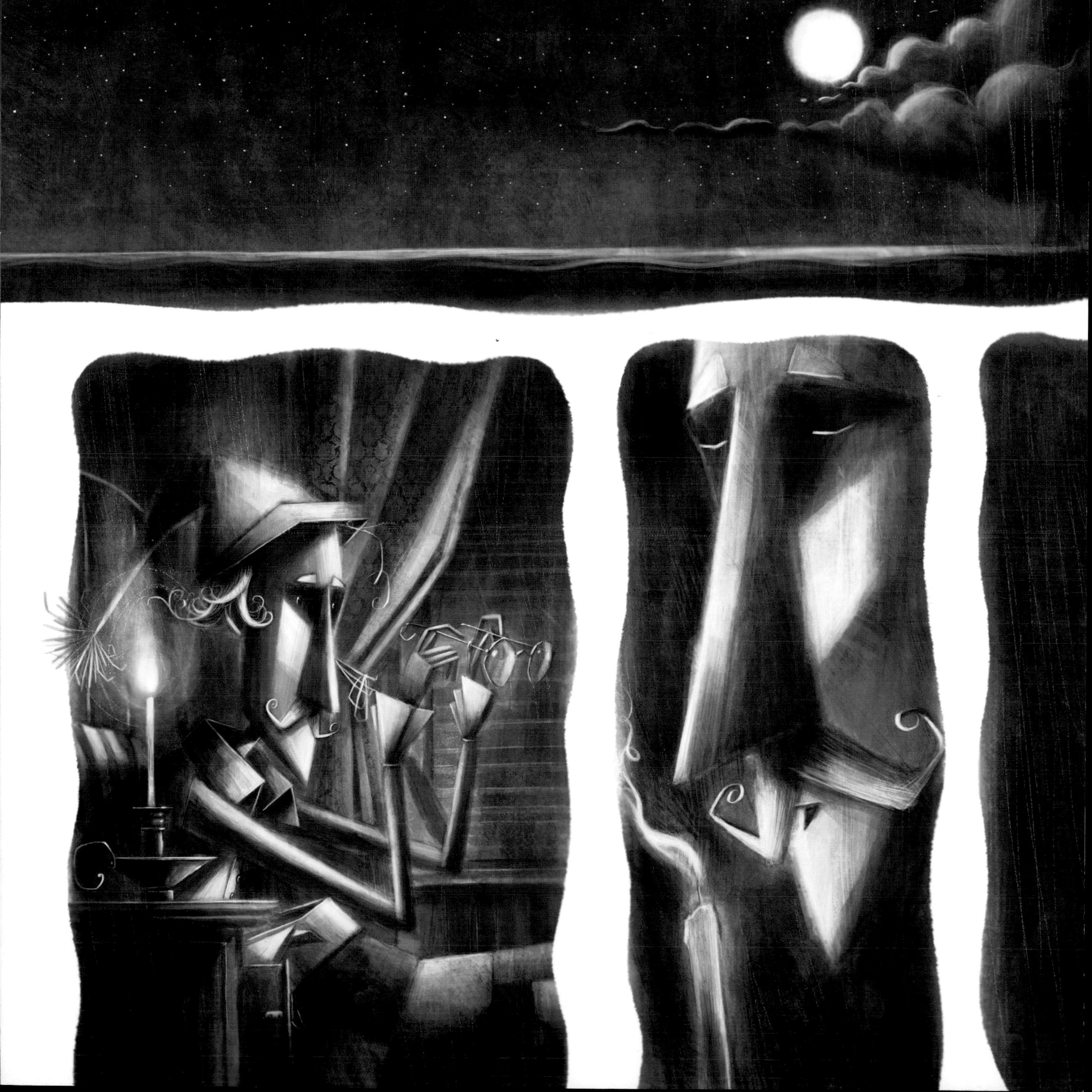

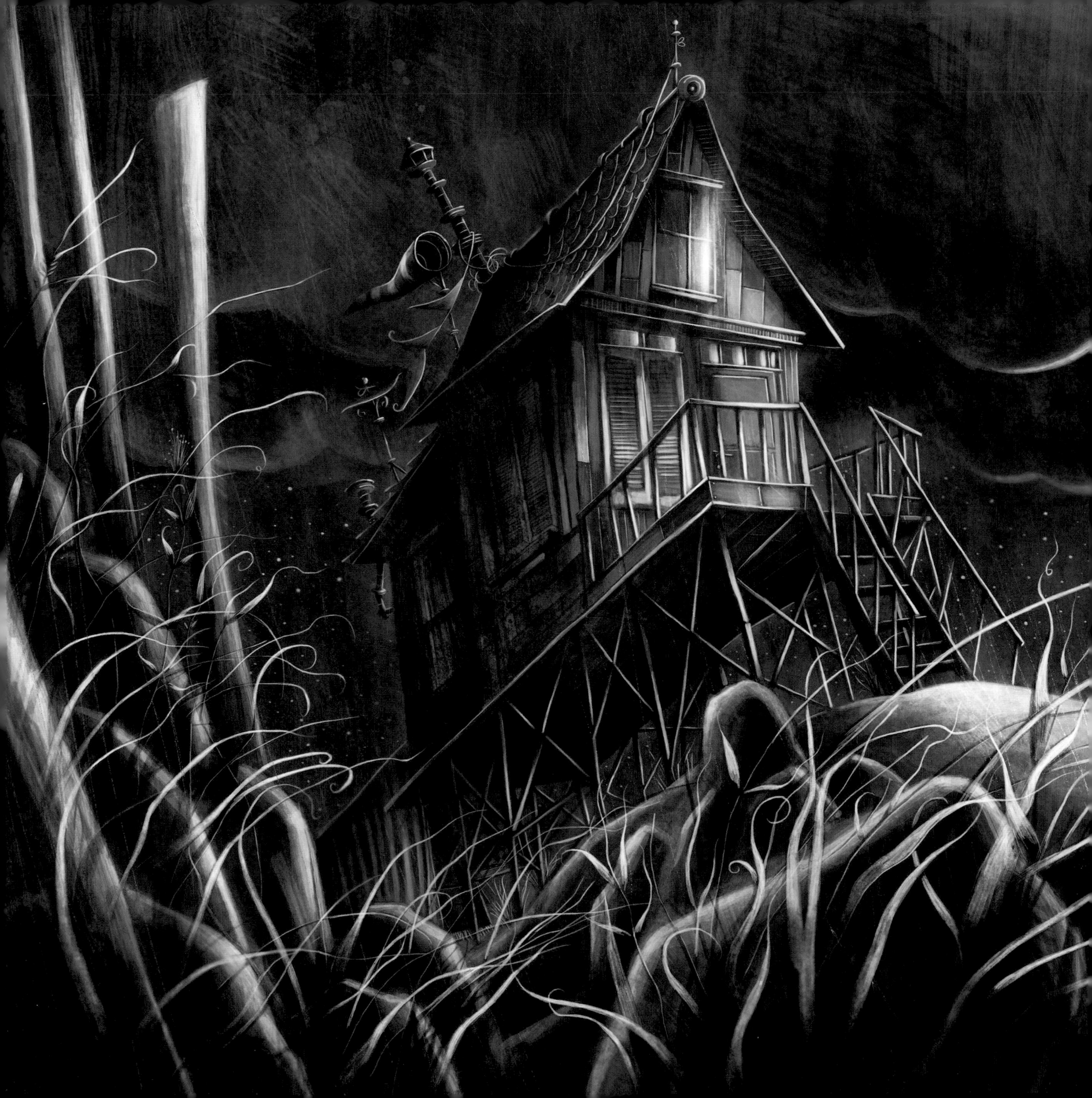

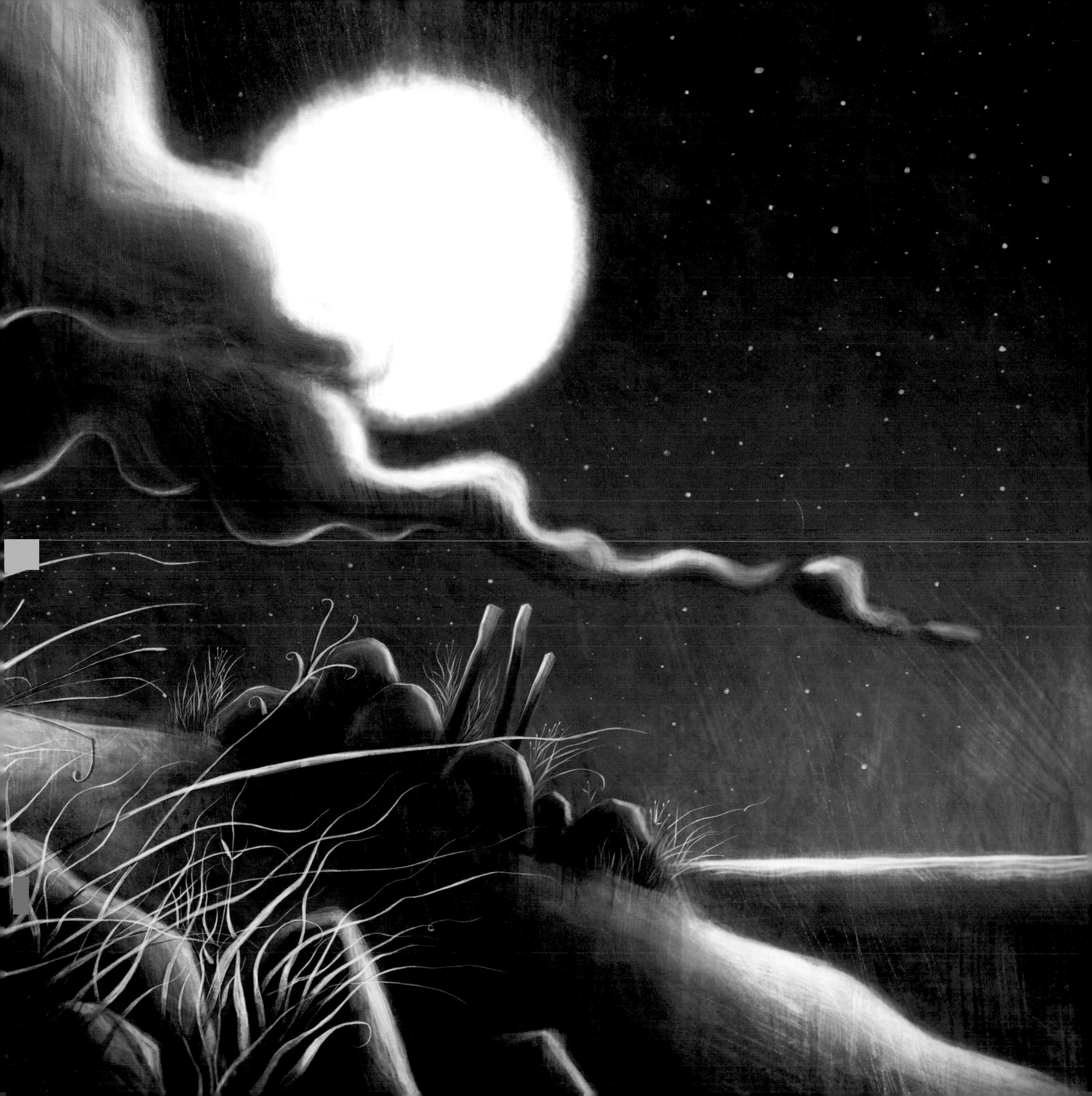

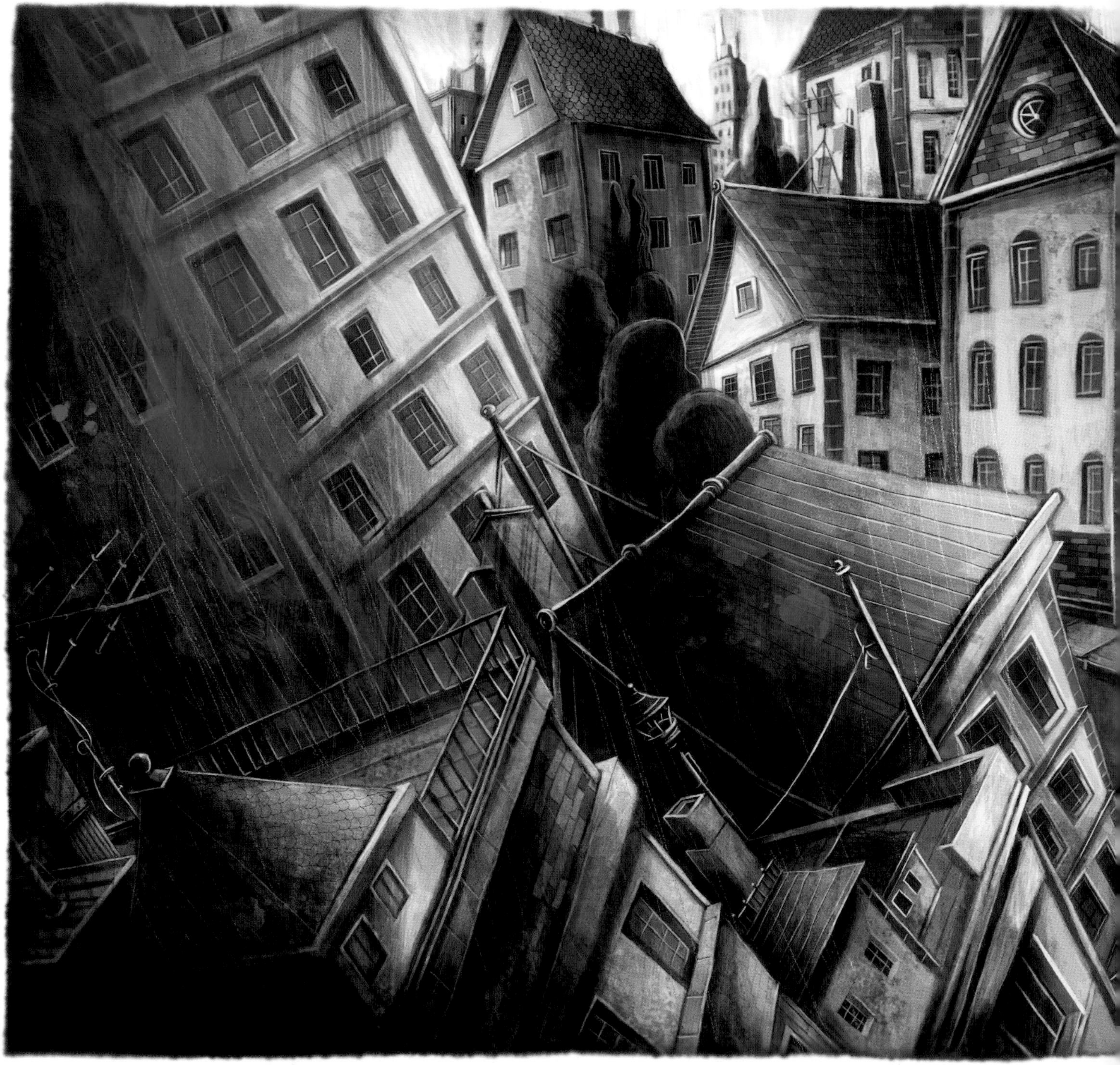

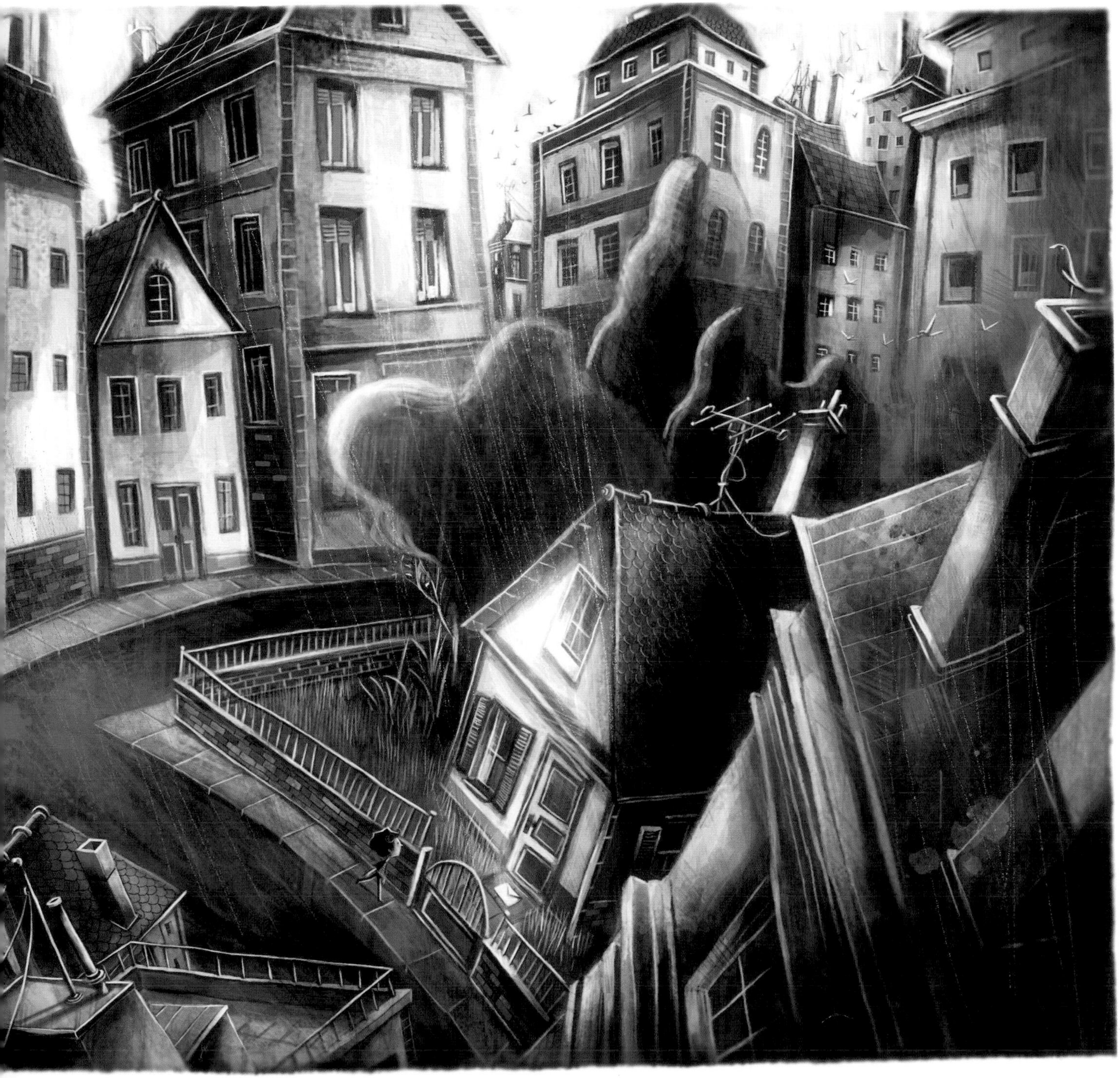

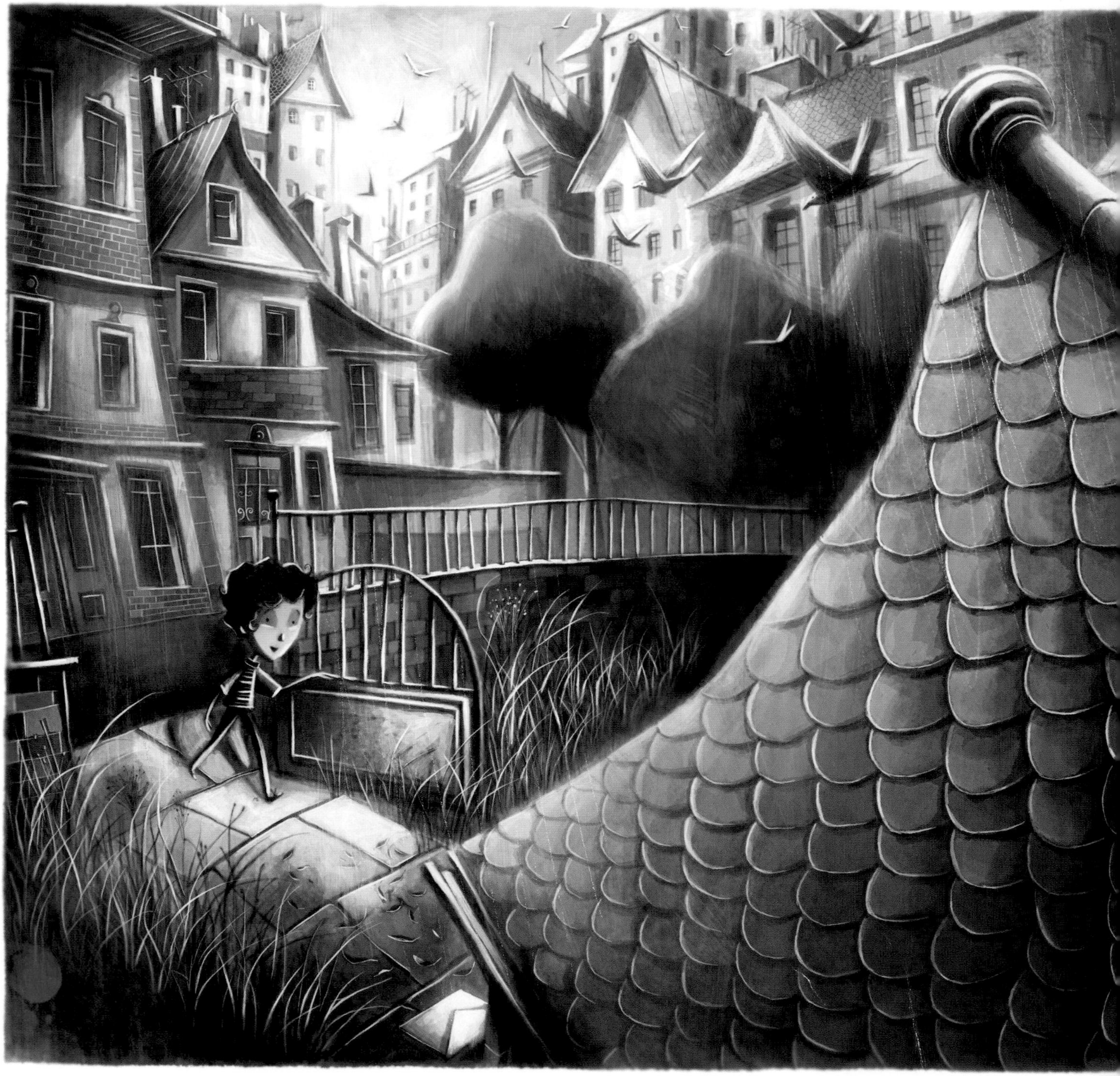

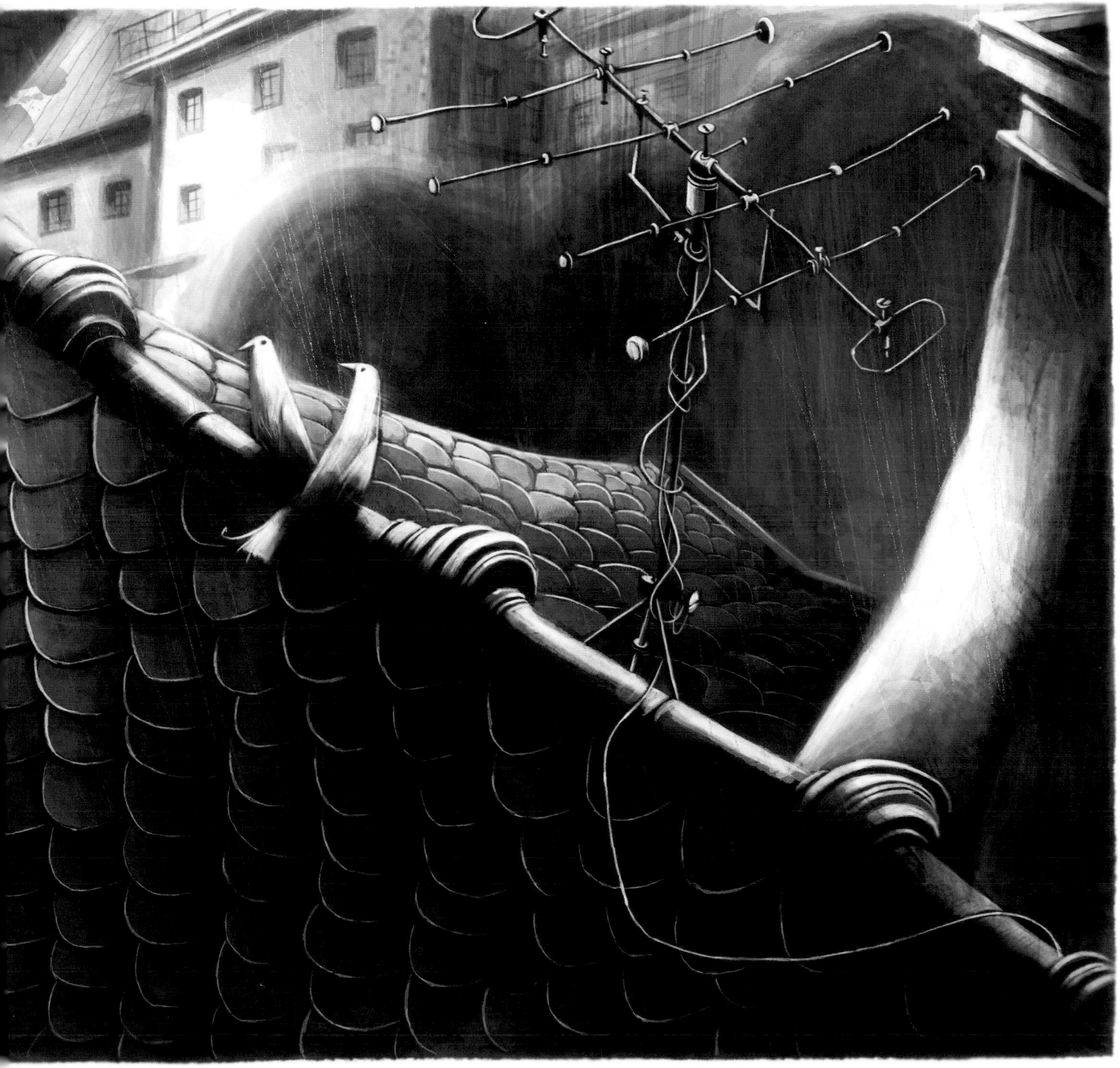

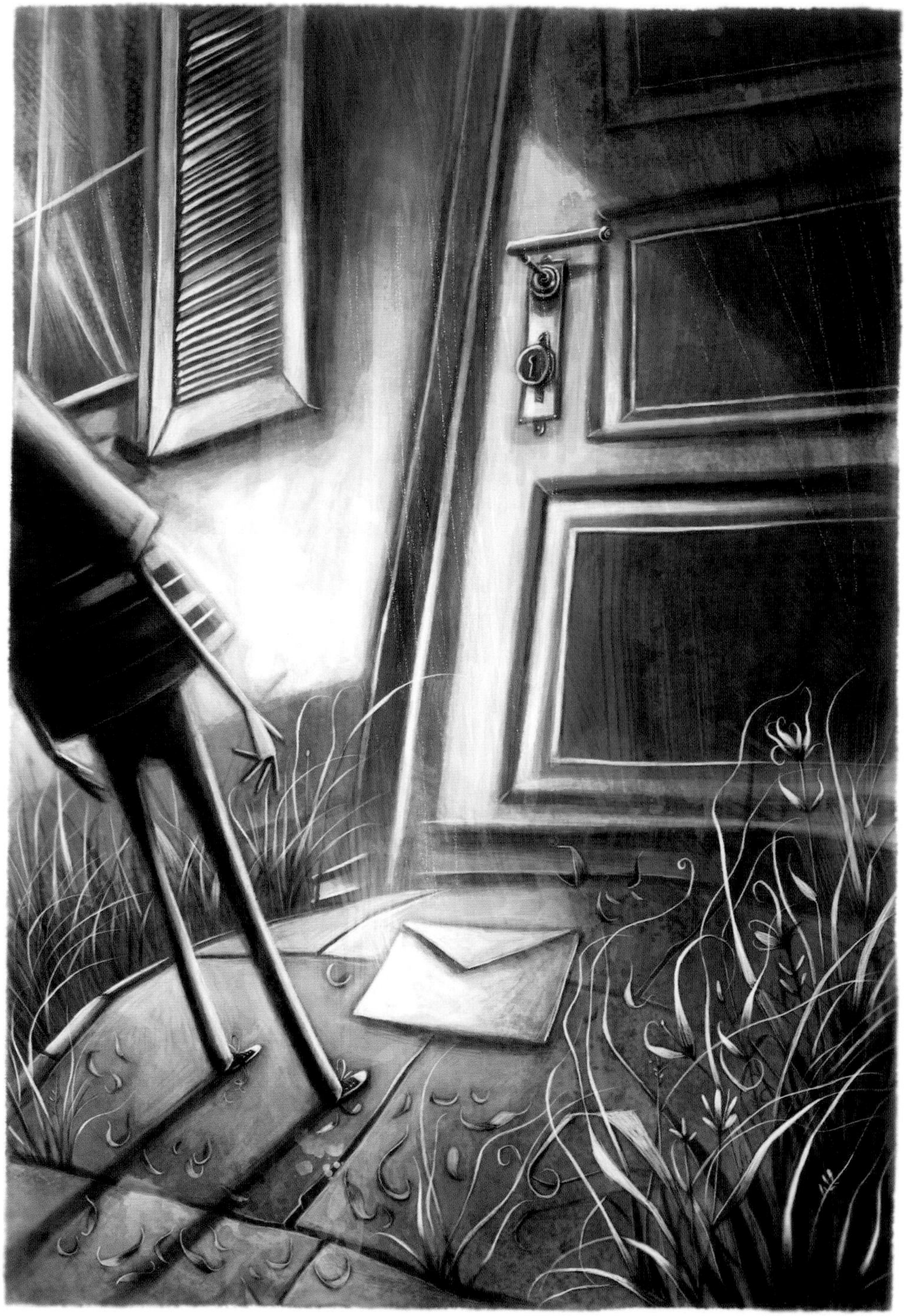
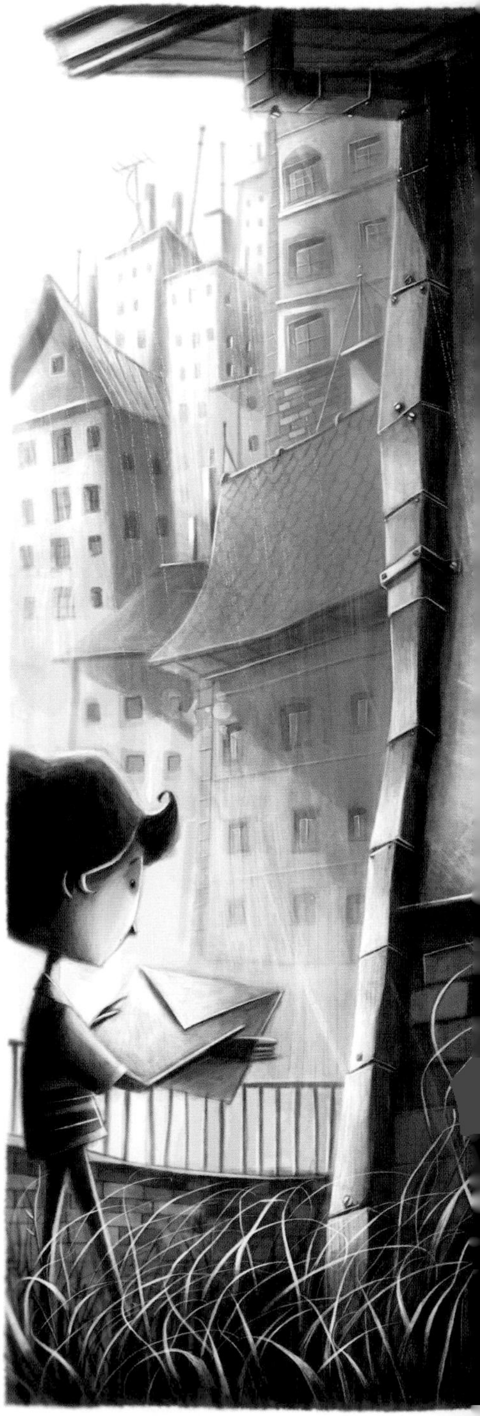

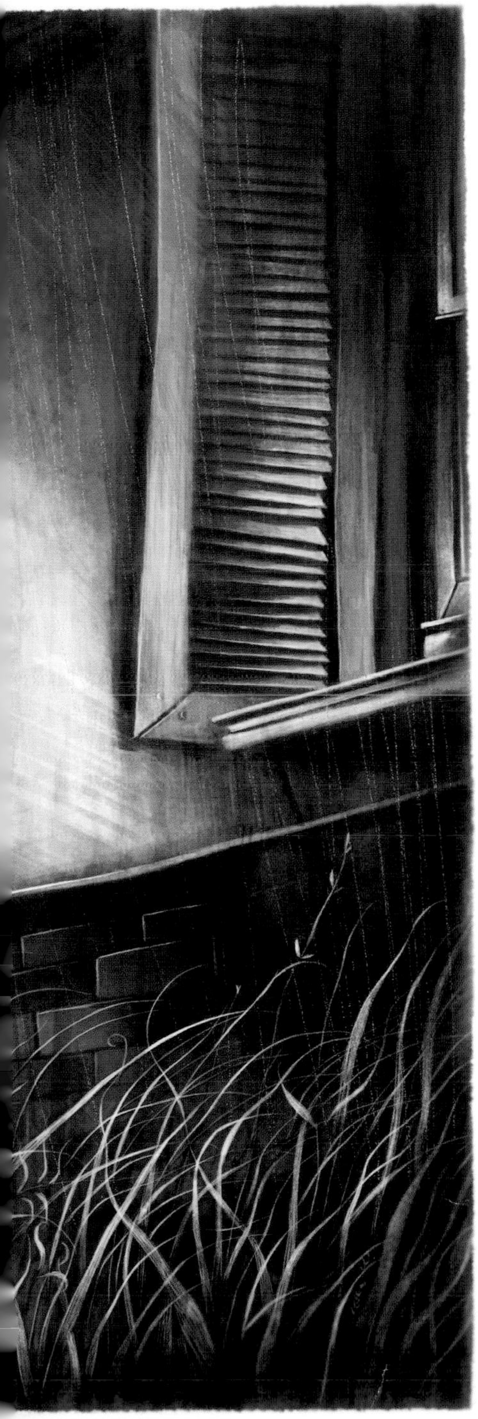
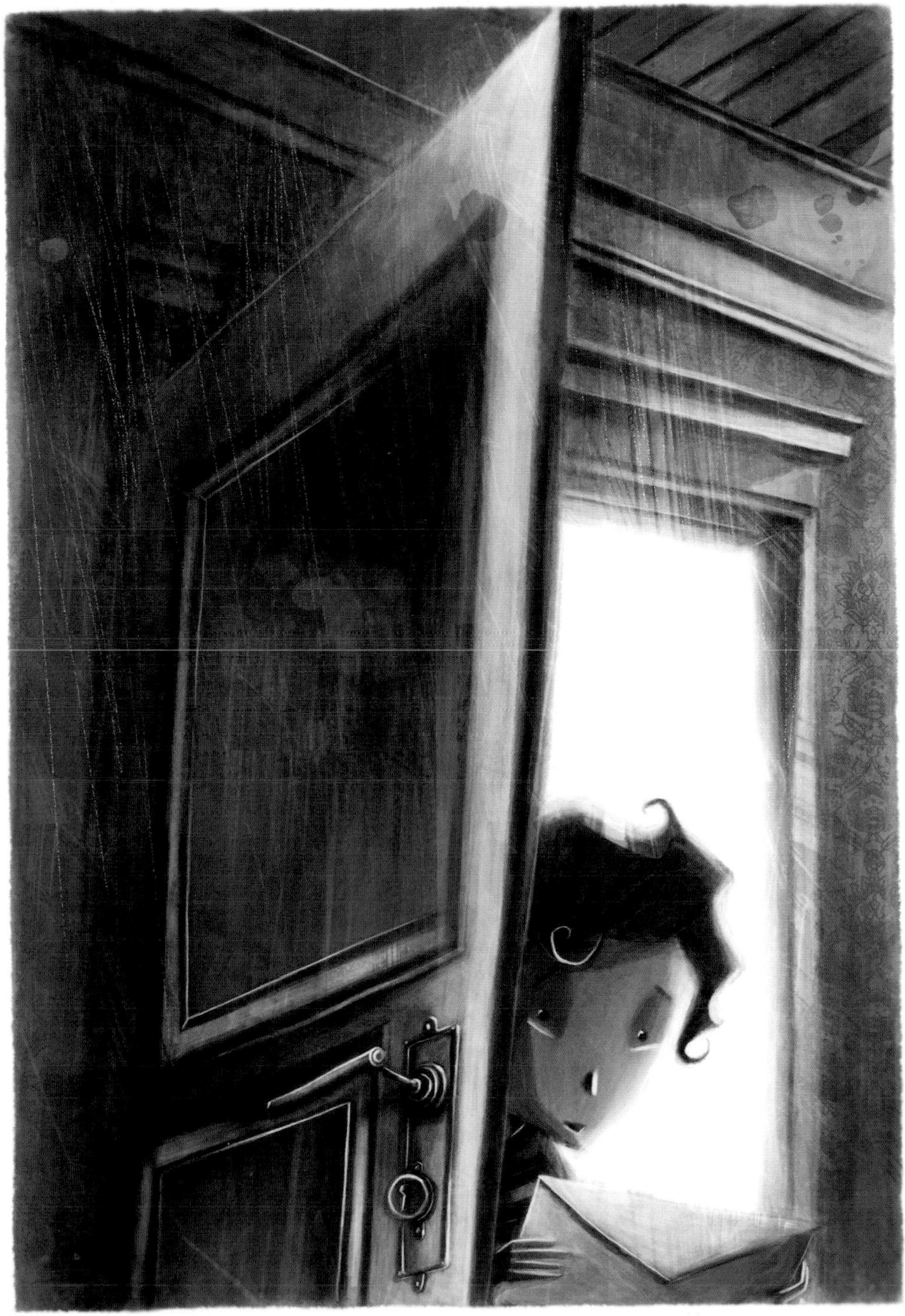

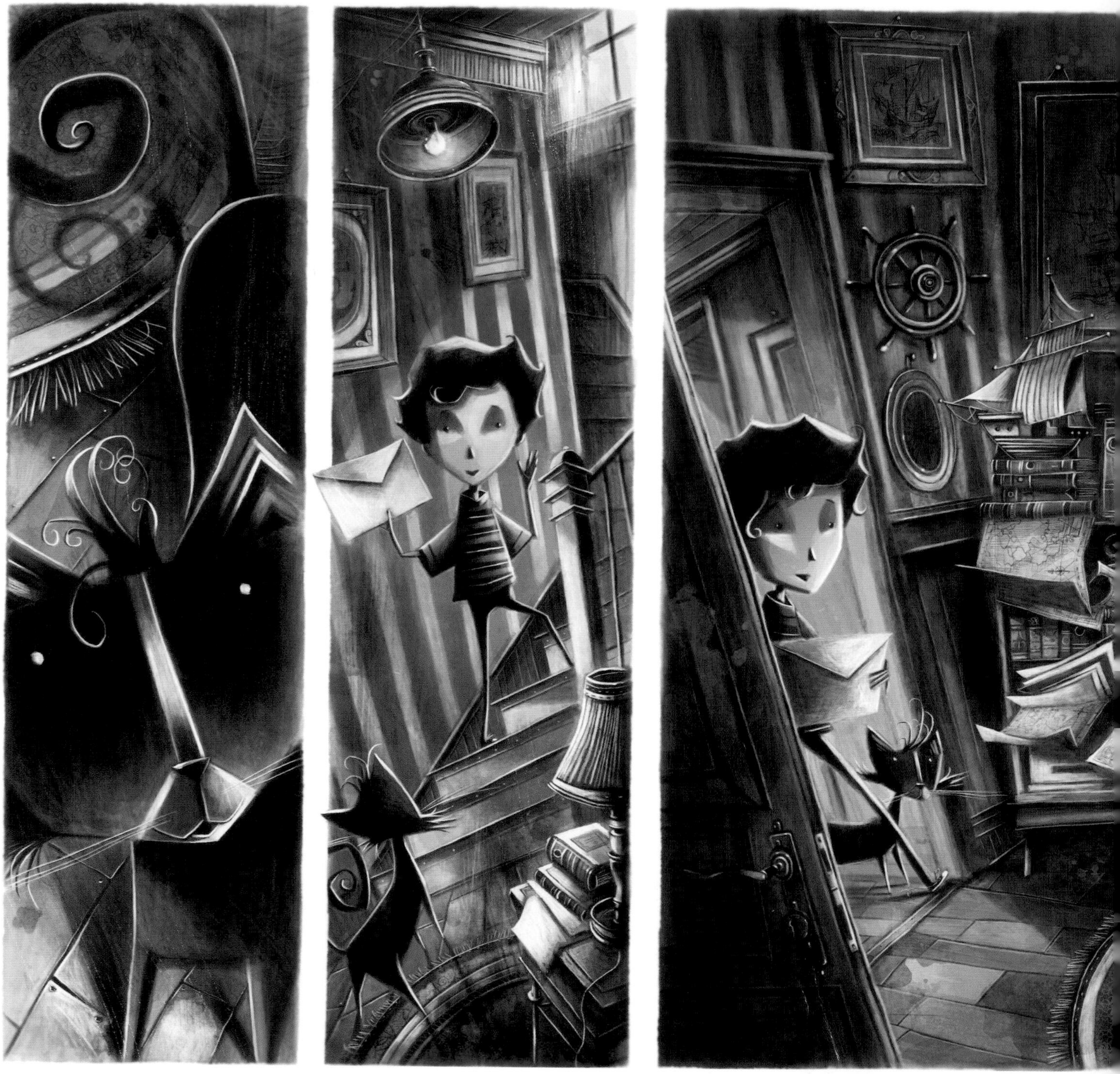

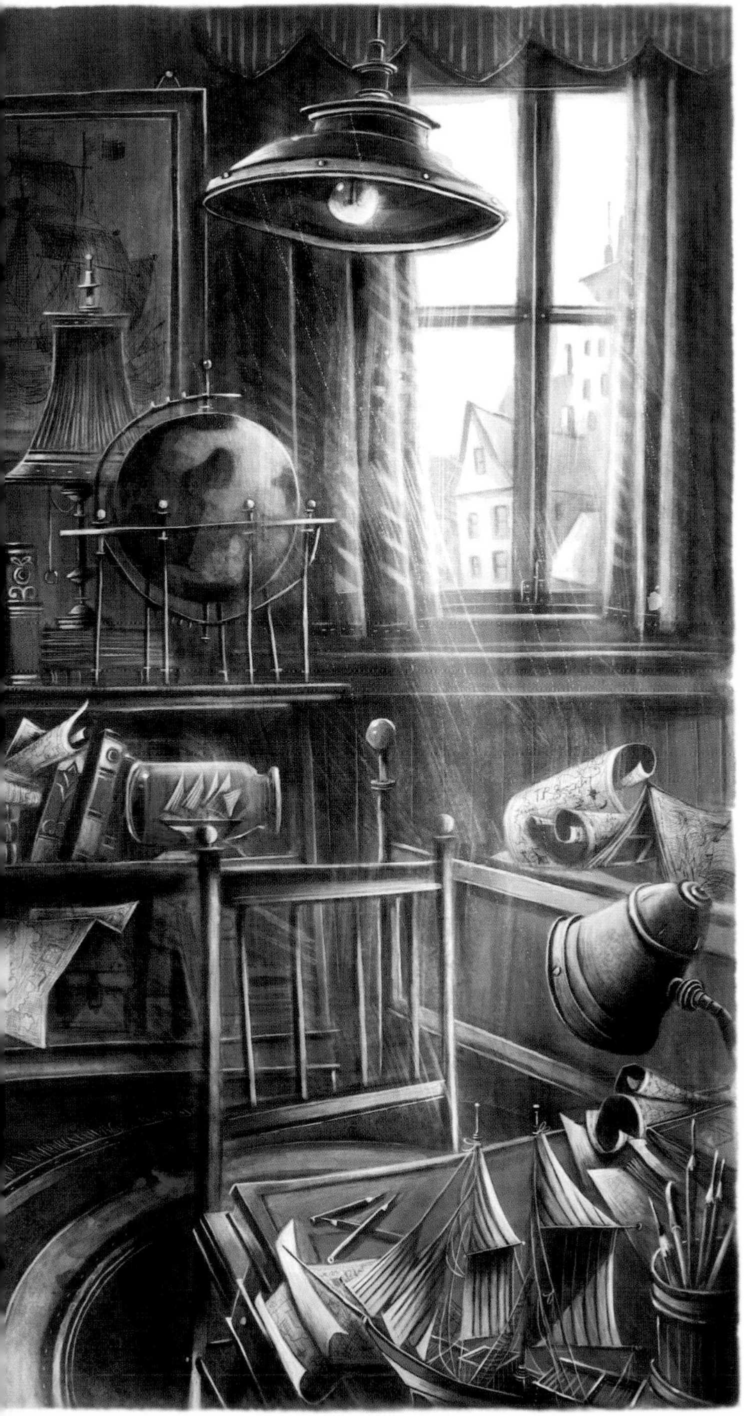

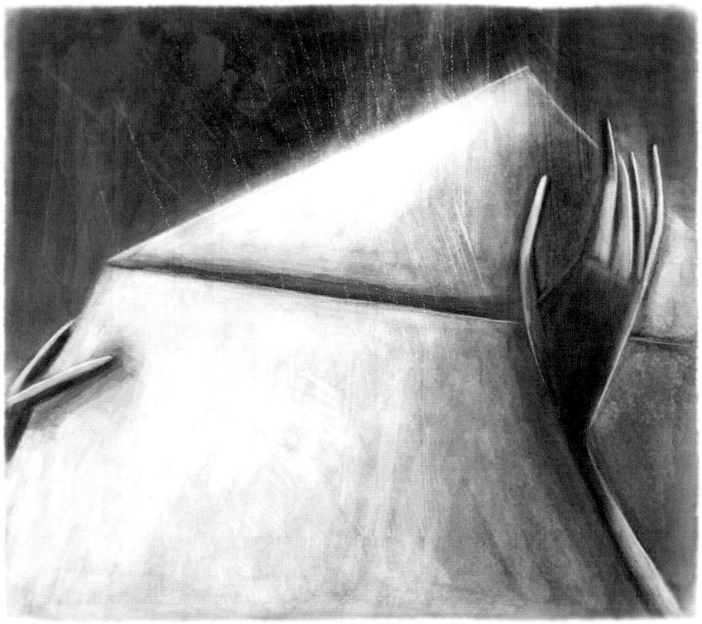

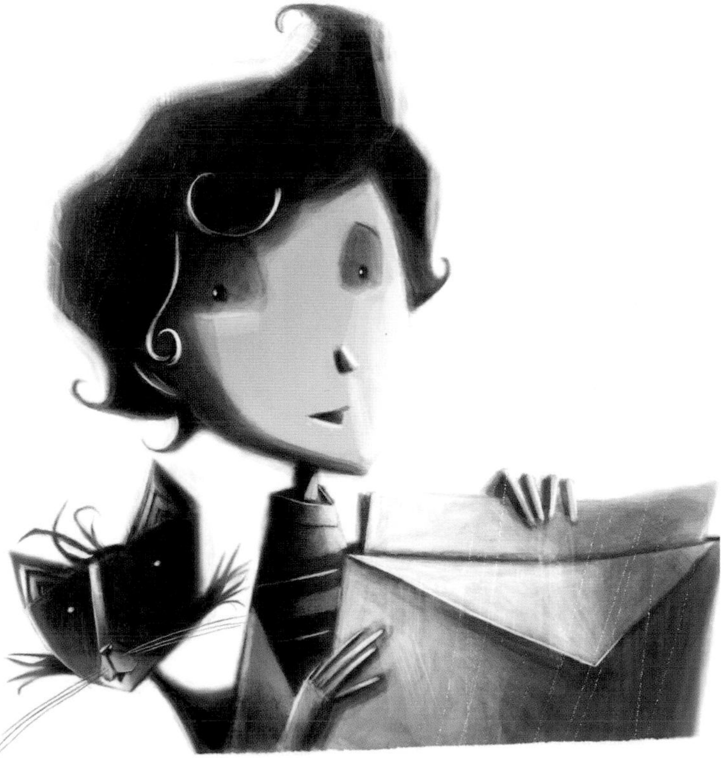

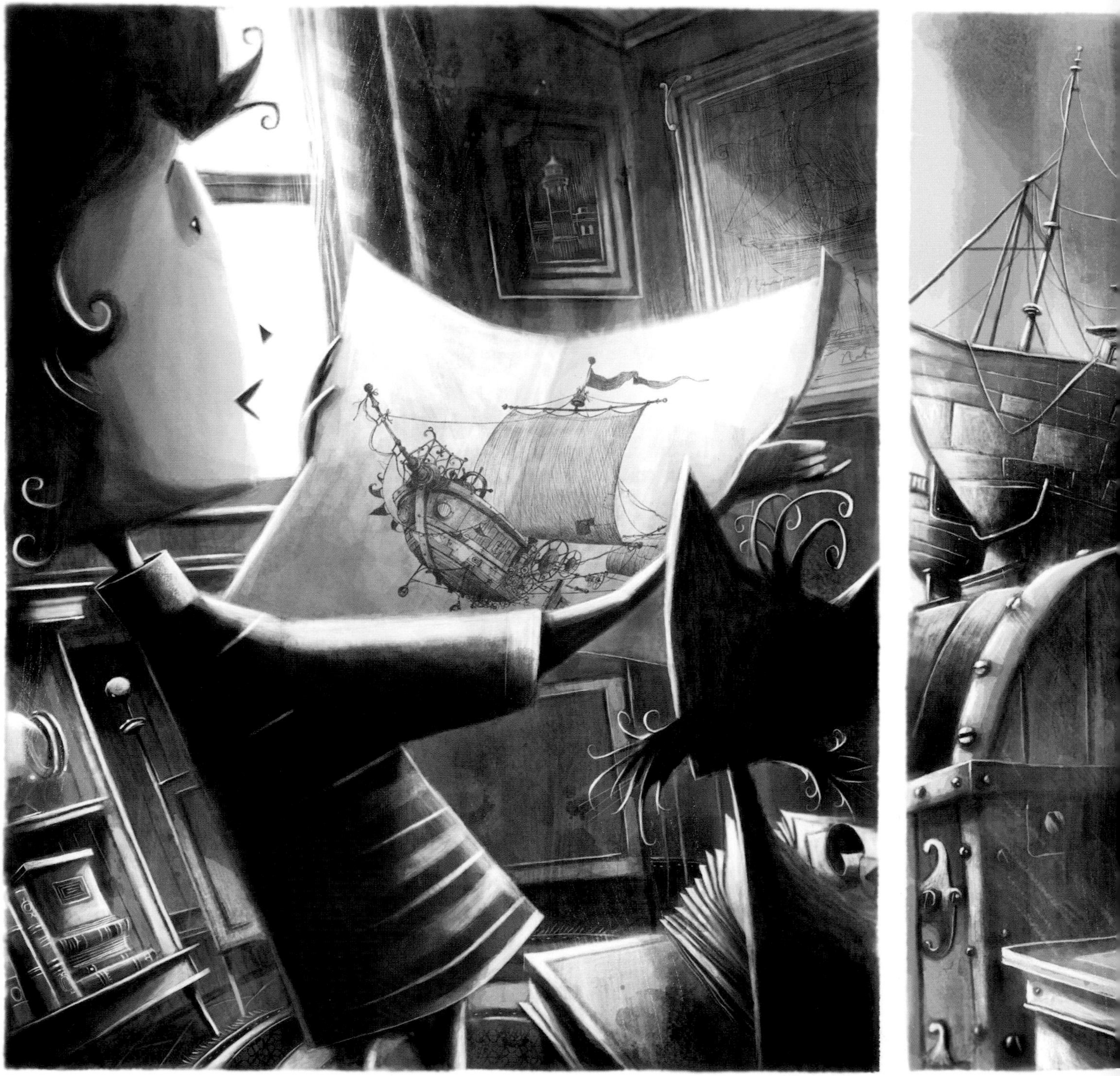

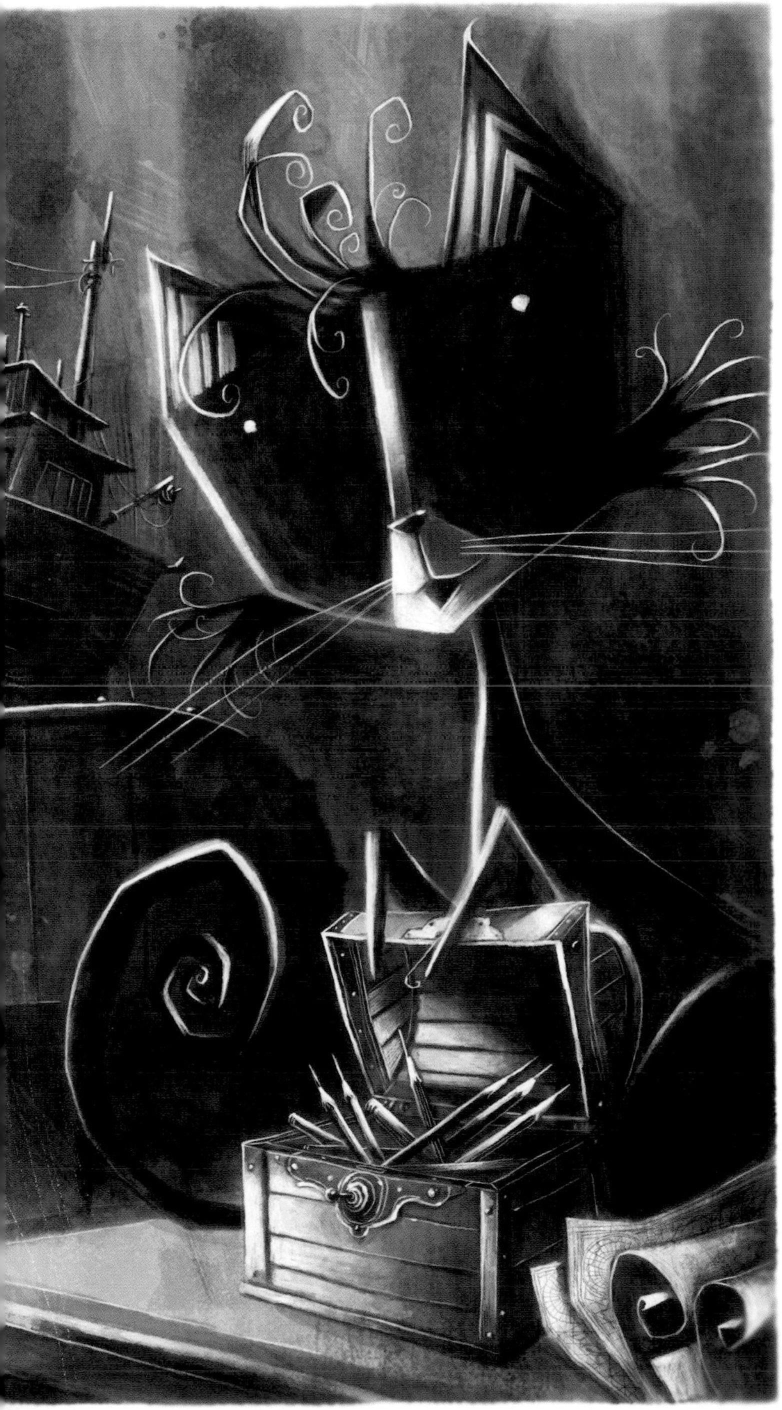
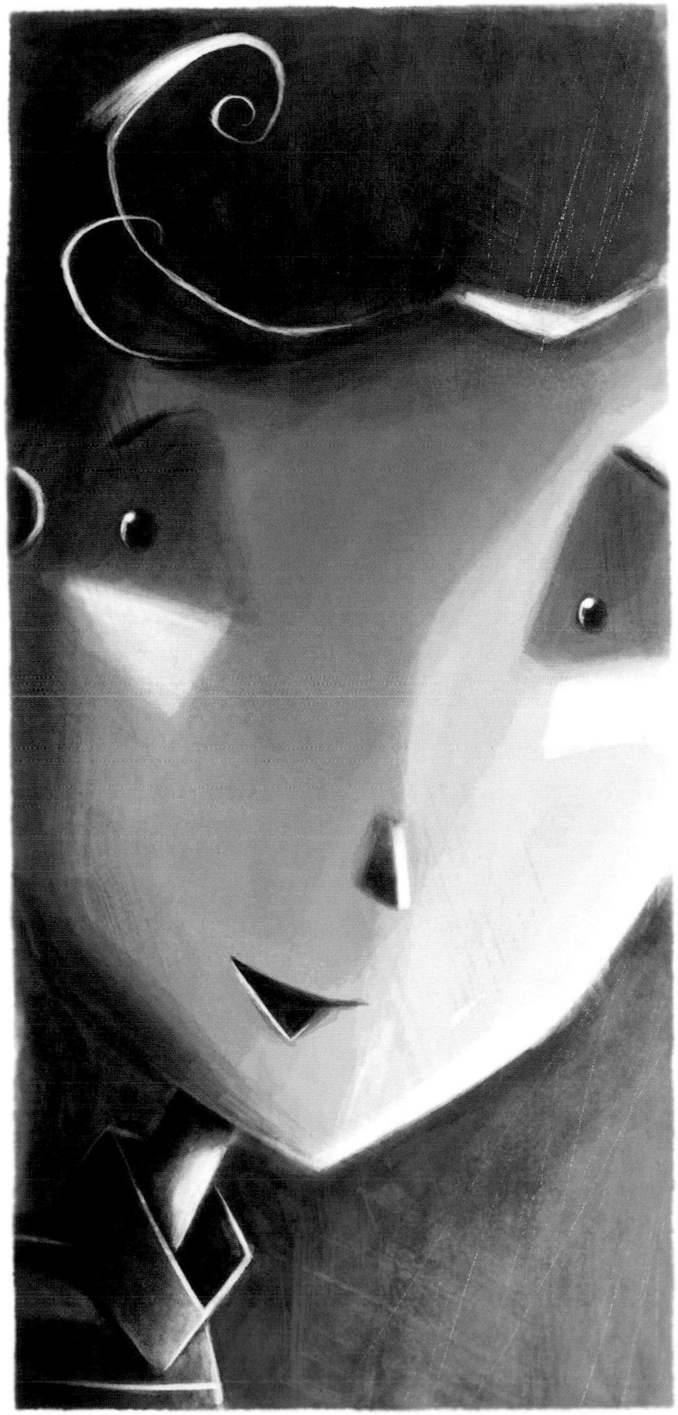

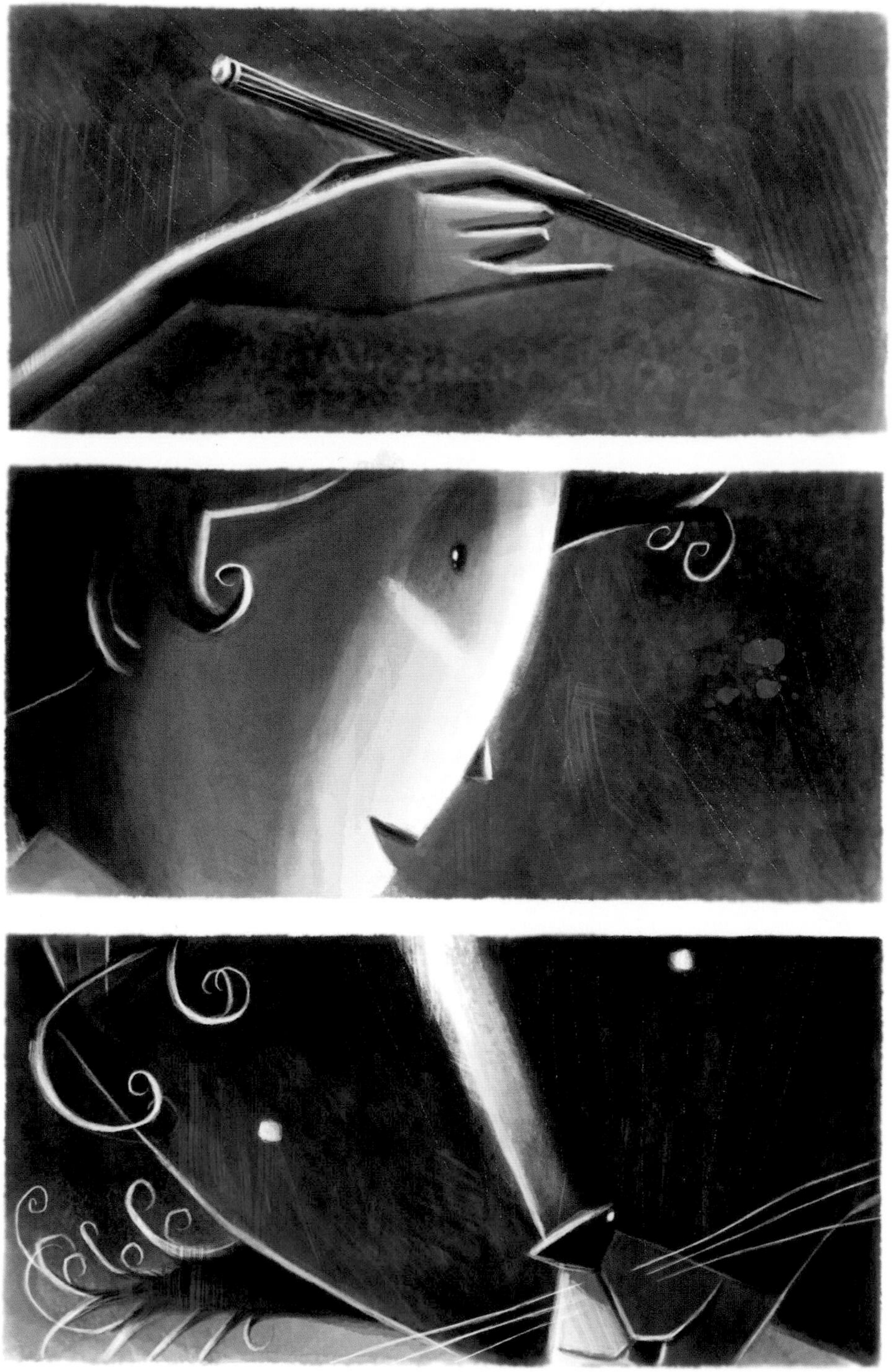

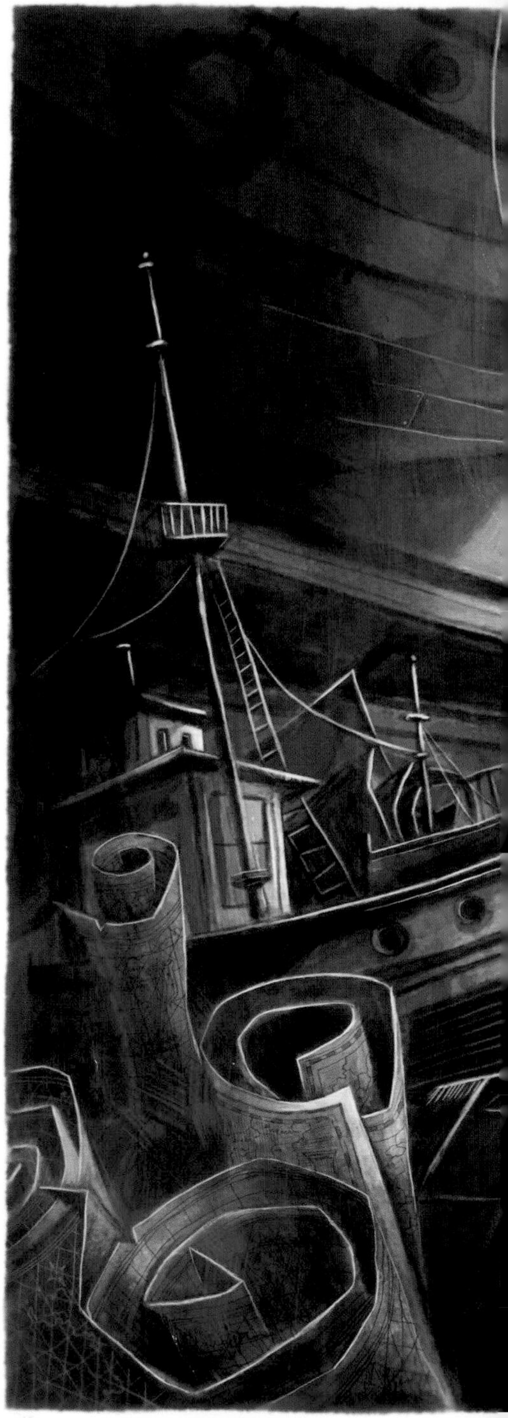

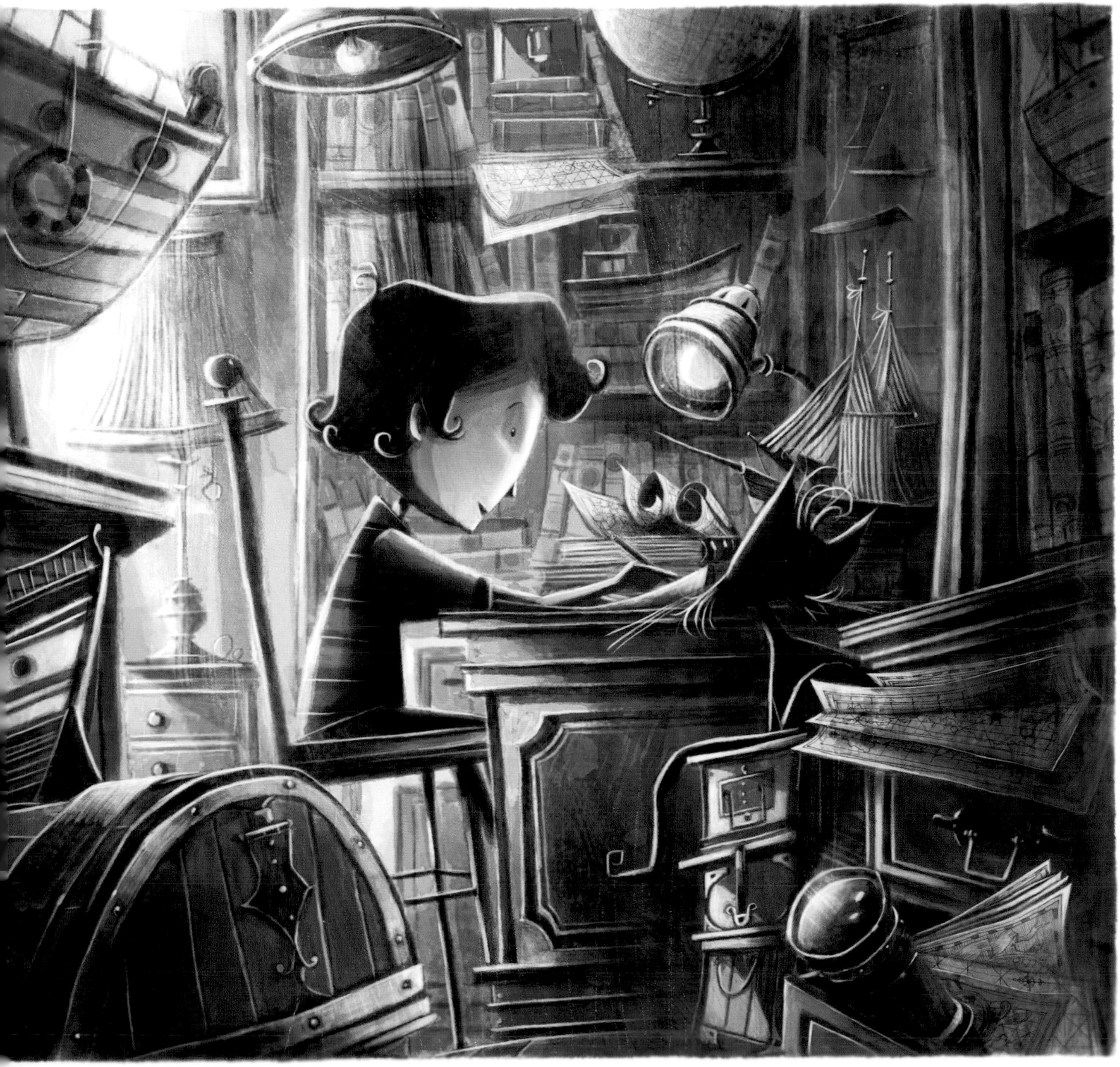

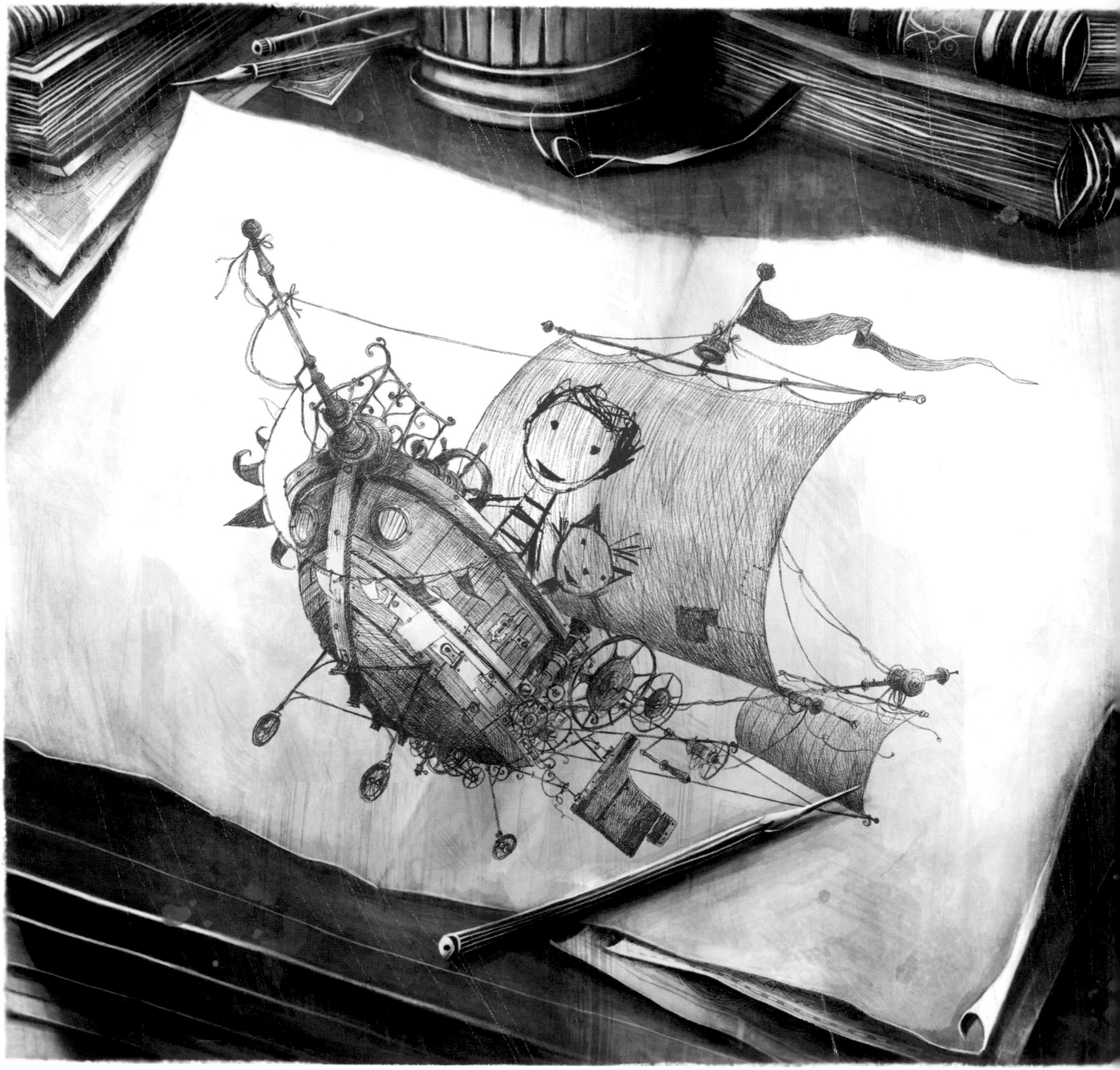

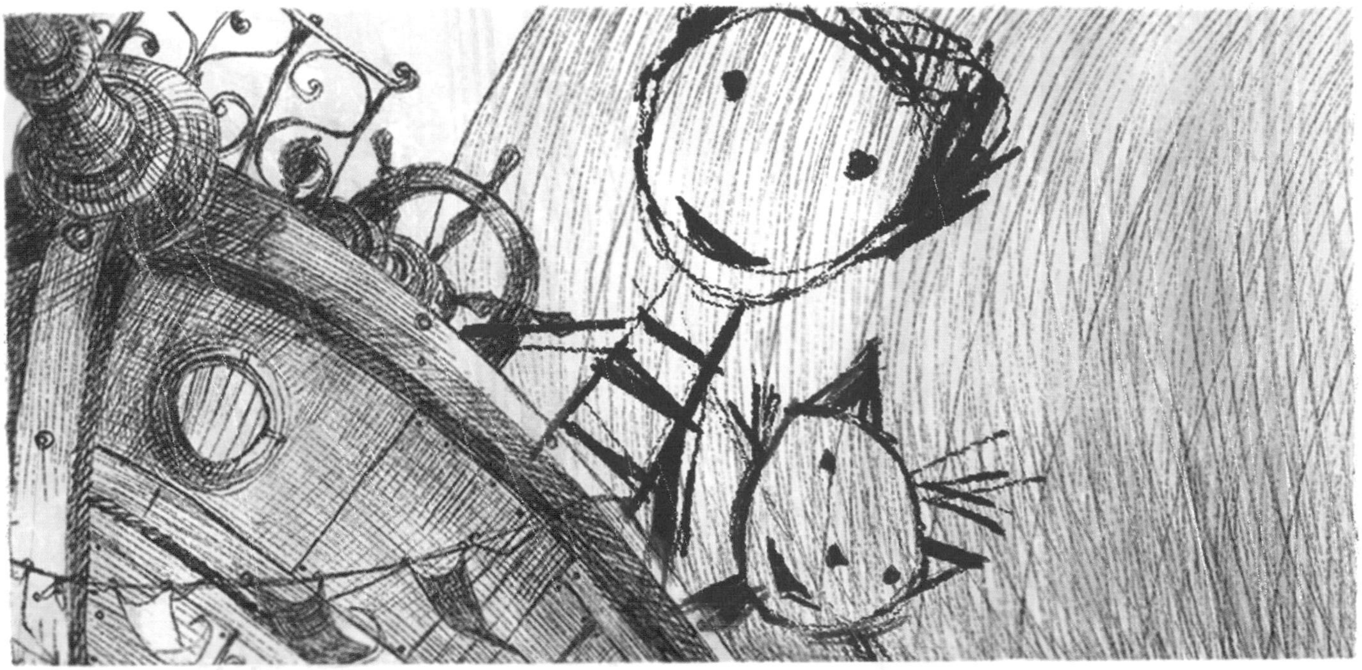

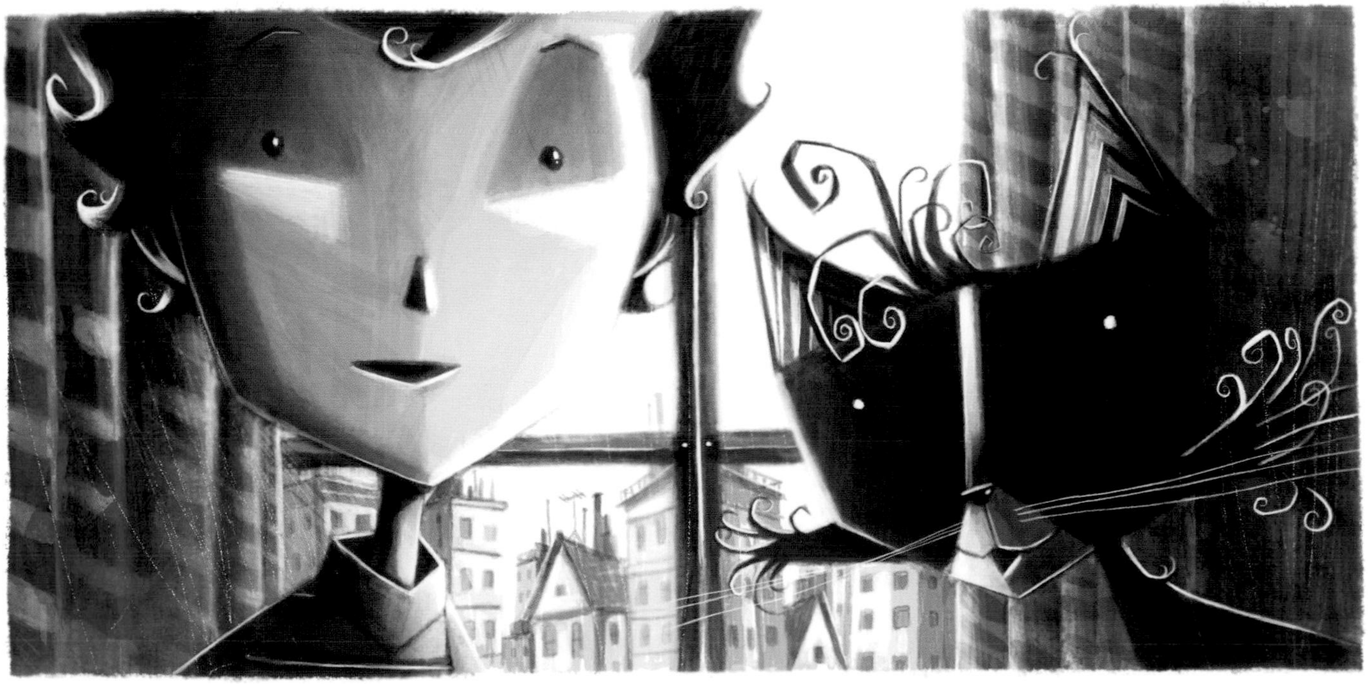

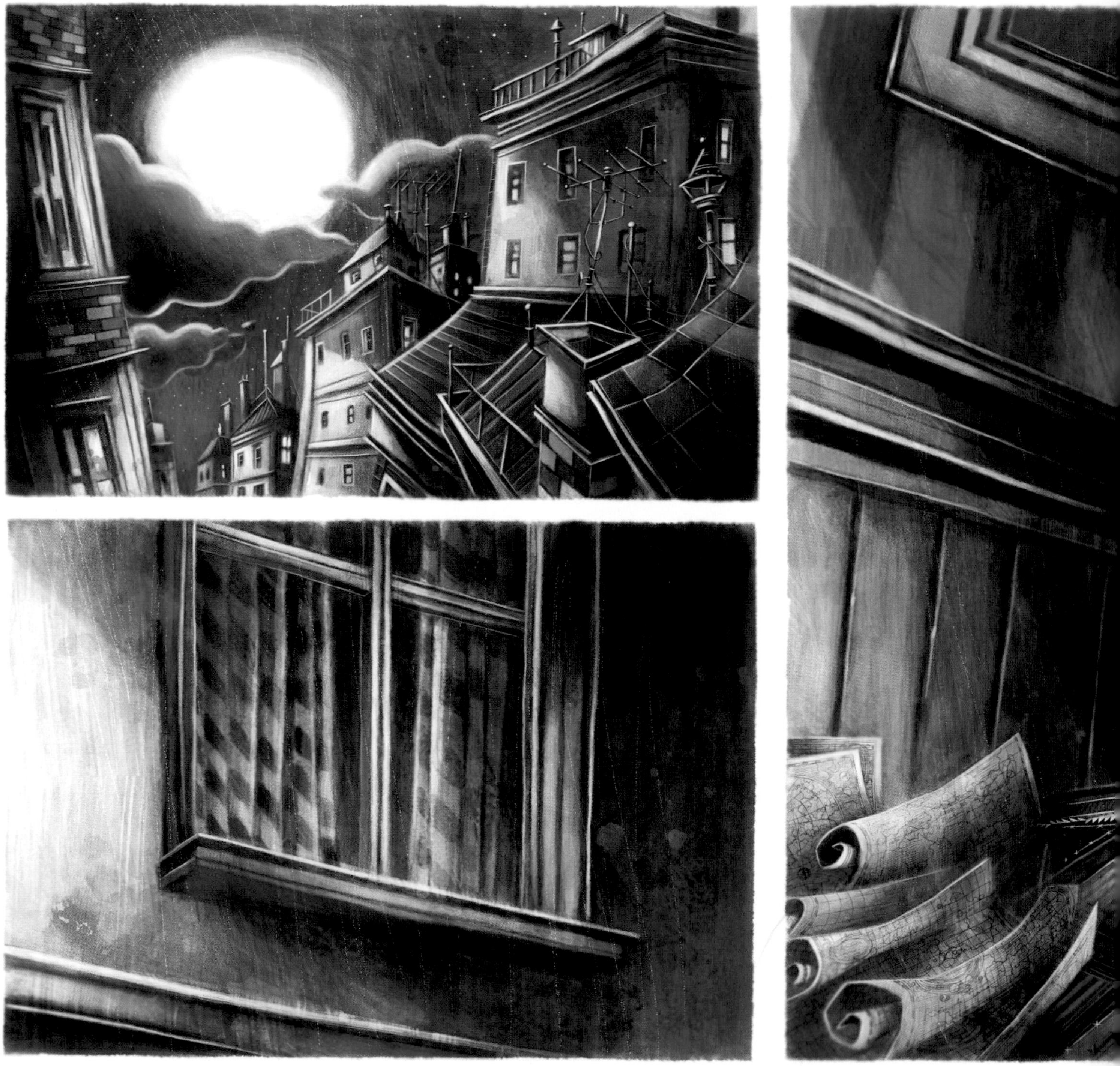

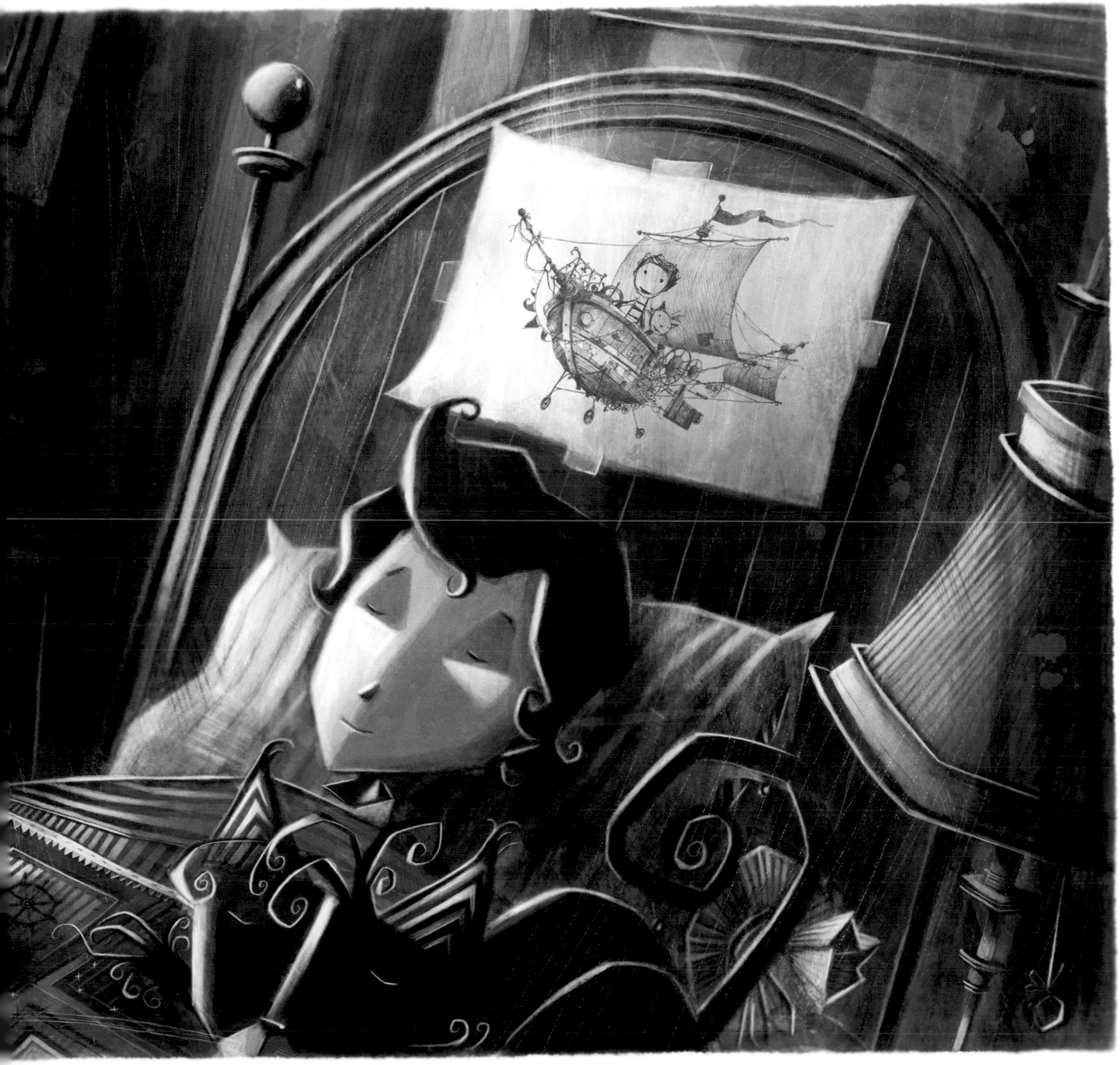

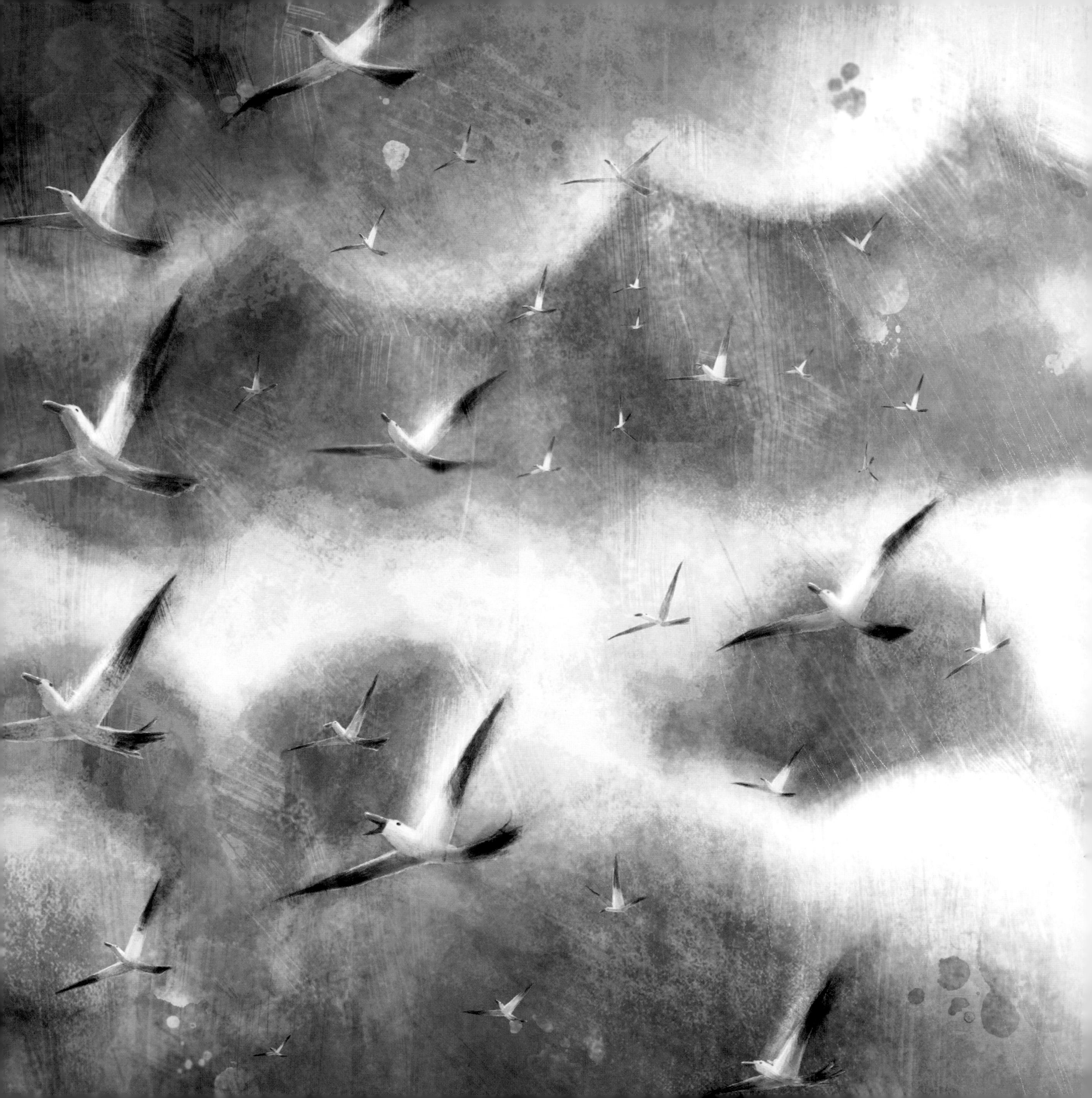

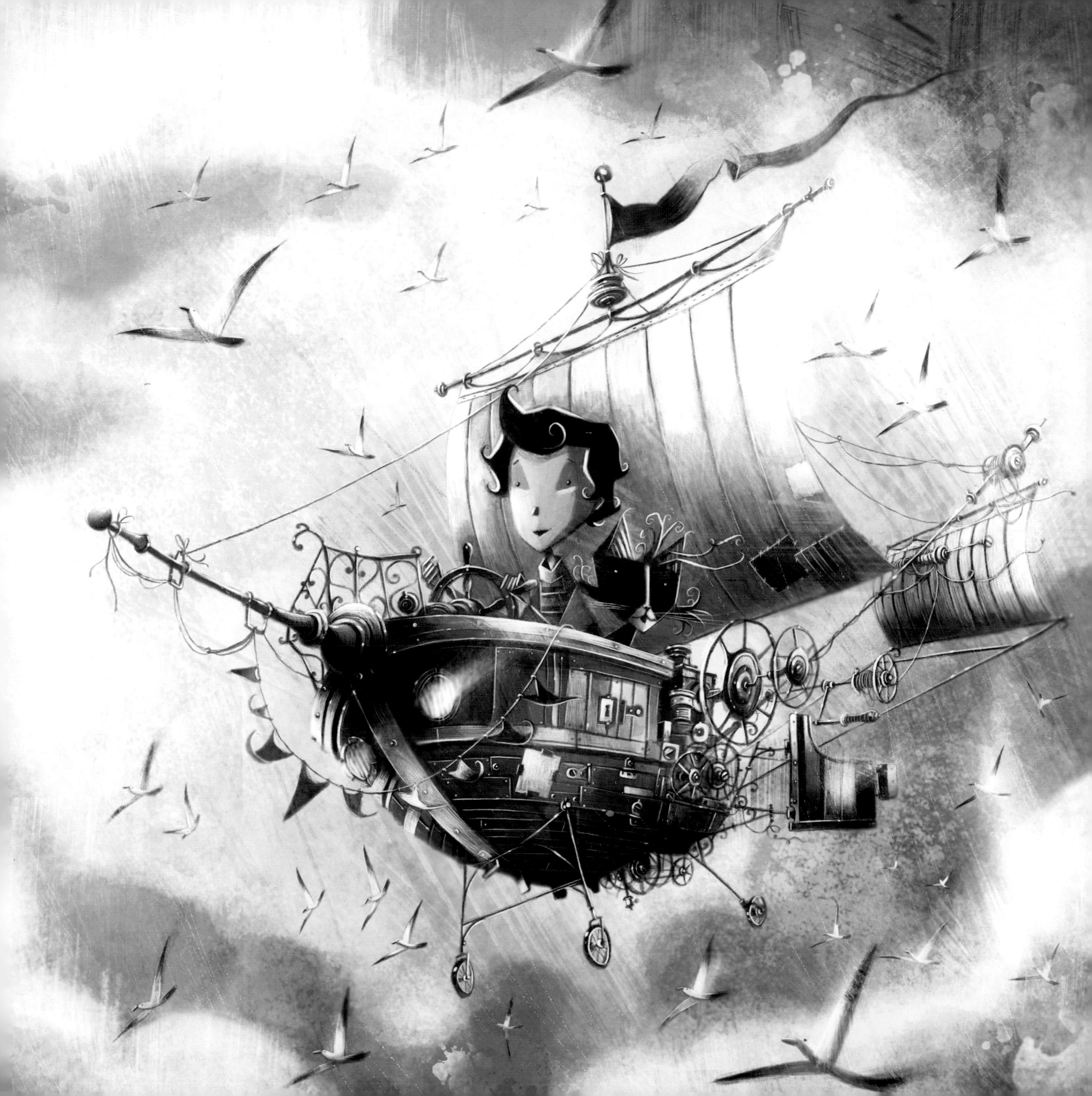

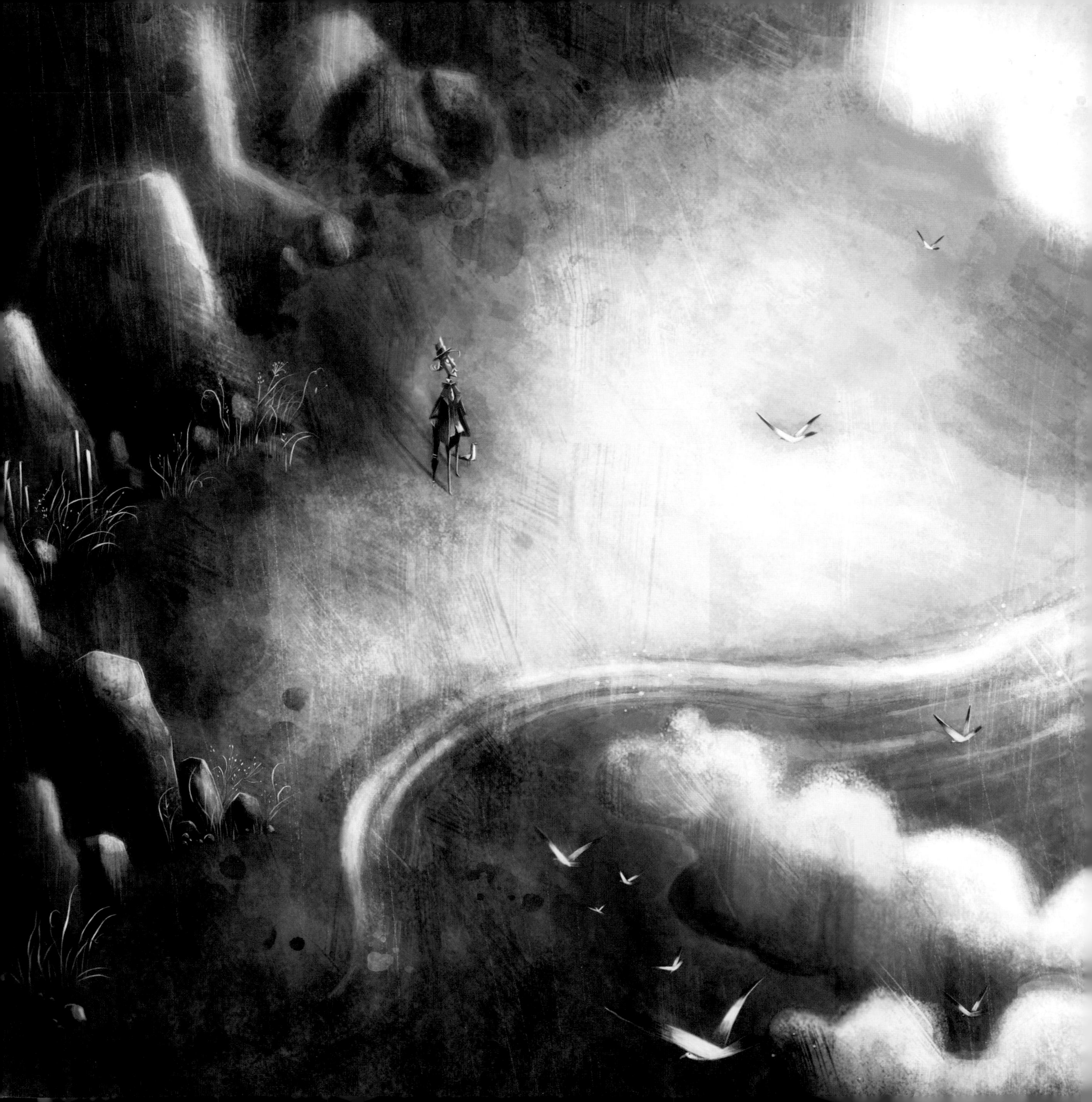

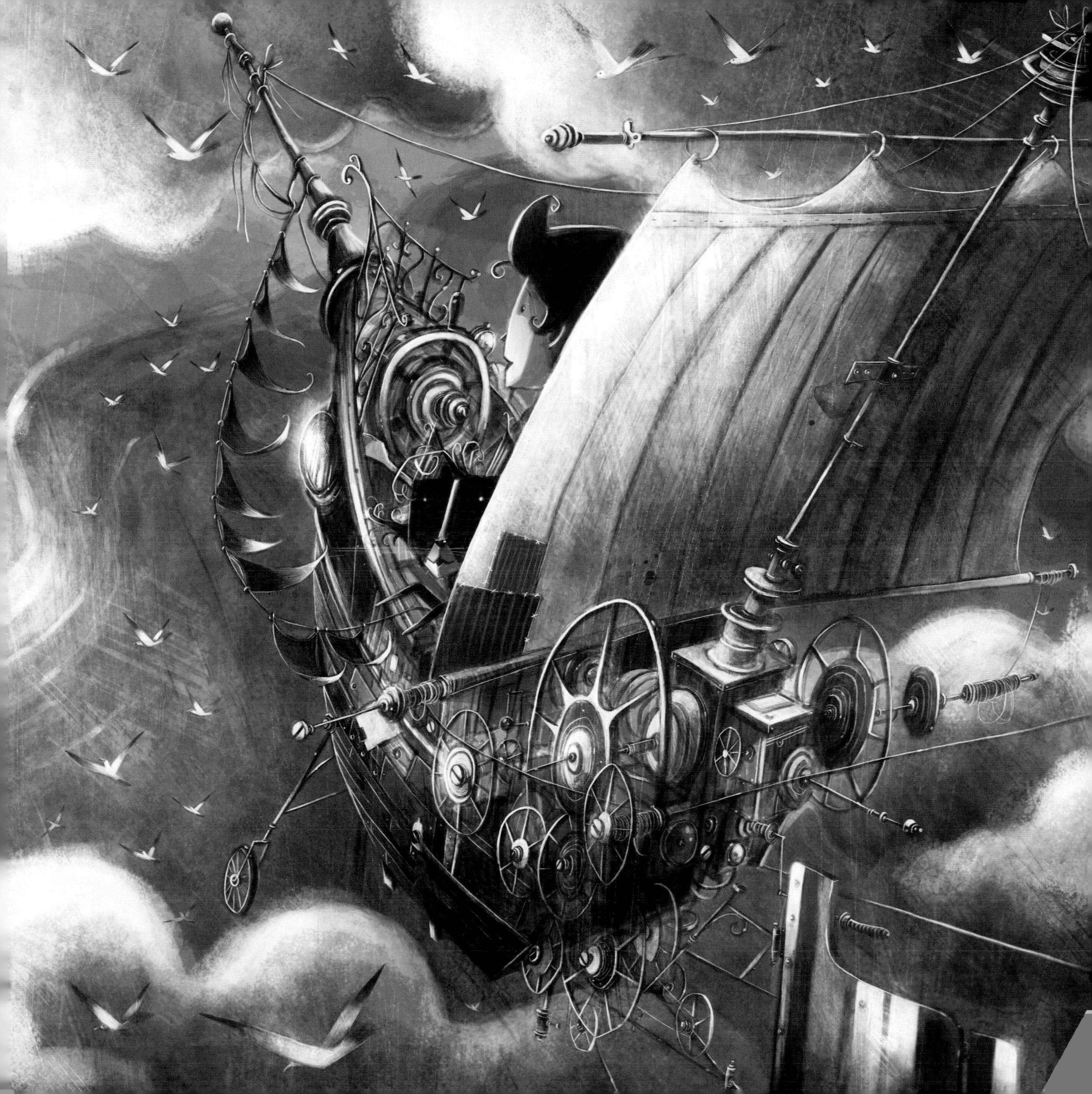

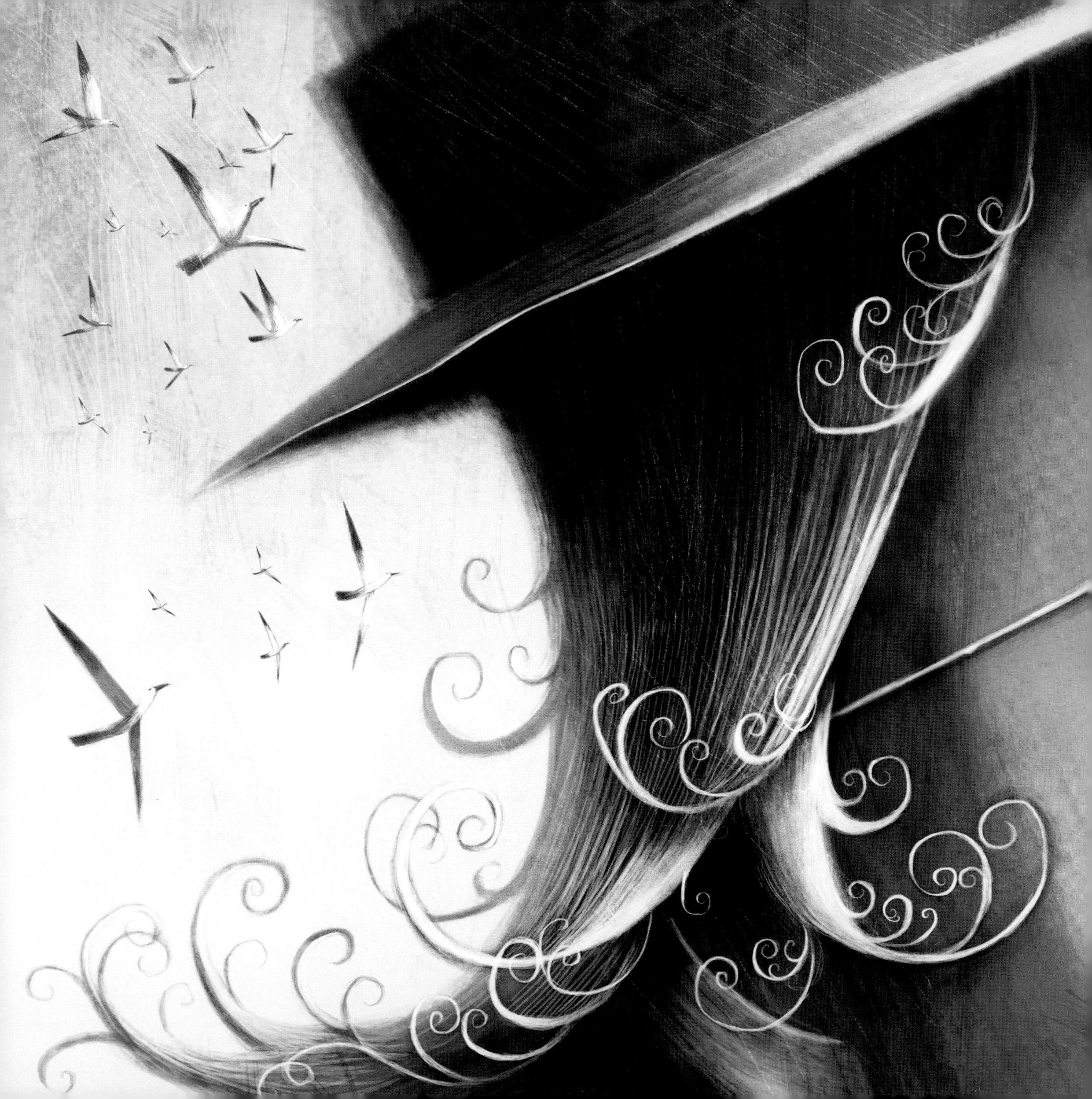

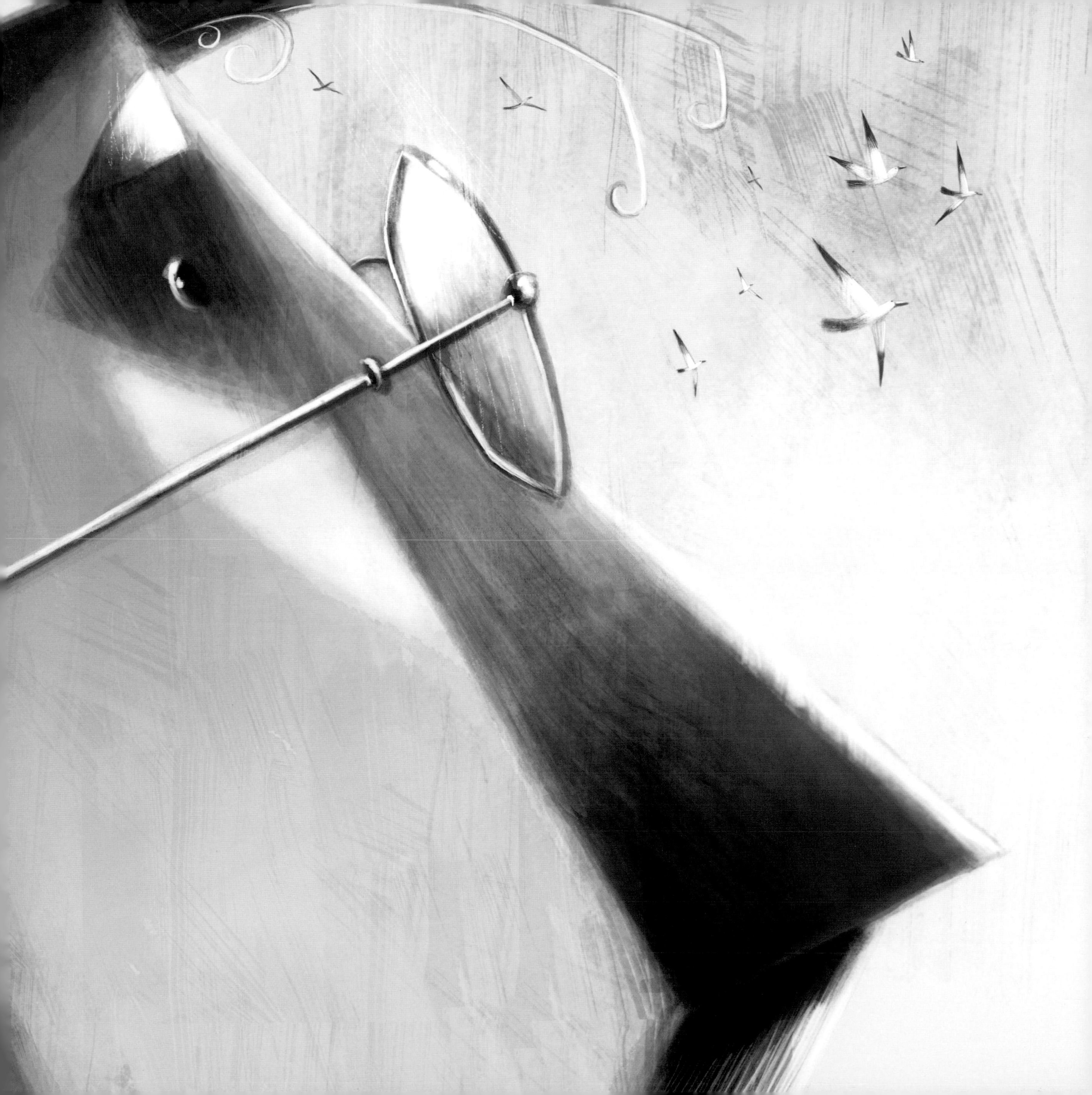

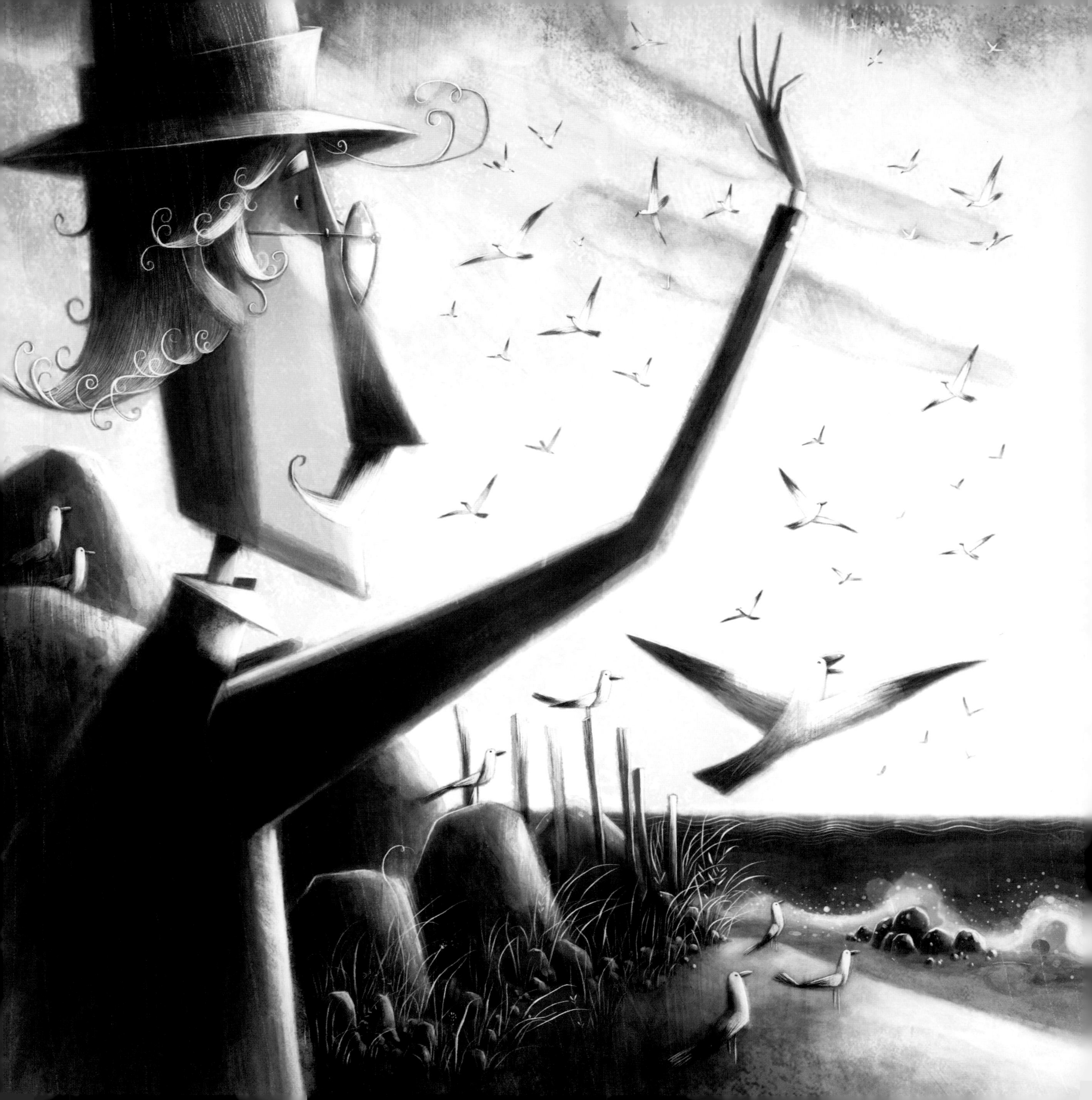

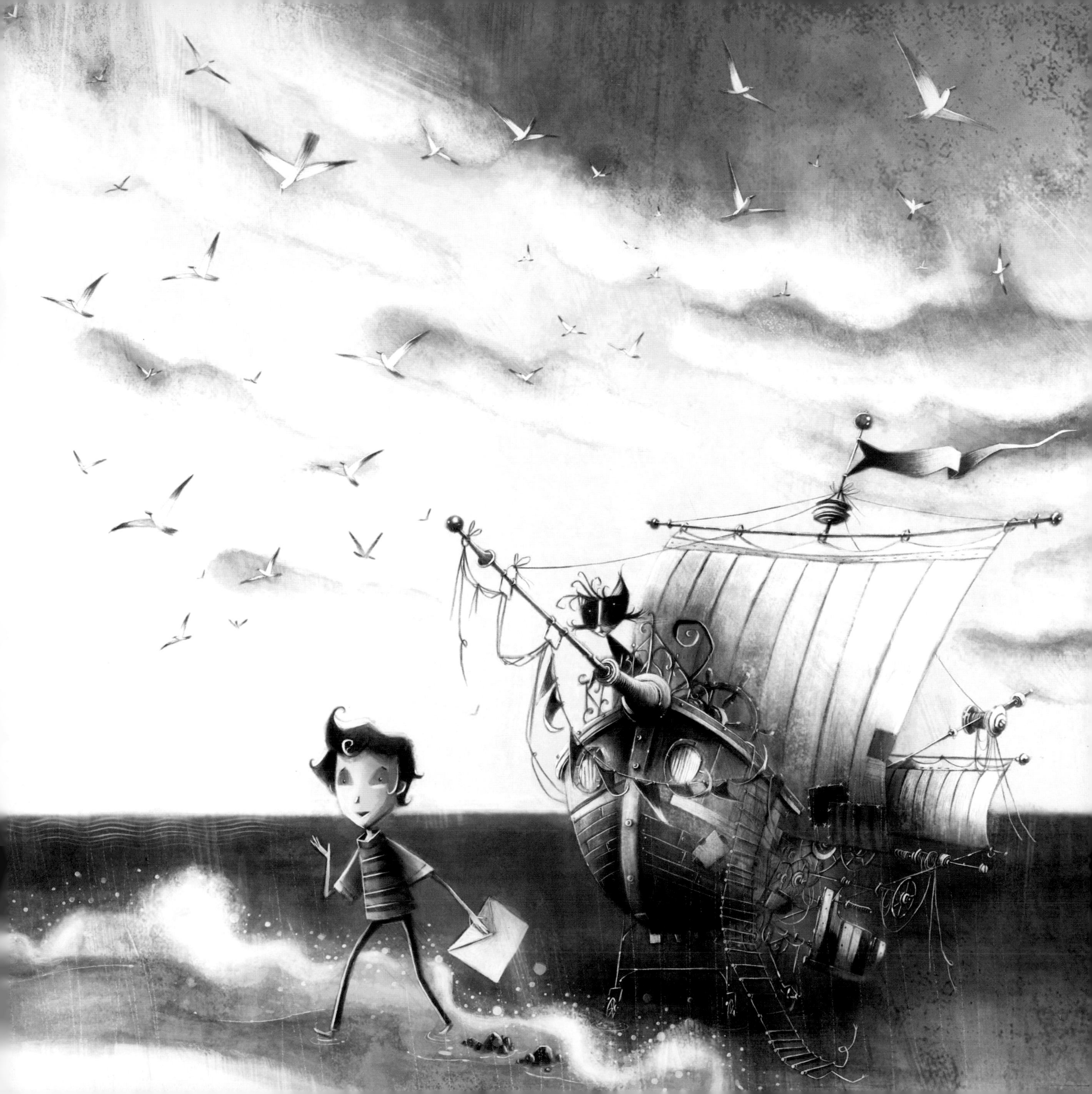

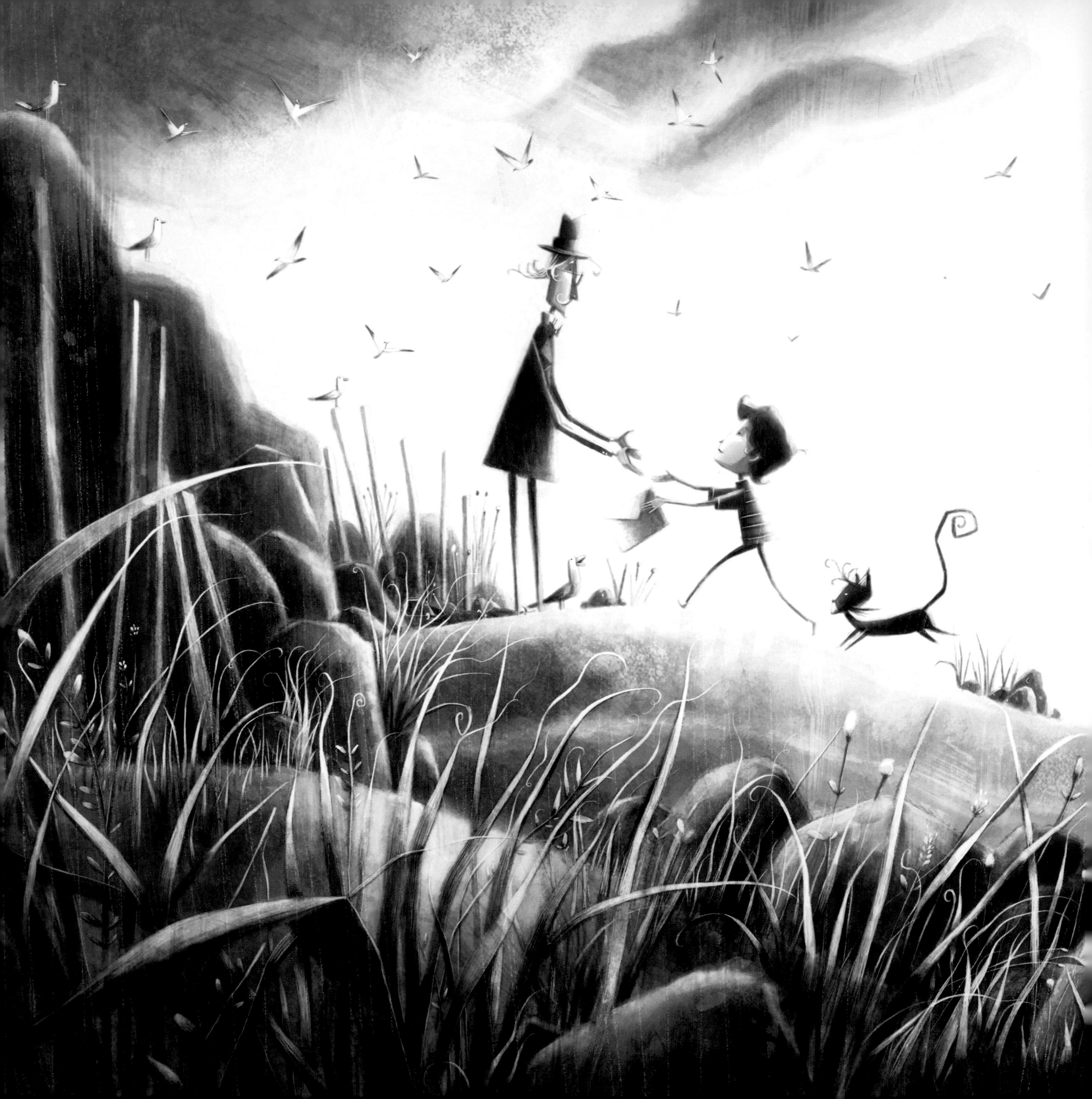

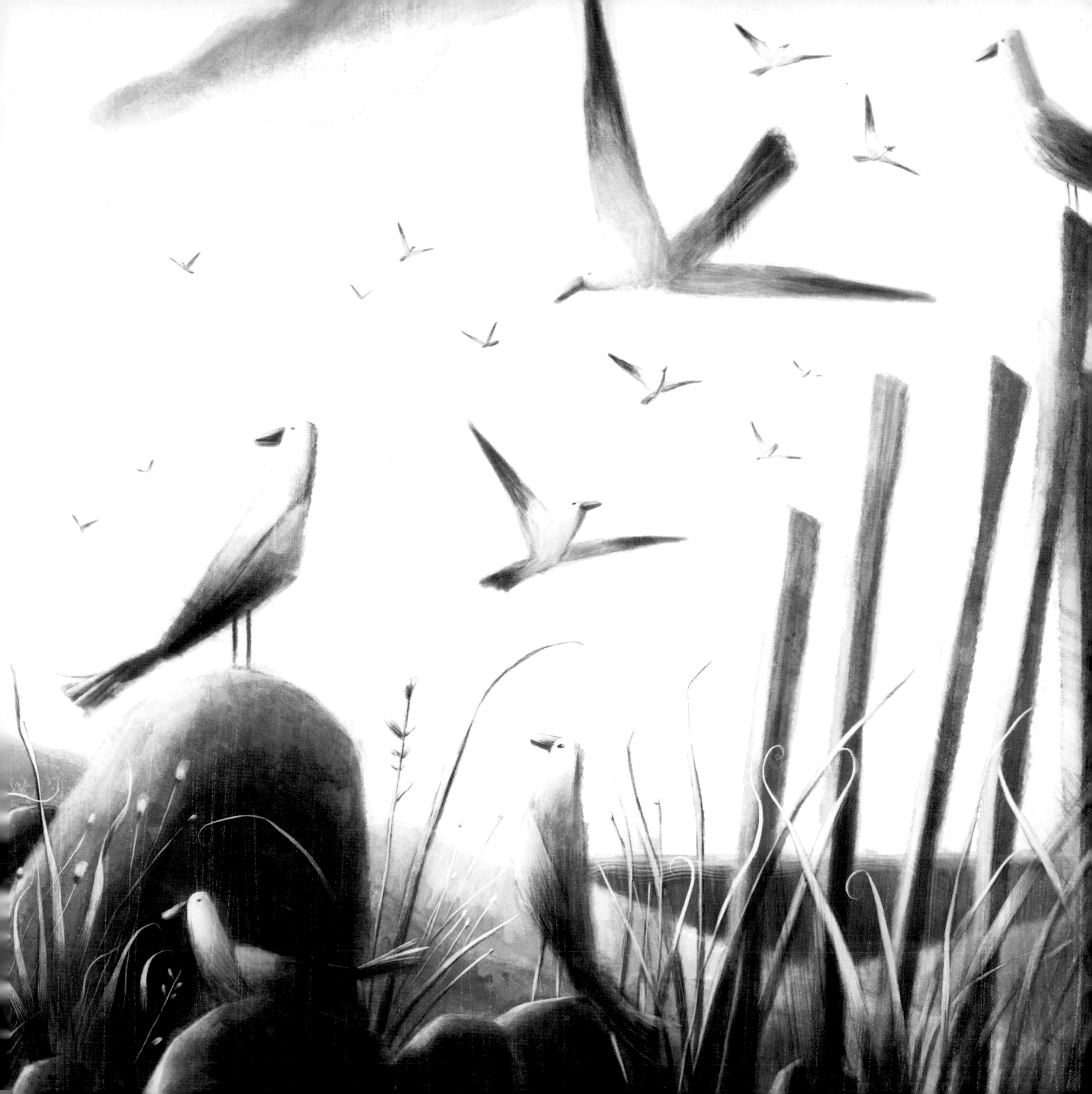

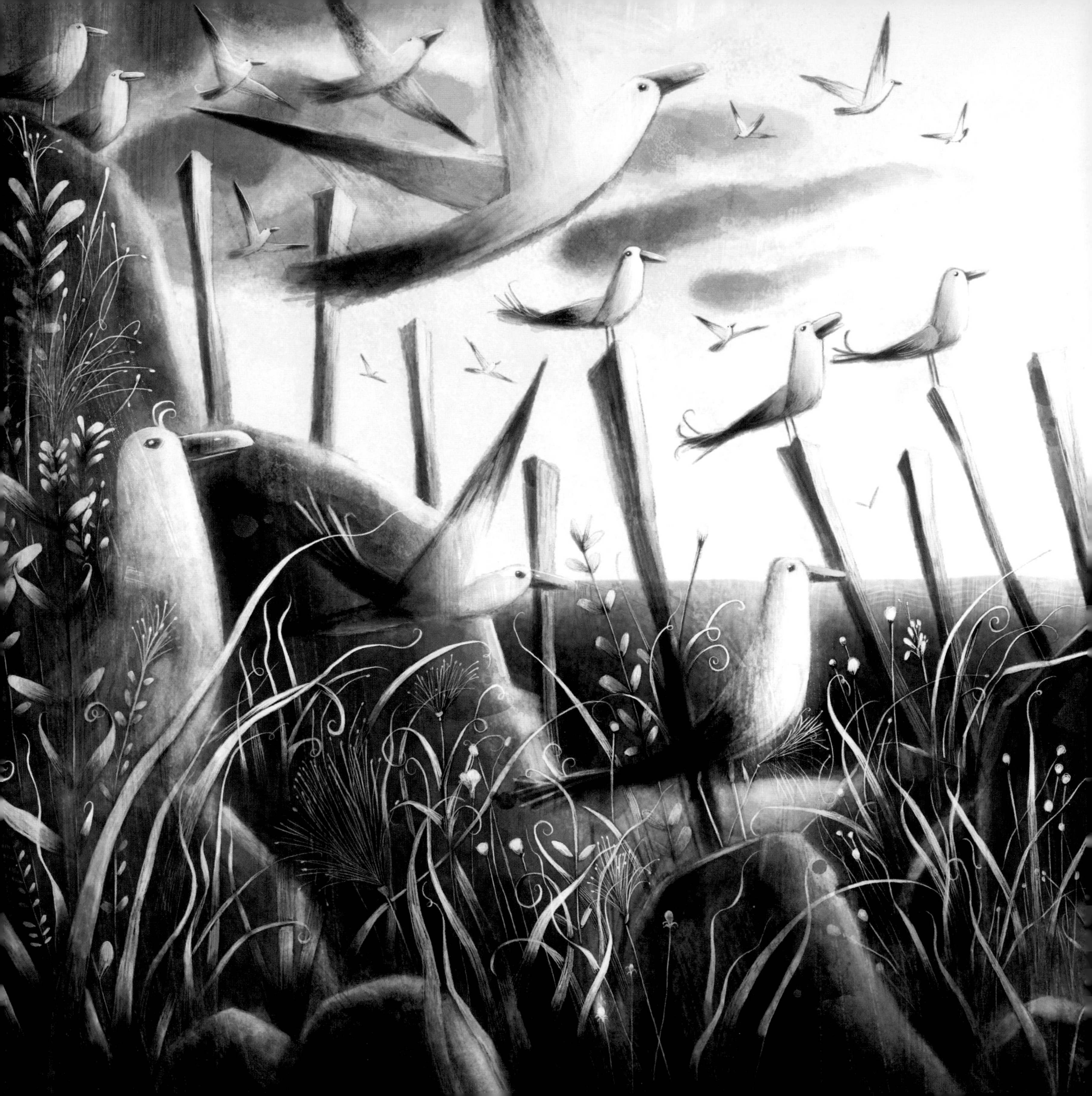

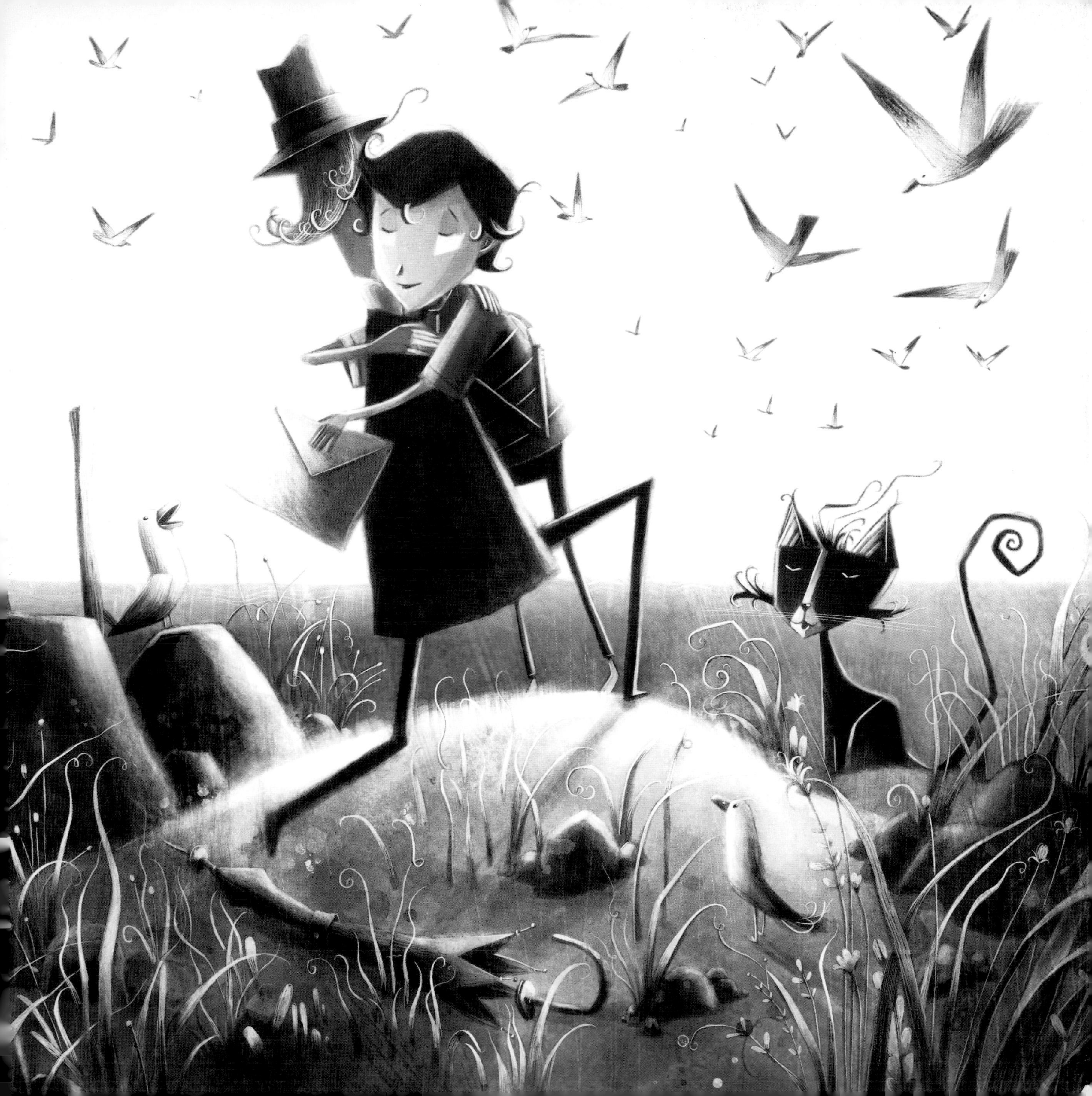

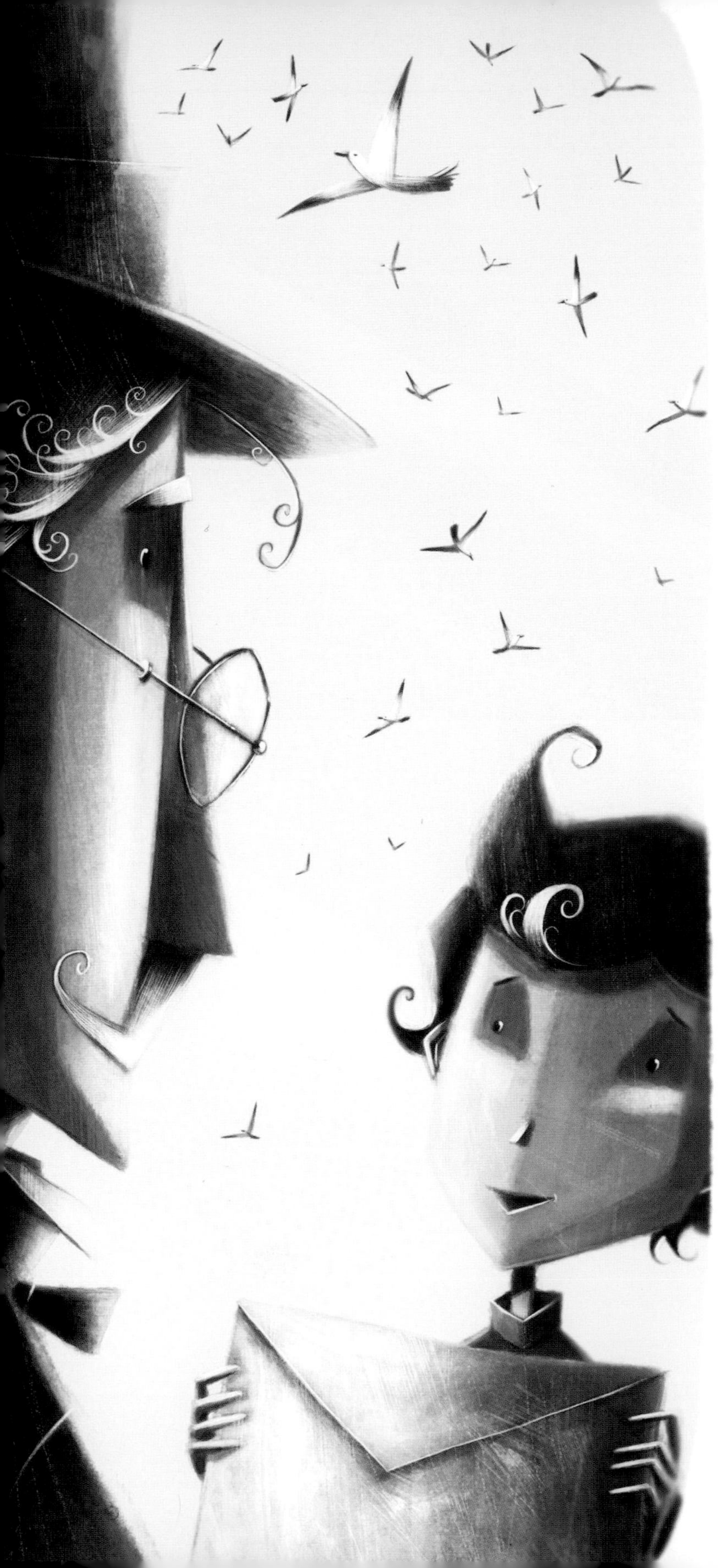

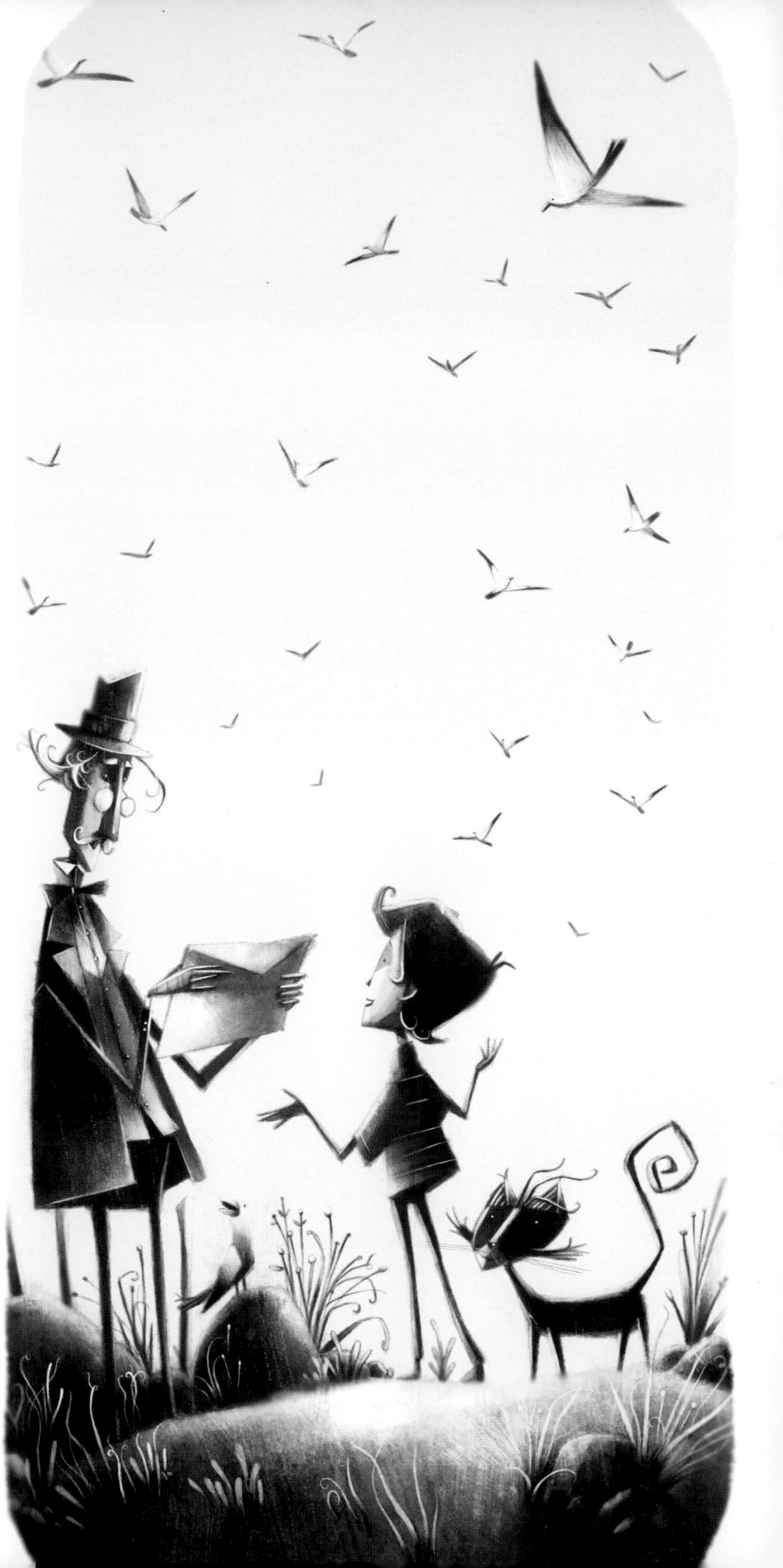

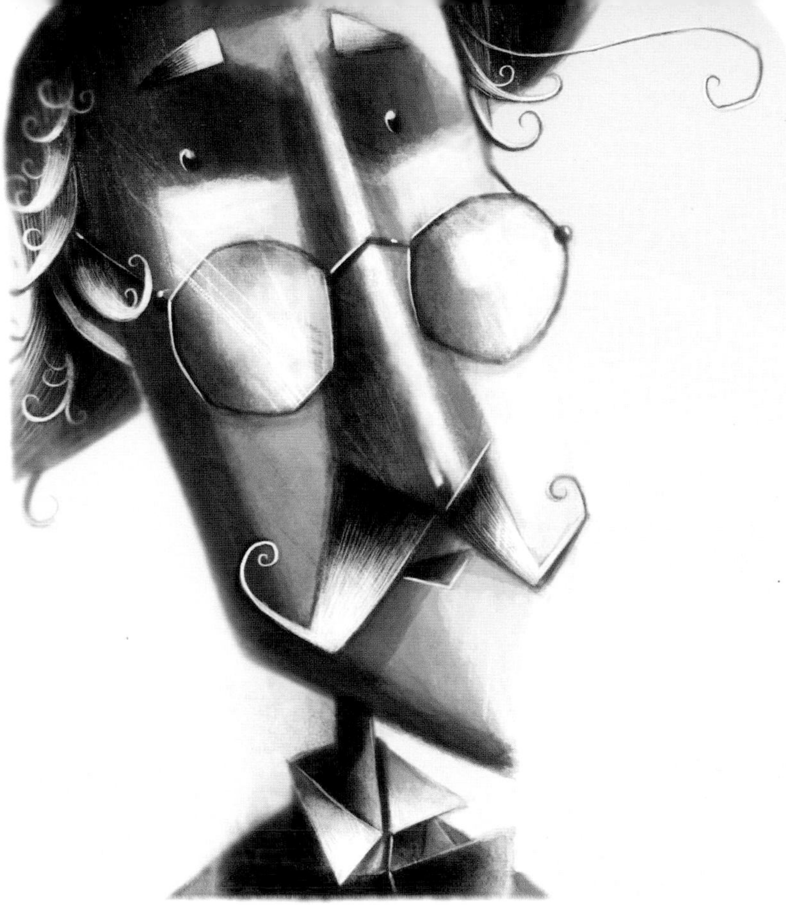

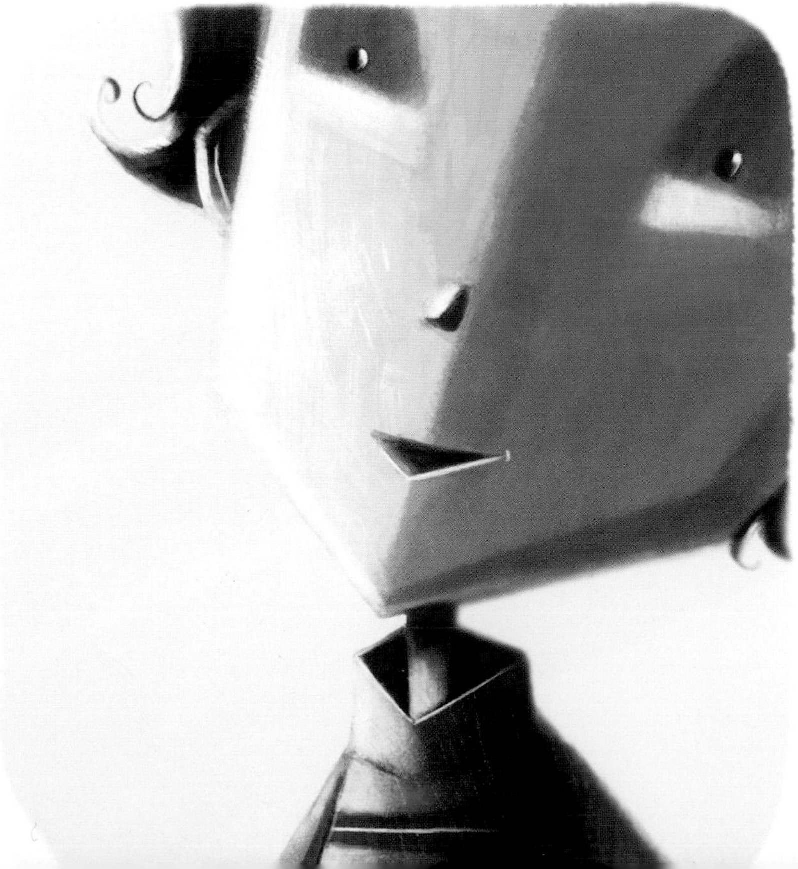

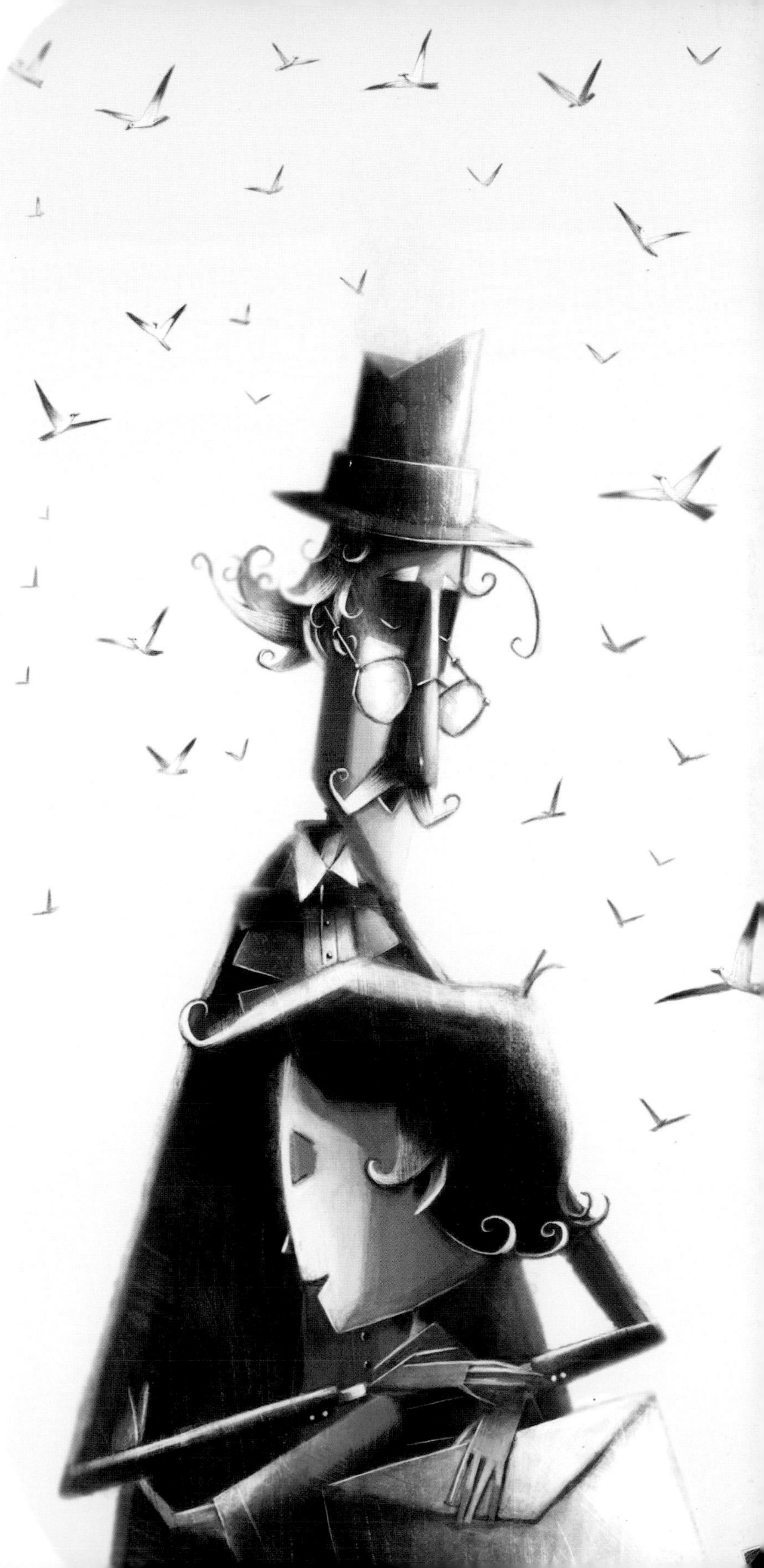

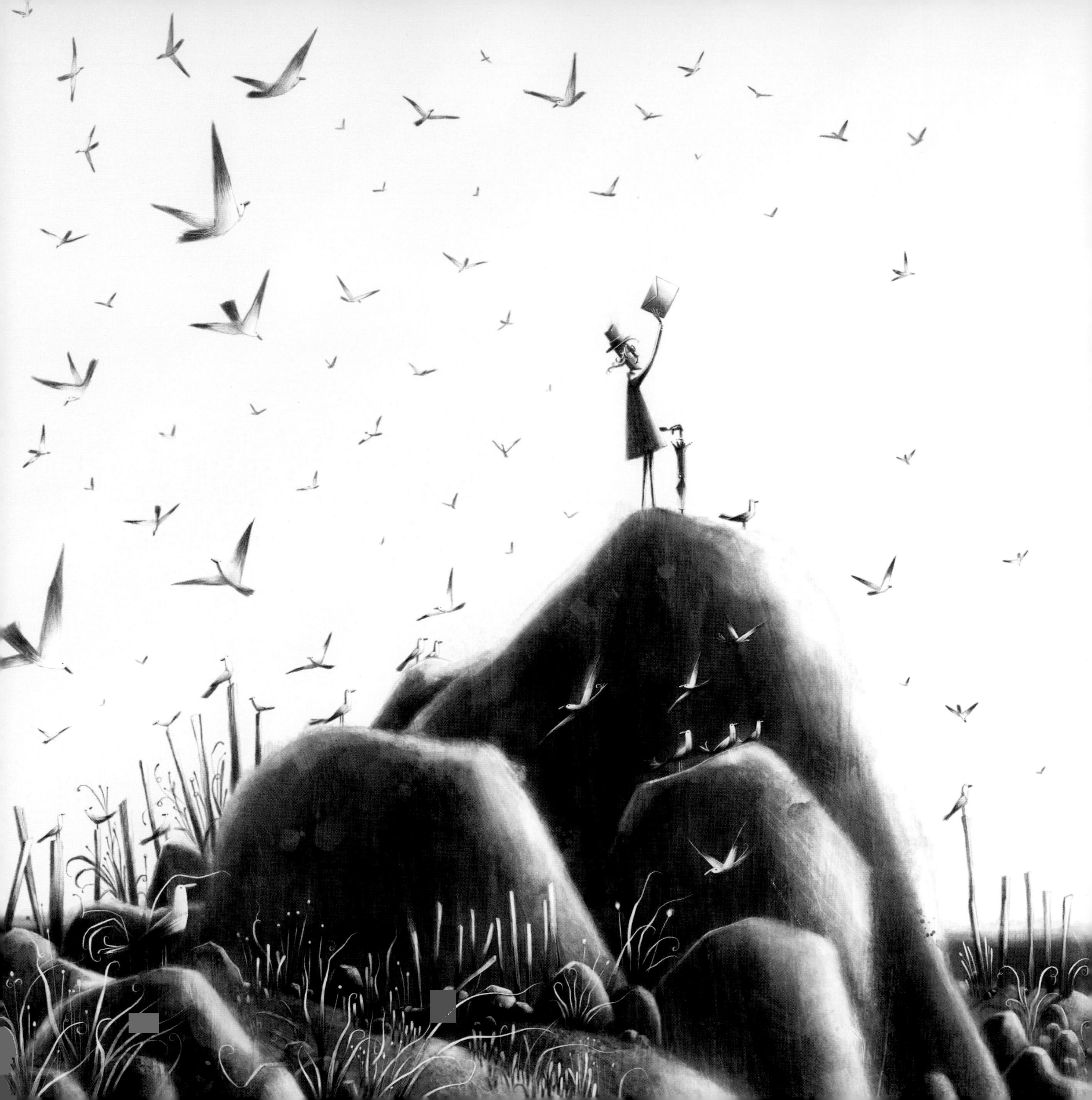

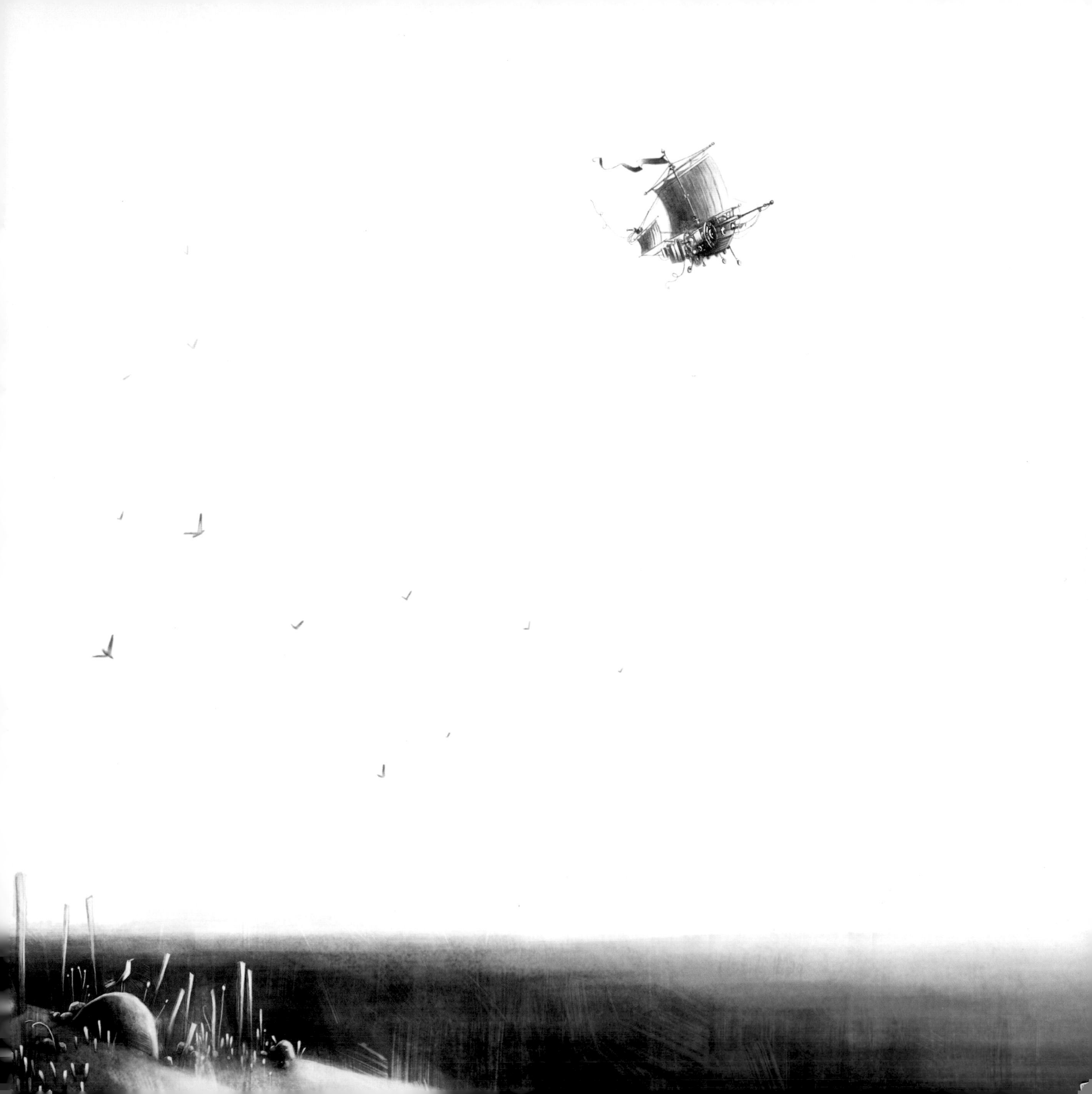

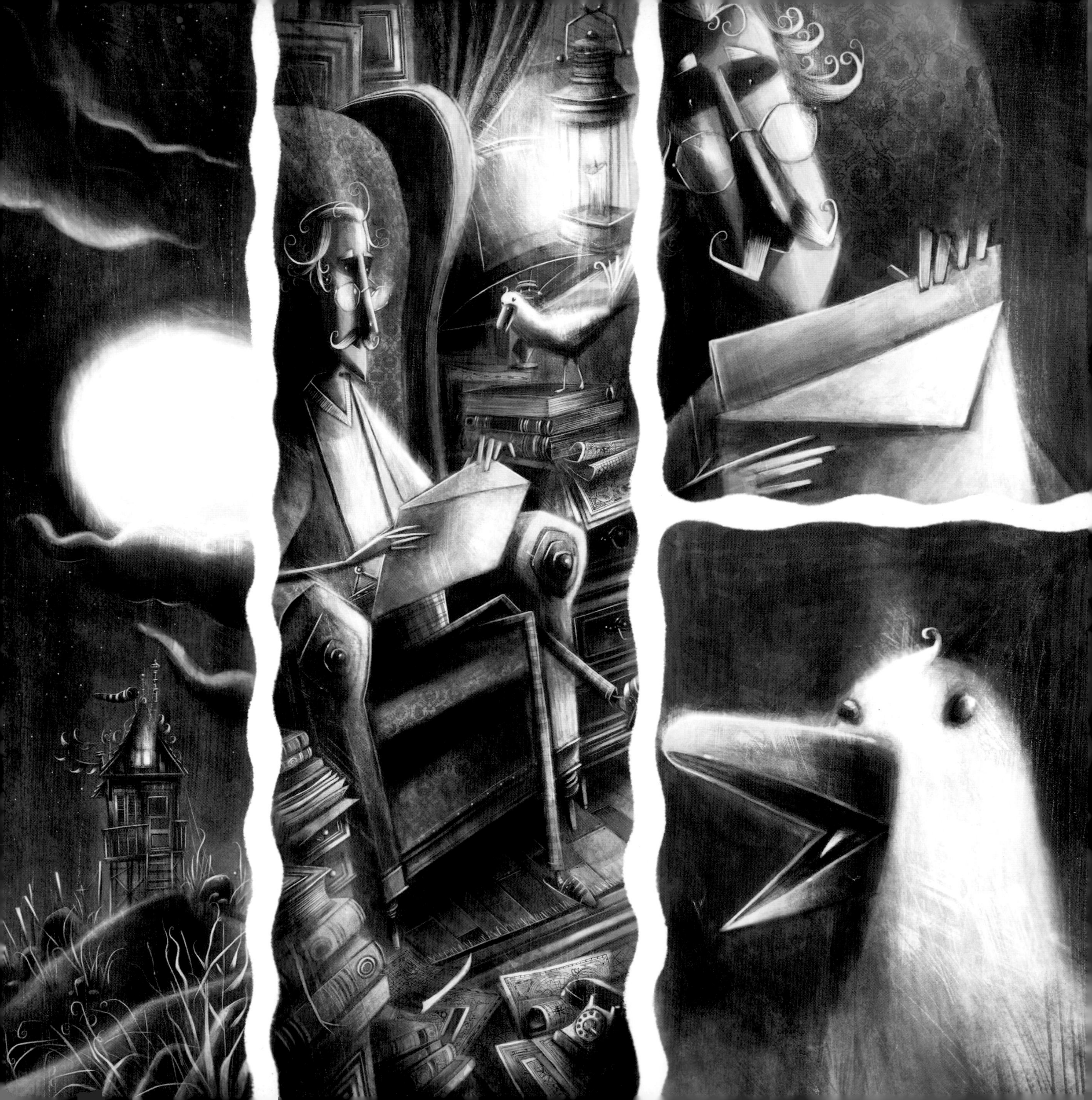

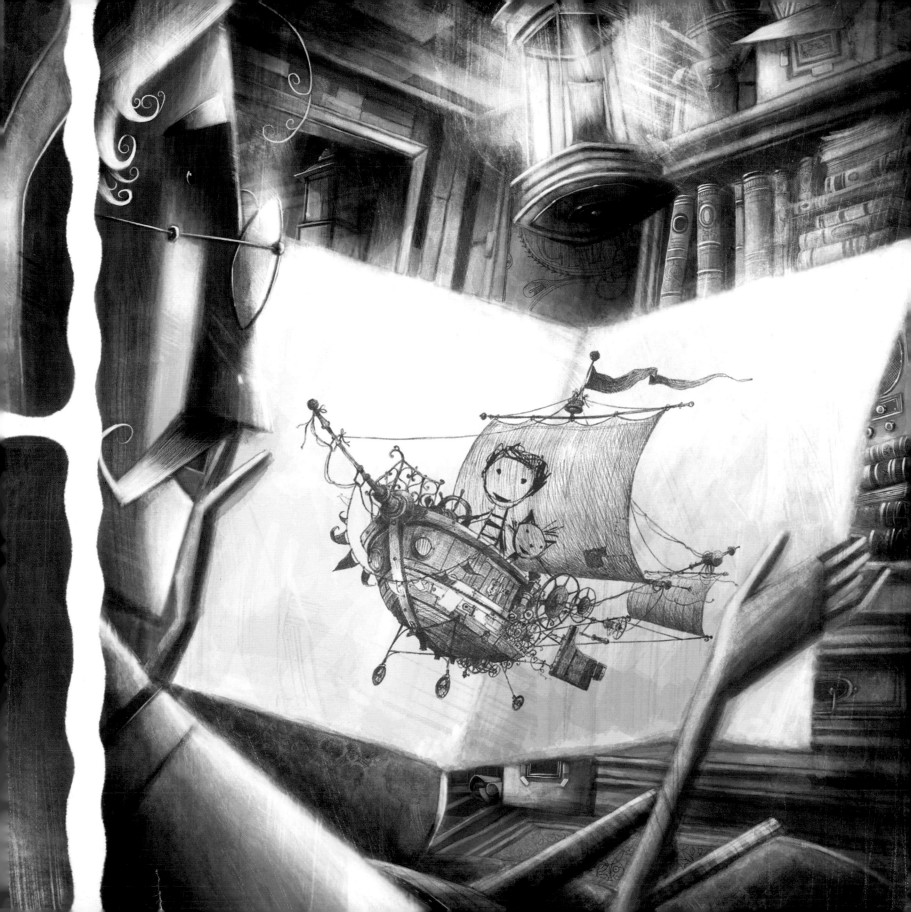

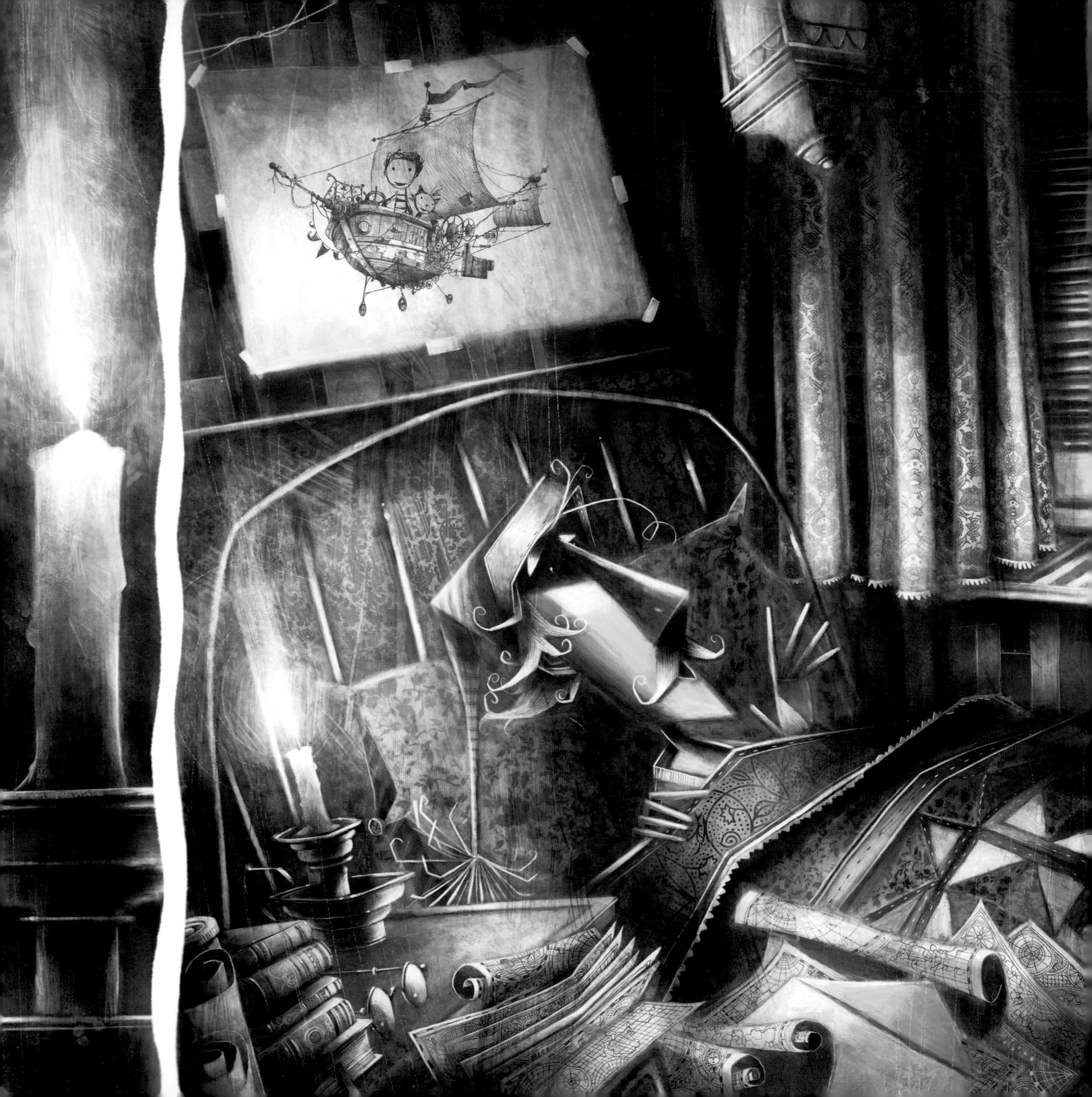

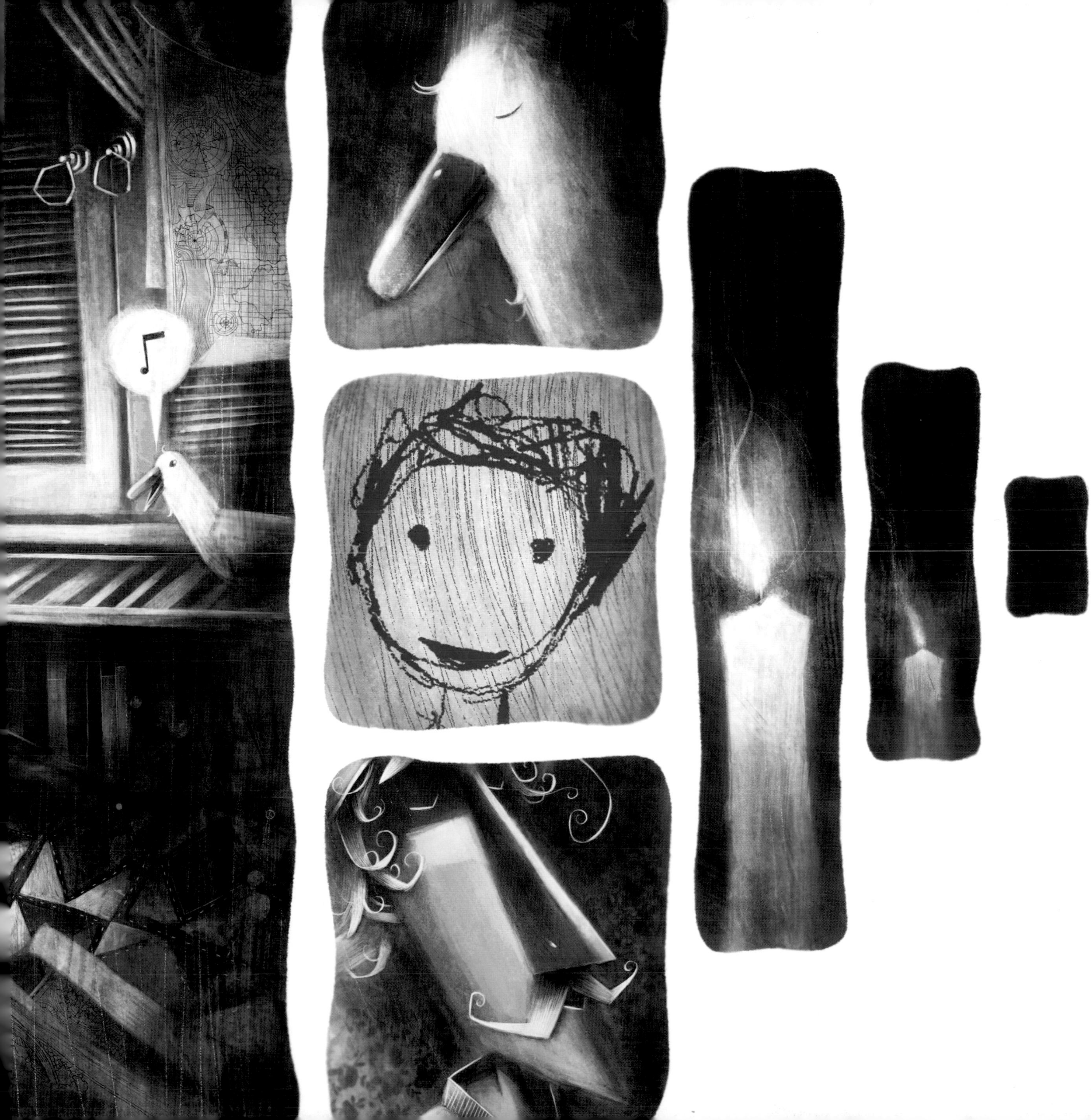

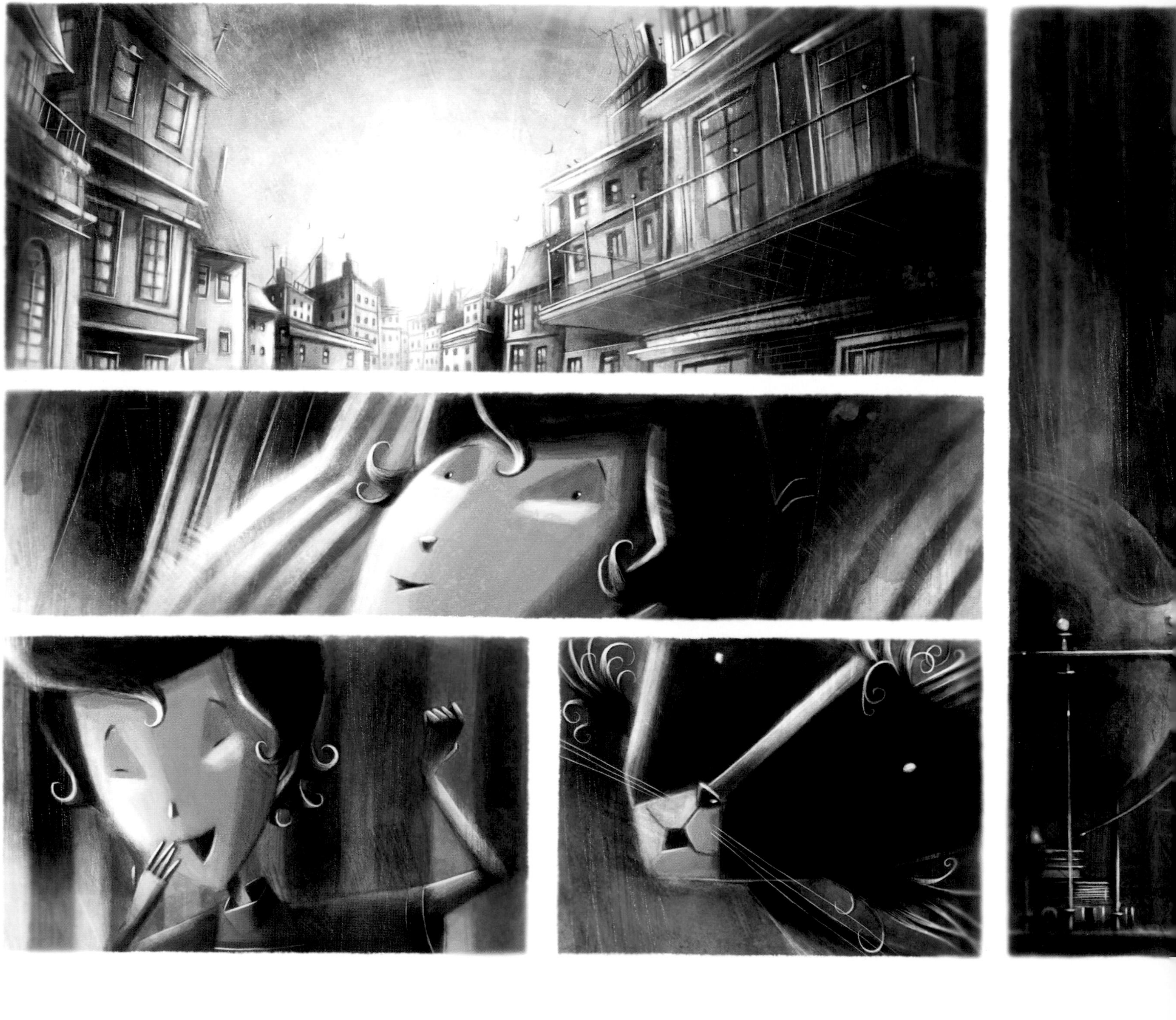

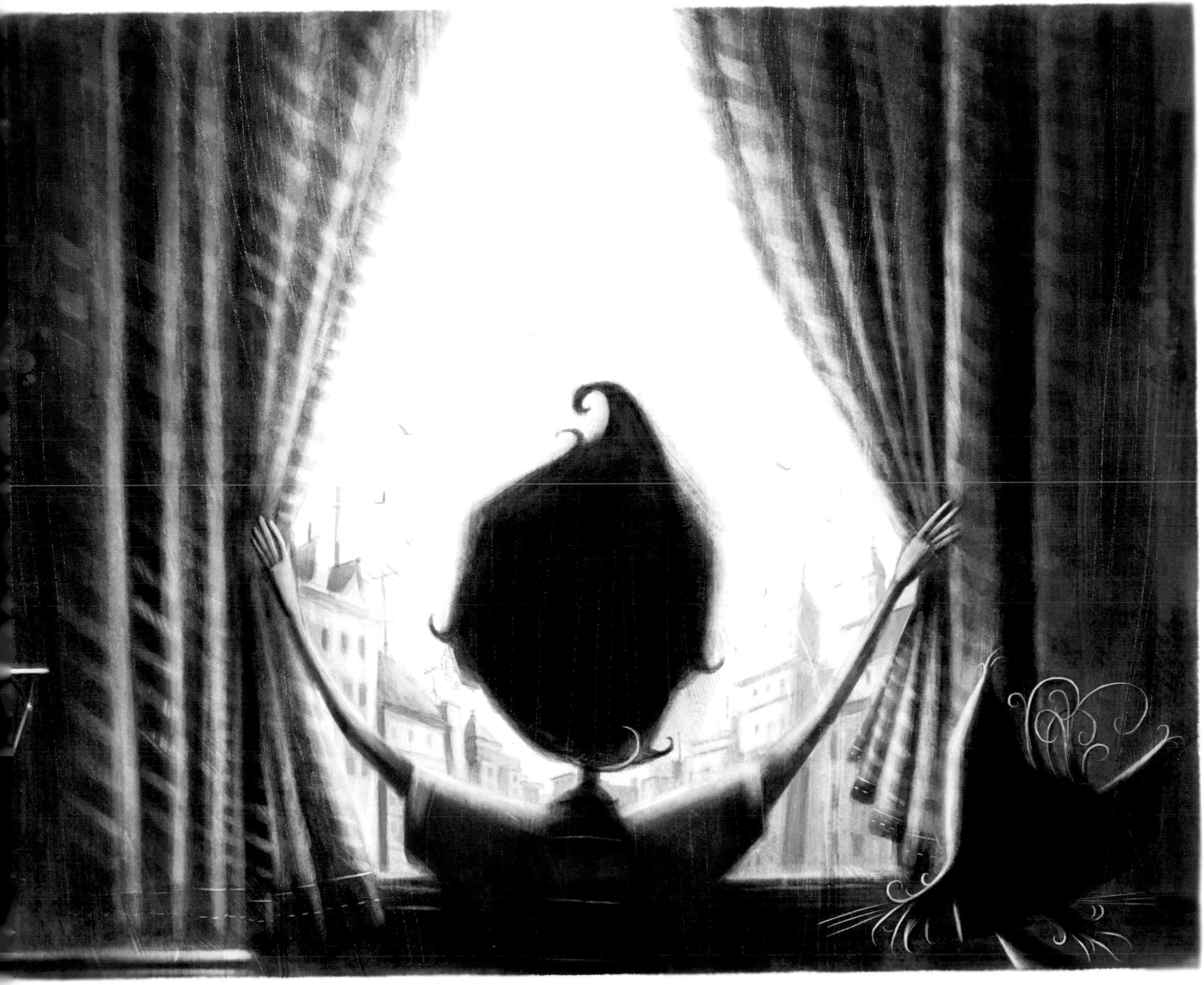

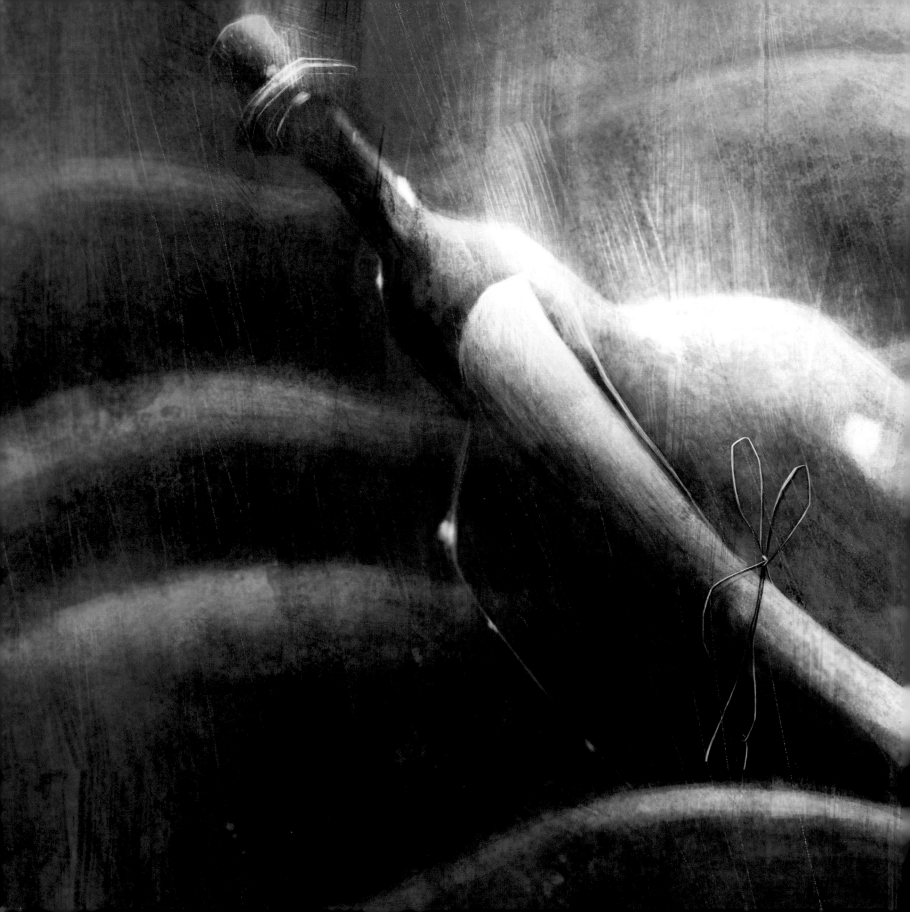

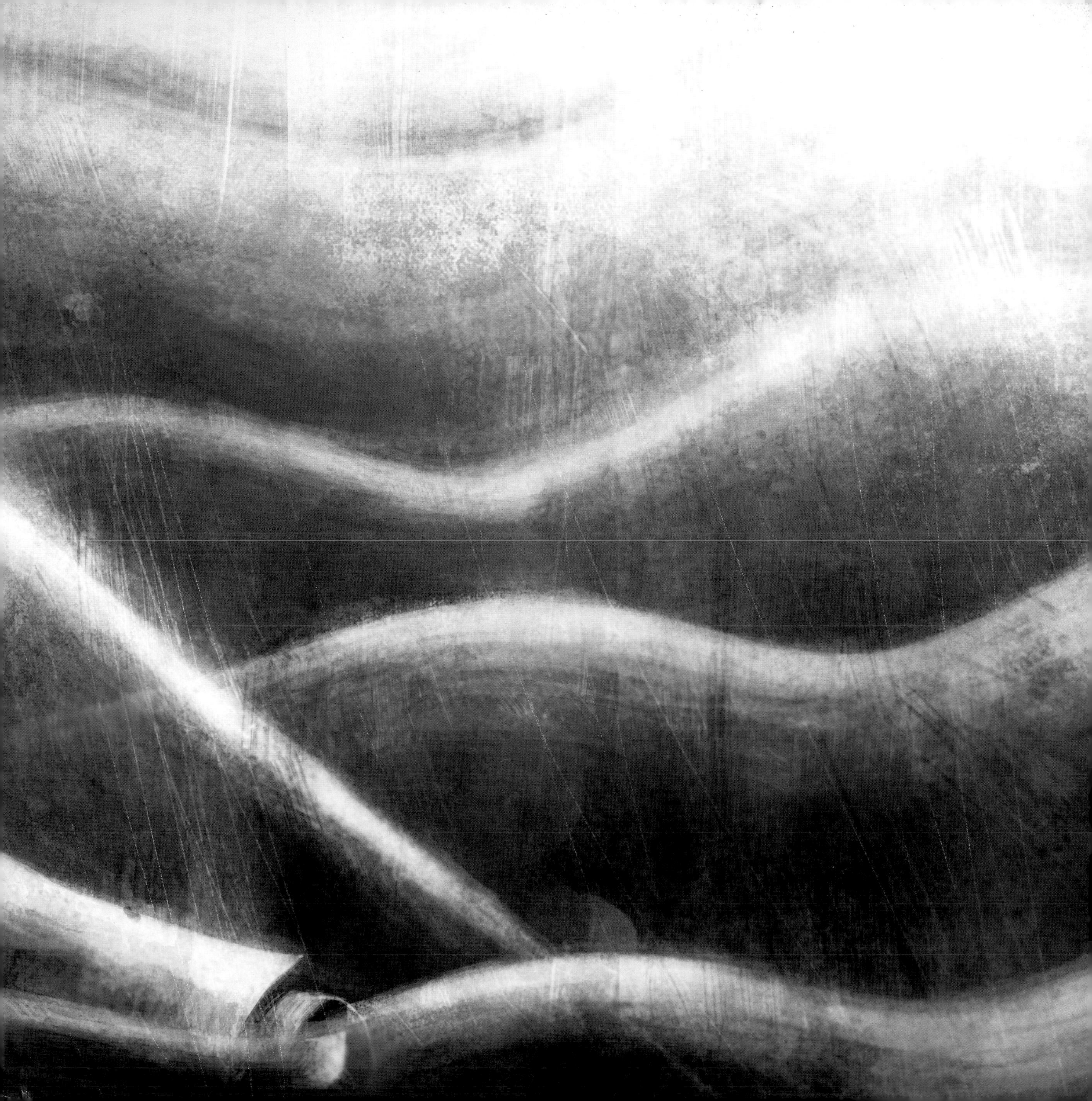

Published by:
Tilbury House Publishers
12 Starr Street
Thomaston, Maine 04861
800-582-1899
www.tilburyhouse.com

Illustrations © 2015 by Rogério Coelho

First North American printing January 2017

15 16 17 18 19 20 XXX 10 9 8 7 6 5 4 3 2 1

Hardcover ISBN 978-088448-528-5
eBook ISBN 978-9-88448-534-6

Library of Congress Control Number: 2016951433

North American design and production: Frame25 Productions
Printed in China through Four Colour Print Group, Louisville, KY

First published in Brazil, 2015, by Editora Positivo Ltda.